RETURN
TO
THREE
SISTERS

Book Two of the
Three Sisters Trilogy

NIKKI LEWEN

JESSICA & BAYLEIGH

May life's meandering path take you places far and near—in eye-opening exploration, safety and, of course, love.

PROLOGUE

Humanity's arrogance and entitlement have killed Mother Earth. The Tri-nami has struck. The polar ice sheets have melted. Earth has been reshaped by flood, earthquakes, and heat. Those who have survived face a barren existence on a planet devoid of life. Food and water are scarce. The Splitter Nation reigns, and human existence is bleak.

Amid a scattering of fog-enshrouded islands of towering redwoods—all that remains of Northern California—a lone woman fights to survive. After years of isolation, she has learned there are others.

May her struggles—and those of her world—not become our own.

ONE

Gus looks at Caleb and sees pain. The man is feeble from lack of sustenance, lack of sleep, and worry.

"How is she?" Gus asks him, moving closer.

Caleb can barely look up. He shakes his head and returns to watching Sadie. She lay still. Gus doesn't know what else to say that hasn't already been spoken.

"You coming to mess?" he asks, knowing Caleb won't answer. "I'll bring ya something..." Gus hesitates, and then leaves—unsure he was even heard.

Alone again with Sadie, Caleb rubs his hand over hers. He notices movement beneath her eyelids. He speaks softly, whispering his words into Sadie's ear.

*   *   *

The trees, ashen and swaying violently, threaten to snap and fall. Yelling while straining to run, Sadie stumbles; falling with momentum, she rolls until striking an object. Terrified to find that it's a dead Splitter with another hovering above, she reaches for her crossbow. It suddenly vanishes as fire erupts and the ground waves in a trembling, lurching disorder.

The fire's heat dissipates as water rushes around her in a sizzling orchestra, the vaporization assaulting Sadie's ears as it deepens around her. Peering over her shoulder, she sees a massive wave offshore, moving with inescapable speed and magnitude. Caught in its powerful surge and thrashing about, Sadie's unable to grasp hold of anything. Debris and bodies cloud the water in an underwater torrent of death. Her vision fades into a shrinking circle until only a pinpoint of light remains.

Sadie snaps awake, escaping her nightmare. Frantic but dry, Sadie wonders, *where am I*? Memories of the Splitter yacht and the flabby albino twins takes shape, but the images don't coincide with any of her current surroundings. A faded poster of Half Dome on the wall clues Sadie in, and turning the opposite direction, she sees Caleb—a mess—asleep at her bedside. Mouth agape, his face is squished into

1

the bed's edge and one hand rests near Sadie's. As Caleb's head slips from its odd position, the movement jars him from slumber. His eyes go straight to Sadie's and, seeing hers open, he stands, and re-clasps her hand in his. Trembling, he kisses it lightly.

"Welcome back," he whispers, looking through her eyes to her soul.

Attempting to sit up, Sadie discovers the extent of her injuries; an ache intensifies behind her eyes and a throbbing pain emanates from her left shoulder. Caleb gently offers aid as she settles into a better position. Noticing untouched water and food sitting nearby, Sadie looks to Caleb.

"How long...have I...been back in the colony?" she asks, her voice raspy and throat dry.

"A couple of days," Caleb answers, retrieving some water and offering it to Sadie.

She takes a long, slow drink, relishing it as the fluid returns moisture to her mouth and lips. The water does more than nourish Sadie's thirst—it awakens concern about the circumstances that put her in the colony's medical clinic. After another long drink, Sadie offers the cup to Caleb and examines her shoulder.

"The bullet went through," Caleb says, seeing her efforts. "We cauterized it after...after getting you to shore."

Sadie's hand moves to her bandaged forehead. It's sensitive to the touch, and she flinches with the sensation.

"You fell...hard," he shares, as Sadie cautiously palpates the area. "And split open your forehead...they stitched it up."

"What about the boats?" Sadie asks, concerned the Splitter vessels that attacked them are now serving as beacons for attracting more members of the brutal Nation. "And...what about, the prisoner... Adam?"

Sadie's mind dashes about in worry. Caleb interjects his frustrations before she can ask anything else.

"Sadie, you need rest. Stop worryin' about everything."

Prepared to challenge Caleb, Sadie abruptly halts her response as one of the medical workers checks in.

"Oh, look who's up!" the lady exclaims. "Everyone will be so excited! They can't wait to see you. Did you see all the gifts?" She steps closer and hands Sadie a few of the cards laying nearby.

Sadie re-scans the room, observing the displays of handmade trinkets and get-well wishes. She's gained local hero status; the Yosemite Colony is thankful and sincere in their words. Reading one of the notes, Sadie smiles and sets it aside. She thanks the woman, who checks the bandages on her forehead and shoulder before offering some pain relief.

"I brought those meds for the colony, not for me," Sadie says, though throbbing in pain. "I'm okay... but thank you."

The woman nods, looks to Caleb, and leaves, promising to check on her again in the morning. As the medical worker disappears, Caleb tries again to get Sadie to take something for her pain.

"No, I need to keep my head straight," Sadie says, looking about. "And...where's my bow?"

Caleb doesn't answer. He doesn't know whether to scream or kiss her. Suddenly aware of it, Sadie reaches over and grabs his hand. Caleb—distraught, exhausted, and relieved—leans his head upon their clasped hands.

"You scared me," he says finally, looking back up at her.

Sadie disregards her concerns. She understands the difficulties Caleb's faced—along with everything they've just endured. Killing for survival is still killing, and the memory never leaves. Troubled by Caleb's poor state, Sadie shifts directions.

"Is that soup?" she asks, nodding towards a bowl.

"Yeah, you hungry?" he replies, reaching for it and handing it to her.

Sadie drinks the cold broth as Caleb offers her a chunk of bread. Halfway through the bowl, she stops.

"You finish it," she says.

"No, go ahead," he insists.

"Caleb, you look worse than I do. Please...I wanna share it with you."

He does feel his appetite returning, and between Sadie's concerning looks and soft tone, he can't deny her request. Taking a sip from the bowl, Caleb catches a glimmer in Sadie's eyes.

"Don't think you can always get what you want," he says, somehow both joking and serious.

"Okay." Sadie smiles, closes her eyes and leans back. "How 'bout... you stay...and in the morning, you tell me all about how I got here."

3

It's the first time Sadie's asked Caleb to stay with her, and the invitation is a welcomed change. Sadie's eyes never reopen and Caleb watches her for some time before also finding sleep.

Weak and dizzy the next morning, Sadie gets Caleb to help her out of bed so she can use the latrine. Failing to coerce Sadie into using the bedpan, he wraps an arm around her waist and escorts her there and back. As she returns to bed, the woman from the night before greets Sadie. She brings in clean bandages, breakfast, and word that the colony is abuzz with news of her recovery. When she leaves, Sadie turns to Caleb, who instantly recognizes her look.

"Ohhhh no...not again," he jokes. "You're not gonna need a notebook...are you?"

Sadie smiles, remembering her deluge of questions when she first learned about the colony and how patient Caleb was about answering all she asked. Even though those sessions were only a couple months ago, they feel like they were from another time. Between interruptions from a steady stream of visitors—each grateful for Sadie's recovery—Caleb shares with her the tale she requested. He answers what she asks throughout his narration; after each guest departs, he continues, exactly where they left off.

"Sadie!" the joyous greeting erupts simultaneously.

"Devon, Derrick, Dom! Oh, it's so good to see you." In a one-armed gesture, Sadie hugs each in turn as they lean over her bed. After the last embrace, her expression changes. "Tell me...why is Delta Force here and not on patrol?"

The team nods in Caleb's direction, and each shake his hand before Dominic explains.

"We were released from rotation...as your escort and for debriefing," he replies.

"So, who's at Oceanside?" Sadie asks.

Noting her focus on security, the team takes turns updating her.

Dominic speaks: "Reinforcements have been added at the coast and all patrol units are locked in current positions until the warning's lifted."

"When normal rotations return, we'll head back out," adds Devon. "Until then, we're assigned colony detail," Derrick finishes, moving closer to Sadie's bedside.

Sadie is grateful for the information and makes a few more inquiries, asking for specifics. The Delta men honor each question with precise replies. Some things the team can't answer because Gus and leadership are still in debate about the recent events, about their consequences—and they eagerly await Sadie's input before moving forward. As Delta Force says their farewells, she notices a difference in their interactions with Caleb. She stares at him without talking until Caleb breaks the silence.

"What?" he finally asks.

"You never said who pulled me out of the water and got me to shore...when I fell overboard." She pauses, staring at him to make certain. "It was you..."

Another visitor enters, breaking their interaction. But Caleb's body language doesn't go unnoticed. As Gus nears, Sadie straightens, reaching to shake his hand.

"How ya feeling?" the colony leader asks.

"Good," Sadie says, ignoring Caleb's concerned facial expression. "I'll be out tomorrow."

Gus drags a chair to sit at Sadie's side, knowing the woman has much to share and that her recollections, more than likely, will add to what he's learned about the thwarted Splitter attack. But as Sadie begins divulging details, he stops her.

"No, not now. From what I've heard, this place has been busy all day with visitors. For now, take it easy. I just wanted to say welcome back and thank you...for protecting and saving us. When you're better..."

"Tomorrow," Sadie interrupts firmly.

Gus smiles and shakes his head. "When you're better...we've planned a full report with leadership. So...until then...rest. That's an order!" He smiles wide, knowing she's not accustomed to being a subordinate.

Sadie returns the smile, enjoying his humor. As he gets up to leave, she stops him.

"Gus, I'd like to move back to that room...at headquarters, if it's still okay?"

"Of course, it's yours as long as you need or want it," he offers, turning to leave.

Sadie knew it would be okay, but thought it proper to still ask.

Grateful and making sure she takes nothing for granted, she adds more. "And…"

Here it comes, Gus thinks as he turns back. He's known Sadie for only a brief bit of time, but senses a plan brewing.

"Can I speak with the prisoner…Adam?"

"Sadie, you're free to talk to whomever you please."

TWO

Sadie does feel better the next day and doesn't need help getting out of bed. After using the latrine, she visits the mess hall, where Marla, the kitchen manager, rushes over, concerned that she's out of bed and walking about. Sadie hasn't recovered all her strength, and the little bit of walking she does serves as a reminder about the necessity of rest. After a quick chat, Sadie returns to the clinic—carrying two bowls—and finds Caleb still sleeping in a chair pushed against the cot. His body is bent over with his head resting on the covers. The sound of her movements wakes him, and he stiffens when noticing the empty bedding. When he sees Sadie standing, he jumps to take her arm.

"I'm okay," she says, handing him one of the dishes.

Sadie sits on the bed as they eat in silence. The warm oats, though soggy, nourish their bodies. When they've finished, Sadie asks Caleb for an escort. He tries talking her into spending another day in the clinic, but Sadie doesn't waiver. She's ready to leave for the colony's headquarters, which will continue to serve as her temporary accommodations. It's also where Sadie stored all of the goods she brought when arriving at the Yosemite camp. The helicopter journey here opened her eyes to the altered landscape of her beloved coast and mountains.

Walking among fallen trees and the remains of the former national park, Sadie can't help but think of the years of environmental disregard that led to this ruin. Unheeded warnings and natural disasters followed by neglect and disinformation accumulated in the world-changing Tri-nami—in which the Pacific, Atlantic, and Indian Oceans simultaneously experienced the onslaught of waves with heights never before seen, in numbers deemed impossible. Each of the tsunamis sent 'Enders' that destroyed everything in their path. With the final devastation of the planet's remaining polar ice, the water never retreated, but rose to unprecedented depths.

Sadie survived the initial impact and rising floodwaters. Even more miraculously, she escaped death for a second time when a final shift in the tectonic plates erupted within the San Andreas Fault. The earthquake and its relentless tremors sunk the remnants of western

California, making the Yosemite Valley, where she now walks, a sea-side locale. Only a few scattered masses of land remain, and one of those isolated islands—her redwood sanctuary, with its coastal fog—is where she lives. The rest of the country dries to dust, devoid of fresh water, infested with militants bent on controlling it.

Sadie's thoughts turn to home, and how long she lived alone on an island. Discovering she wasn't, in fact, alone, was only the beginning; now an adopted family back home prays for her safe return, and an entire colony of survivors is grateful for her existence. The opportunity to spread her father's legacy and save even more lives now seems possible.

Walking side by side with Caleb, Sadie grows more appreciative. She loops an arm through his to aid her weakened state. Finding comfort, she knows that he, too, is there for her.

Approaching headquarters, they find it deserted except for a lone guard, who snaps to attention in salute of Sadie as she enters. She nods in response—intrigued by the feeling of prestige—and passes the room used as a holding cell for the Splitter prisoner. Leading Caleb to her room, Sadie shuts the door. She finds her belongings and piles of supplies untouched, and her crossbow leaning safely against the wall. Its presence has a calming effect, and she breathes deeply.

"Caleb, would you take these," she says, tapping two bulk bags of food with her toe, "to mess?"

He nods as she moves to sit on a cot against the wall.

"Thank you. I need to rest. Can you come back later and…take me to dinner?"

"Of course!" Caleb says like a teenager, encouraged by another invitation to be with Sadie.

He leaves, feeling more alive than he can remember. Even under the strain of the two heavy bags, his steps are light.

As he disappears, Sadie quietly gets to her feet, removes the sling immobilizing her left arm, and retrieves her knife. Stepping out of her room, she approaches the guard with authority, and orders the prisoner's door open. The young guard hesitates, but a raised eyebrow from Sadie has him hurrying to open the door.

"I'll let you know when I'm ready to leave," she says, entering the cell and immediately shutting the door.

Adam—the captured Splitter—jumps to his feet. Sadie steps one stride closer. His initial optimism deteriorates as he doubles over in pain from a powerful right uppercut that lands just beneath his diaphragm. On all fours and gasping for air, he's aware that he's at Sadie's mercy. Sadie drops to a knee and grabs Adam by his hair. With her other hand, she places the sharp blade of a hunting knife to his throat.

"You took women, to the Captain…men, to those…cannibals, and kids…" She trails off as the knife's pressure increases, threatening to break the skin's surface. "How could you let that happen?"

Sadie's rage attempts to escape. Clutching Adam's hair, she yanks his head further back to glare into his eyes. Unfazed by his struggle to breathe, her silence terrifies the young man.

"When I come back…you're gonna tell me everything." She releases her grip and stands tall. She bangs on the door and the guard opens it. She leaves Adam alone to recover from the experience.

The guard relocks the door as Sadie retreats to her room—nauseated by the ordeal. She collapses into the cot, physically exhausted and mentally drained but unable to sleep. Sadie's mind wanders until its unease forces her to pace back and forth in the small room. Then, she leaves, bound for the cell. This time, Adam is cautious and keeps his distance. Displaying a body language that demands respect, Sadie sits in the chair across from him and begins to talk.

"You're here because I sent word…I wanted another chance to talk with you. Otherwise…" She doesn't finish, allowing the silence to speak.

Adam, ashamed and unsure of his fate, slowly proceeds to talk.

"The kids…" He pauses, afraid of the anger he sees building in Sadie. "It's not what you think, they weren't harmed, at least…*that* way." He cowers beneath her glare. "They were only transported on that boat…Cookie made sure no one harmed them."

"Cookie?" Sadie's eyes are steel, asking about the deceptively innocent sounding name.

"The giant…black guy." Adam swallows and softens his tone. "The Maji Wanga." Then, at a whisper he adds, "The witch doctor."

Witch doctor? Sadie thinks, her eyes narrowing in memory, memory and fear. Adam nods slowly. "Start talking. From the beginning."

"Okay…first off…those two boats, and what they do, are infamous. They say Cookie's a genuin' Creole witch doctor from deep in the Louisiana bayou...and the twins are his cursed cousins. I don't know how they ended up teamin' with the Captain, but they work in unison." Adam can't stop as a burden lifts with each word he shares. "Da Cap had an insatiable appetite for women and...the others, well...a taste for men."

Sadie doesn't appreciate his choice of words. She makes this known by resting the hunting knife atop her thigh, pointed at her prisoner.

"Ahhh hem." Adam clears his throat and then continues. "Cookie and the Captain are, ahhh...were...notorious in their abilities and methods. They were untouchable, travelin' the waters, takin' what they wanted when they wanted." He pauses, looking at Sadie's blade. "I crossed paths with 'em about...three years ago and...sort of... lucked out. If you can call it that. They were short a man ...needed someone who could repair the outboards on the zodis." He shrugs his shoulders. "I could...it was that or be the next victim, so...I joined 'em."

"The kids." Sadie reminds him, holding her ground.

Adam stalls, knowing she's not going to like what he has to share. His fingers caress the tinged area along his throat from Sadie's knife.

"We've been explorin' the Pacific's new boundaries lookin' for fresh water and...a suitable location for a new training base." He swallows nervously. "To build an army...an army of firsties."

"Firsties?" Sadie asks, unconsciously tapping the blade, one fingertip at a time in an eerie rhythm that resonates deep into Adam's soul, echoing across his past transgressions.

He swallows. "First generation flooders. Kids born after the Tri-nami."

"They're training children to become killers and you've been helping!?" Sadie's grip tightens on the knife, barring the whites of her knuckles. Adam's nerves tense.

Adam drops his vision and stares at the floor, knowing the role he played was worse than wrong.

"So where are the kids?" Sadie asks, undeterred by his remorse.

"On an island...southwest of here."

The mention of an island in the direction of her homeland, grips Sadie in fear.

She stands. "How did you get on that island!"

Worried by Sadie's demeanor, Adam doesn't hesitate. "With the zodis. We anchored and brought 'em ashore...just like we did here."

"Where'd you anchor them?" she asks.

"On the northwestern side...near the ruins of an old bridge or somethin'," he answers, unsure the direction of Sadie's questioning.

The landmark doesn't match Three Sisters—her island—and Sadie feels relief in her veins. She stares at Adam with such length and intensity it forces him to break eye contact.

"Tell me more," Sadie adds finally.

"We just left there, after deliverin' a batch of firsties." He pauses, seeing Sadie's hardening facial expression and decides it's best to continue. "The site's still being prepped. We're supposed to keep command updated, continue our travels...and gather more..." His voice fades. He doesn't want to induce Sadie's rage by mentioning more kidnappings of children.

Sadie's mind races with an avalanche of questions and thoughts, but a light knock on the door pulls her attention away. As it opens, Gus sticks his head in, looking them over.

"My guard said you were in here," the colony leader says. "You ready...or...do you need more time?"

Sadie answers, staring directly at Adam. "No, we're done...for now."

Out of the holding room, Sadie notices a group of men at the table and moves to join them. Besides Gus, Delta Team is present along with the other two senior council members. All of the men rise to greet Sadie, curious what transpired between her and the captive. With formalities out of the way, Sadie peers over a chart laid out between them. "We got it off the Captain's boat," Gus says, as Sadie stares, amazed.

The exquisite detail and craftsmanship depict areas that the Splitter vessels mapped. The reshaped coast and adjusted Pacific boundaries leave Sadie mesmerized. They look alien, transformed to such extremes that it challenges the images engrained in her memories. But it's the depiction of several islands—specifically, a nearly perfect representation of Three Sisters—that forces Sadie to realize their safety is jeopardized.

Pulled from studying the map, Sadie provides a complete report on all that occurred before her injury and bout of unconsciousness. The men are impressed, and, in turn, the group fills in the days that followed and a discussion on possible strategies begins—mostly in regard to the two Splitter yachts anchored off the Oceanside camp. During their talks, Caleb quietly enters, gets a few nods and, with silent approval from Gus, joins the group's dynamic.

"No," Sadie boldly states as the men grow quiet, "there's a reason we got 'em, and it's not just to sink or burn their remains. Those boats might just be our salvation."

Confused, the men watch closely as she traces a finger over the chart still laid out among them. "Look, this is where we are," her finger moves, "and this is Three Sisters, and…over here," she traces further south, "I believe, is where the Nation is building their new base."

Intrigued by the information, Gus asks for clarification—allowing Sadie an opportunity to share what Adam's just provided. She leaves out no details; the group is equally impressed and disturbed with the intel she provides. It's unanimously agreed that Sadie will continue gathering information from the prisoner until it's decided what's to become of him. In the meantime, Sadie directs the conversation back to her thoughts on the Splitter yachts.

"We can't just let those kids be turned…into killers. We have to do something about it. They'd never expect an attack from their own ships." She looks at Caleb, already showing his clear signs of disapproval, but she continues outlining what she feels is necessary.

Until it's time to depart for dinner, the group debates strategies, personnel, and the probability of success and failure for such a dangerous mission. Nothing is decided—too many variables are yet to be sorted.

One by one, the group leaves until only Sadie and Caleb remain. Drained from the day's events, Sadie suggests eating in as she retrieves a food supply bucket. Caleb takes it from her before locating her sling and carefully helping Sadie immobilize her arm. Noticing the newly broken skin on the knuckles of her other hand, he gingerly examines them—but the only information Sadie offers is a light shrug of her shoulders.

THREE

Sadie lightly knocks on the door of a rusted-out, modified, and barely functional RV that serves as home to a beloved colony member. The rig sits on blocks; its sides warped and bloated from years of use are far from linear and covered in patches, giving the place a feel of decrepit functionality. The entrance, also covered in ragtag repairs, is held by wires that keep the door on its frame. As it opens, Sadie half expects it to fall off.

"Oh, what a nice surprise!" says Auntie T, the owner, genuinely happy by the visit. "Welcome," she lightly pats the RV's faded brown and tan exterior, "to 'the Moose.'"

Sadie's eyes turn to glance at a fairly large dent just below the woman's hand. Her look invokes an immediate explanation from the teacher.

"Years ago, I lived in Alabama. During my first ever hurricane, a log smashed into it, but that's a story for another time. Please... come in."

Accepting the offer, Sadie looks around the humble abode. The electric range top is long outdated, but surprisingly most of the burners still work, along with the tiny refrigerator. An old, portable solar panel provides the home's energy—one end of its cable comes in through a broken kitchen window, while the other stretches to the roof to gather the sun's rays. The interior walls and ceiling, even more warped, add to the structure's oddity. The 70s brown and green décor is accented by children's artwork.

"I'm making some mint tea. Would you like some?" says Auntie T, who picks a couple leaves from a plant growing in a small window box atop the dashboard. Going about her task, she continues talking about the run-down RV. "My husband and I bought it used, and...it served us well. We traveled cross country multiple times, both east to west and north to south. Every dent, repair...and broken piece comes with a story. Now," she says, gesturing, "the Moose is home, and...it's all I have left of those days."

While they wait for the kettle to boil, the two women sit at the small dining table, that doubles as a bed when folded down. Besides

Auntie T, two others, who take shifts working with the kids and staying at the nearby orphanage, share the home. Each week they rotate, allowing them a break from the routine and some personal freedom away from the demands of work. It's a system that serves both them and the children well.

"I wanted to thank you for the other day," Sadie says. "Meeting all the kids and seeing the orphanage was a highlight...something I'll never forget."

"It was Luna's idea," the older woman says, referring to the Sadie Larkin Day celebration they hosted for the colony's newly trusted hero. "She talked all the kids into it...their excitement leading up to your visit was remarkable to witness. They kept coming up with ideas and things to make."

"Well, I was surprised...and honored," Sadie says humbly. "I haven't been able to stop thinking about them since."

As the teakettle begins to whistle, Auntie T gets up and returns with two steaming mugs. "How are your interviews going?" she asks, sitting back down across from Sadie.

Sadie blows softly on her steaming tea. "I'm almost done," she says, "but...it's a little overwhelming trying to decide who gets to relocate. I wish there was a way to take all those interested, but Three Sisters just doesn't have the resources to sustain large numbers." She pauses, sips her tea, and carefully broaches the subject she intended to discuss with this visit. "What about you? You don't have any interest in relocating?"

"Me?" Auntie T says, caught off guard. "I can't leave the kids."

"Who said anything about leaving the children?"

Sadie's reply changes the elder woman's demeanor and dilutes the lightheartedness between them.

"Alright Sadie, exactly...what are you proposing?"

"Well, first off...you know I meet regularly with leadership council." Auntie T nods as Sadie speaks. "There's information that has yet to be shared, but...I've been given approval to talk with you. However, at the moment...it's still strictly confidential."

Sadie pauses, waits for the woman's nod, and then divulges the Splitter's plan of creating an army of firsties. Sickened by the news, Auntie T's hand covers her mouth.

"I'm worried about their safety. There's already been two attacks on the colony and next time...we might not be as lucky. If they get the kids..." Sadie trails off, not wanting to think about the youngsters in the hands of such evil men.

Auntie T stands up then sits right back down, more concerned about the children's safety than ever.

"I need you to speak with your co-workers," Sadie says. "In private, and share what I've just told you...all of you can relocate...all the teachers and kids..." Sadie hesitates before adding more. "Three Sisters has only two accessible spots, both difficult to navigate, but easy to secure and defend." Understanding Auntie T's dilemma, Sadie makes sure not to push too hard. "Please...weigh the options, see what the others think, and...we'll meet again."

Auntie T nods slowly and sips her tea as a silence settles between them. Sadie stands, drawn to a particularly interesting depiction of toothbrushes.

"Luna?" she guesses.

The older woman allows a soft chuckle to escape. "Yeah, she draws them all the time. She's taking the job you gave her very serious."

Sadie finishes the tea and thanks her host before departing. Back outside, Caleb stands to join Sadie as she exits the site. Pulling a small pad from her back pocket, Sadie makes a notation while checking her list.

"What?" she asks, looking up at him and noticing his expression.

"You," Caleb says, shaking his head and smiling, "and your seemingly endless supply of paper. My god...do you own every last surviving piece?"

Sadie returns the smile, ignores his comment, and leads them to her next stop. Again, she enters a makeshift living quarters as Caleb finds a place outside to sit and wait. This time, she returns fairly quickly. Sadie's sudden exit worries Caleb.

"Changed his mind," Sadie says, crossing off the name. "Decided on staying here...thought there were others more deserving."

"Wow, that's mighty big," says Caleb.

"Yeah, I thought so too."

"Okay so...who's next?" he asks, watching Sadie scan her notes. "Well, there're only a couple left, but...I think I'll finish tomorrow. Instead, let's head back for an early lunch. Then, I've got more questions for Adam." She grows silent as they walk among the campground's homes.

On cue, Caleb leaves early in the afternoon as Sadie enters another round of interrogation with the colony's prisoner. Afterwards, as becomes routine, she meets with Gus and the council, adding details to their ongoing debate on how to best serve the colony. At the meeting's conclusion, Sadie announces that her last interviews will be in the morning; she makes a request regarding the upcoming gathering. Her motion is quickly approved and the group disperses, hungry for the evening meal, where the mood is jovial as stories of Sadie's heroism are told.

Between the kids and their questions, Sadie is bombarded with attention while waiting in line at mess. During the meal, nearly everyone makes it a point to come over. Sadie's table remains full. Any time someone departs, another person fills the seat until it's time for the evening gathering. At the camp amphitheater, the benches are packed. Standing between the two fires lighting the area is Sadie, who knows the crowd is there to hear her announcement of who'll accompany her back home. As the crowd quiets, Sadie begins.

"I know you're curious about who will be invited to leave, but...there are a few of you I still need to meet with." Sadie slowly scans the crowd. "And for anyone else who might be interested... this is your last chance to speak up...so please, after we finish tonight, if you've changed your mind...one way or the other, let me know."

A murmur travels through the crowd, but before it grows too loud, Sadie regains everyone's attention. "There's more..." Her hesitancy doesn't go unnoticed. The colony dwellers still and lean in. "There are details about the Splitter Nation we've recently discovered that need to be shared. And once we do...it may change some of your minds about relocating."

Sadie looks to Gus, who nods. He stands and takes over.

"They've begun building a new base," he says, standing at Sadie's side, "and unfortunately, it's not far from here..." He pauses, not liking the news he's sharing. "It's designed for...training...for training child soldiers."

His words ignite the crowd into an explosion of comments, profanities, and questions. Between Gus and Sadie, they manage reining in control by taking turns adding details, explaining what they know, and answering what they're able to. An army of firsties isn't something they want the colony's children to fall prey to, let alone, be forced to contend with.

As the evening wraps up, the people are unsettled by the news, but hope tomorrow's meeting goes better. They've never had back-to-back gatherings, but then they've also never had anyone relocate or a Splitter holding so near.

Walking back to headquarters, Sadie is surprised as a lone woman appears. Sensing the woman's need for privacy, both Gus and Caleb leave quietly.

"What can I help you with?" Sadie asks, knowing this particular colony member normally doesn't interact with anyone but Gus.

The woman looks long at Sadie before speaking. "I'd like to talk… about relocating?" she finally says.

Sadie nods, noticing the woman's discomfort. It's obvious she wants to meet now, so Sadie motions her inside and over to the table, where they sit across from one another.

"My name's Cameron," she begins. "I've been livin' in the colony since the first Splitter attack last fall. Do you know…about me?" She pauses, gauging Sadie's reaction.

Sadie is well aware of Cameron's status as an outcast who joined them after helping stop an invading Splitter group she was traveling with at the time. As for the details that led up to her actions, only Gus knows them, but looking at her, Sadie reads the hardships etched into Cameron's face and answers honestly.

"I know you eliminated the Splitters you traveled with, sought sanctuary here, and have an agreement to only speak with Gus. As for the circumstance that led to your actions…I can say, I know nothing about 'em."

Cameron's eyes have the hollow look of a woman who's suffered beyond the boundary of the human psyche. A survivor and a fighter, her face exhibits a glimmer of determination before it fades quickly to sorrow. She starts to tell her tale. She speaks with brutal honesty, sharing accounts of the years of monstrosities forced upon her, starting at a very early age. Sadie listens, never interrupting, knowing that talking about it now may offer some form of therapy for Cameron.

"I finally decided that being with one, was better than being… passed around. So, I found the biggest, baddest asshole…and managed to survive. It wasn't pleasant…" Cameron fights her emotions. "But I lived, and…when the chance finally arrived, I took it." Her eyes glaze with hatred. "I killed that fucker and all those cocksuckers traveling with him. I'll never fall victim again."

Cameron stops talking, and Sadie honors the woman's silence.

After a few moments, Cameron looks back up. "I don't fit in here. I thought…Three Sisters might be a chance to…heal, and live without constant fear of being found." She looks directly into Sadie's eyes. "I know there are lots of others wanting the same chance, so…here's what I offer. First…I don't need *anything*…I can manage on my own and fend for myself. Second, anytime those bastards come around… you can count on me to fight. And…I'll make you the same deal I made with Gus. Any information I have about the Splitters, their methods, modes of operating, or…anything you want, I'll share. You have my word."

Sadie senses the truth behind Cameron's words. Without responding, she gets up and makes them tea before returning to her guest. The silence that settles between them allows both women to contemplate all that has been shared. Halfway through her cup, Sadie's mind comes nearer a decision.

"Cameron, your story will stay with me forever," Sadie says thoughtfully, reaching over and placing a hand atop hers. "I believe you've survived such…horrific circumstances for a reason. What you've endured and suffered should never be allowed to happen…I'd proudly fight side by side with you against the Nation. But…as you said, a lot of folks want to go…and I can't take everyone."

Cameron's hopes fade.

"After speaking with you, though," Sadie continues, "I'm thinking about adding one more option. On the southeast corner of Three Sisters…completely isolated and far from others…there's a narrow peninsula, sort of a tail…that draws my curiosity. There are views out into the ocean on both sides and…I'm contemplating stationing someone there, to observe and keep watch." Sadie gauges Cameron's reactions and body language, finding confidence in her gut feeling.

"There's nothing but empty woods, cliffs, and coastline. I've camped there enough to know it's possible to make a permanent camp and…maybe…you're the perfect fit for such an isolated area."

Cameron's eyes show light for the first time. Sadie finds joy seeing it can still happen.

"Obviously, there's a lot more to discuss and agree upon, but... wha d'yah say? Should I put on another pot of tea so we can continue talking?"

FOUR

Adam jumps out of his cot, surprised at Sadie's sudden appearance.

"Yer here awful early," he says, staggering in an attempt to put on pants.

Dressed more completely, he moves toward Sadie, curious what she carries. On approach, he's handed a tray and uncovers a hefty serving of food. It's more than he's gotten the entire time he's been held captive. Adam digs in, devouring handfuls at a time. Suddenly, he stops and looks up at Sadie, realizing this unexpected meal and visit may not be as welcoming as originally thought.

"Is this...my...last meal?" Adam trembles.

"I'm leavin'...for home," says Sadie, not relieving his concern. "These are leftovers from a farewell dinner last night."

Adam looks from the plate back to Sadie. "So...should I be... savorin' this food...as my last...or..."

Sadie doesn't answer and Adam becomes increasingly nervous. He swallows, but the food catches in his throat. He coughs uncontrollably. When it subsides, a loss of appetite and a building anxiety take over. He regrets much, realizing how miserable a life he's been leading.

"Is there anything else you want to tell me," Sadie asks. "Anything else that we should know?"

He stares blankly. He's shared more details of his life with Sadie than he'd ever thought possible. Everything she asked, he answered, usually at great length, including responding to all of her follow-up questions and endless inquiries about everything concerning the Splitter Nation.

"I...guess...ahhhhhhh...well, I'd...like to...'pologize...for...my... poor choices." Adam looks up, weary-eyed and broken. "I could've... done better." His head drops with the wisdom of his failures.

Sadie's gut instinct, reinforced once again, leads her to the same conclusion.

"Adam..." she begins, "this is your last meal." He cringes with the confirmation. Sadie hesitates with a long pause. "It's the last food the colony will share with you."

"I'm gonna be starved...to death!" he shrieks while pacing the small quarters.

Sadie shakes her head until he grows calm and sits back down. She gets up, knocks lightly on the door—and as it opens, several boxes and food containers are slid into the room.

"You're not gonna be starved to death," Sadie says, sitting back down. "People aren't supposed to inflict cruelty upon others." She keeps her tone neutral. "We've debated...and we've decided..." She pulls a large box over. "Your fate will depend on the usefulness and accuracy of the information you've provided. Until it can be veri-fied, you're to remain imprisoned here." She opens the box, showing Adam its contents. "You won't be eating from the colony's supplies. I'm leavin' enough food to feed you until I return...next spring. Then, we'll decide what's to become of you."

Adam isn't sure how to respond. He's grateful to learn he won't starve and has an entire year, but the thought of being locked in such a tiny room has him sweating.

"What happens if you don't return?" he asks.

"Better hope I do," is all Sadie offers, while lightly knocking upon the door again.

Gus enters and nods at Sadie. Seeing the supplies she's provided, Gus looks from them to Adam. Enough food to feed one man for a year is a substantial amount. The colony leader is still a little leery of keeping a prisoner for that long, but he agreed to it, and time will tell whether it will be beneficial or not. He hopes so—God, does he hope so!

"Adam," Sadie starts, "in my absence, Gus will take over meeting with you. I hope that you're as forthcoming and honest with him as you were with me. Make sure he doesn't regret this arrangement." She turns to walk out the door.

"Wait," Adam says, standing again. He slowly approaches and reaches out to shake Sadie's hand. "Thank you, Sadie. And...good luck."

With his words, Sadie leaves. She hopes for more than just luck, but her thoughts are cut short by Caleb's approach.

"All ready?" he asks.

Sadie takes one last look around, nods, and heads outside to join the small group that has gathered for her. Most are present to begin a new chapter in their lives, excited at the opportunity to relocate. Others are there to say a final farewell to her and the other travelers. Kind words and warm hugs are exchanged. Then the caravan sets off on the trail to Oceanside, where Sadie's return to Three Sisters will be by boat rather than helicopter.

The journey is hot and slow, especially with all the kids—two *and* four-legged. The young goats, separated from their mothers for the first time, prove difficult to manage. Tied to the back of a cart pulled by a pair of full-grown goats, they've tangled their ropes so badly that the caravan's forced to stop and rearrange the lines.

As for the children, they started off with eager energy, but faded quickly after the initial excitement wore off and the drudgery of heat and constant walking took over. Between bouts of encouragement, regular rest stops, and turns riding on the cart, they've managed; and late into the second day, as the group crests one last slope, the ocean comes into view, brightening their moods.

Auntie T and the other two teachers make a point to excite the children about its presence and point out the seascape's features for the kids. Sadie's vision darts directly to the two Splitter boats anchored just offshore. A shudder runs the length of her spine at thoughts of what occurred upon those yachts. But she smiles for the children.

"Sadie!" one of the Delta men yells, jogging towards the group.

Devon and Dom follow Derrick and join the caravan, greeting everyone and offering help. As the first leg of the journey comes to an end and everyone rests, Sadie finally finds an opportunity to meet privately with Delta Force, who departed days ahead of everyone. She wants updates and specifics on the progress with the boats.

"The Professor's out there now," says Dom. "He's been tinkering with the solar-electric system, but I think he's about done."

"The Captain's boat has been thoroughly searched and inventoried." Devon halts, uncomfortable mentioning all the items Sadie wanted removed from it. "We also took care of...the master stateroom. Everything's ready."

"What about...the *Maji Wanga*?" Sadie asks in a lowered voice.

"Ahhh...no one's really...comfortable going aboard, and workin' out there is...it's just..."

"Hauntingly evil," Sadie finishes.

All three Deltas nod in full agreement and then take turns filling in the details of what's been left or removed from the boats.

"Well, let's get out there before it gets too dark," Sadie says as the guys wrap up their report.

The zodiac zooms toward the yacht Sadie will travel in, but she points to the other and its course is redirected.

Climbing aboard the *Maji Wanga*, the same eeriness lingers, and with each step, Sadie has to force herself to remain calm.

"What's that?" Dominic asks as Sadie retrieves a small pouch from her daypack.

"It's sage, from a friend's garden," she answers, holding up a small bundle of the dried plant. "She gave me this…said it was for just in case…I'm hopin' it'll help."

"What does it do?" asks Derrick.

"It's used to cleanse and purify, and…hopefully…ward off evil." Sadie lights the bundle, washes her hands through its smoke and has all three Deltas do the same.

As the sage's aroma fills the spaces they travel, Sadie silently offers peace to any and all energy that may be present. The torture, cannibalism, and witchcraft that once filled this vessel is still palpable. The Deltas show Sadie a few necessities aboard, but they don't stay long before hastily returning to the zodiac. Making sure to extinguish the remaining sage bundle, Sadie sets what's left aside, to save it for another use. As they tie up to the Captain's boat, the Professor appears ready to depart for shore. He nods to each of the men and awkwardly shakes Sadie's hand.

"I never thanked you," the Professor says, before abruptly turning around and explaining a couple of key features and areas of concern on the vessel.

The Delta boys shrug their shoulders at the Professor's gruffness and follow behind Sadie. He talks rapidly, but Sadie absorbs the information and asks questions for clarity. Her thorough nature impresses the former educator. He wraps up what he feels obligated to do, doesn't say goodbye, and begins to leave, mumbling about checking on the recently repaired desalination equipment back on shore.

"I'm done here," Sadie says quickly, "and…I'd like to look at those repairs."

Sadie's attempt to pause the Professor works. He turns to look at her, nods once, and disembarks. Not far behind the Professor, the second zodiac reaches shore where the Delta crew is instructed to load up the animals and additional cargo. Sadie's excited about securing goats and chickens for Three Sisters and can't wait to see the looks on the faces of Clara and Anna.

"Let the others know that we'll meet briefly as soon as I return," Sadie says, walking off in the same direction as the Professor.

Looking over the operation, Sadie holds her comments to allow the Professor uninterrupted speech, which he finds to be a valuable quality of her demeanor. By the end of his tour and his explanation of the recent repairs, Sadie closely examines the parts—taking notes and measurements, which further intrigues the man. Scribbling additional details, Sadie can tell the Professor isn't exactly sure what to think.

"I've gotta barn full of equipment," she begins. "When I return… there might be some parts I'll be able to find."

"Well…in that case, if you've got any copper tubing, gaskets of various sizes, sheet metal, or tanks…they'd be helpful," the Professor says.

"Anything else?" she adds.

The professor judges whether Sadie's serious or not. "I'll put together a list," he says finally.

Sadie pulls out another small, unused notepad from her daypack and offers it to the Professor, along with a pencil and pen. He takes the items, struck by their newness. He's been out of real paper for years, and down to one last nub of pencil for months.

"Maybe…add to your list more writing materials?" Sadie suggests.

The Professor finds her more and more to his liking, and is surprised with each word.

"Professor, I've got…a considerable amount of resources and the means to survive quite comfortably." She pulls another notebook from her pack. "My father was a self-educated man of incredible talent, and his work…" She composes herself, thinking carefully about her next words. "Well…I believe his work can help here."

Although intrigued by the notebook, his attention stays fixed with Sadie as she talks.

"As I'm sure you know," she continues. "I've supplied quite a bit to the colony, including lots of seed." Finally getting to her point, Sadie makes sure to hold his focus. "The amount of water rations the colony will save due to the relocation effort should provide a larger supply for the garden, which should increase crop yield...maybe even help establish some new ones." She hands over the notebook. "This is a copy of my father's research and his experiments with biofuels. Please examine it and decide, if...the colony may be able to do more than just feed *itself*."

The Professor opens the work and is immediately impressed by its organization and detail. As the sun dips into its final descent, he is so engrossed by the research that he fails to hear Sadie say goodbye or even notice that she's wandered away.

With the relocating group congregated, Sadie reiterates the importance of sustainability and reviews specific guidelines for life at Three Sisters. She reminds everyone that they have a one-year commitment to getting things ready for the possibility of bringing more colony members over and for making sure that those going now are a good fit.

After a year, they may either stay or return to the Yosemite colony. Sadie also offers them a last chance to opt out and tells the small crowd it's not too late if anyone feels they'd prefer to stay. Even though many have concerns and fears, none take the offer; and in the lengthening silence, Sadie finds solace that they're sticking with their decisions.

"Okay, then," she replies, turning her attention toward the youngsters, who have behaved exceedingly well, "Auntie T will lead you to the zodis. You get to go first...and spend the night on the boat!"

The children cheer and squirm with anticipation. As they're escorted, Sadie offers a thanks to the Delta crew, knowing that, once again, they'll take care of matters aboard and have everything situated as directed. Their aid and dependability have been invaluable; she's blessed that they volunteered so quickly to escort the group to Sadie's home—and, then, to take part in the daring rescue mission of the firsties.

As the remaining group disperses, another gathers. All the people stationed at Oceanside, along with the newly appointed security team, arrive. Most of what needs to be addressed has already been shared, but Sadie finds it appropriate to thank them for their efforts and to encourage the work they've undertaken. Noticing the Professor's absence, Sadie begins anyway, talking about the horrifying yacht still lurking off their shore.

"I know you're prepared if there's another attack by sea…and keeping that vessel as bait," she says, nodding in its direction, "although dangerous, may be an incredible advantage…especially for us in the future." She scans the audience. "I want to thank you… again, for all your efforts and say how much I appreciate what you do."

The gathering ends and most people make it a point to talk with Sadie before departing, to express their hope of seeing her again soon. From the corner of her eye, Sadie watches as the Professor approaches from his work station. Without a word, he hands over a list, folded in thirds. Opening the paper, Sadie notices it was folded intentionally to designate three separate spaces for three distinct lists: each labeled and recorded by order of necessity or preference.

"What do you think…Miss Sadie?" the Professor asks, in a slightly sarcastic manner while she stares at the document.

"Very meticulous," she responds without looking up.

"So…can you fill it?"

A wry smile crosses Sadie face. "I'll guess we'll find out."

FIVE

"Any response?" Sadie asks, getting to the fly bridge and joining Delta Team around the captain's helm.

"Yes," Dom replies, handing over a small scrap of paper while Devon monitors and reports the solar charges on the batteries.

Sadie smiles, reading the simple message. Taking the radio controller, she sends a final, brief Morse code. The communication is returned almost instantly; she's not the only one anxious for their safe arrival.

As the fog thickens, the crew's concern of being sighted by passing Splitter vessels is replaced by a fear of miscalculating their position—and running into one of the many sea stacks protruding along the coast of Three Sisters. With yells from port side, the crew navigates safely around the first stack. They drop anchor and wait. Sadie and Caleb board the zodiac for a look around. They maneuver the small harbor mouth and skirt toward the shore.

Sadie and Caleb arrive to waving hands from three natives excited for their return. They tie up along the *Intrepid II*, anchored just off the cliff's edge. Scrambling aboard the former Coast Guard vessel—owned by the young José—they are greeted by a slathering of hugs and questions.

"What happened to your hair?" Anna says, the young girl running a hand through the short mess of what remains on Sadie's head.

"Did you…get stitches?" José asks, a hint of mustache on his upper lip as he peers closer at her forehead after a hearty hug from Caleb.

"And what about this shoulder?" Clara asks. The grey-haired woman breaks from her embrace, sensing that Sadie's guarding her left side.

Sadie shrugs and gives each of them another hug as Caleb offers a brief overview on what happened to Sadie.

"Oooohhhh, child," Clara says, squeezing Sadie's hand. "Later, when we get the chance, you're gonna tell me the whole story…but for now…what do you need us to do?"

After informing them of the number of people waiting just offshore and outlining a strategy, it's decided José will return with Sadie and Caleb to help the new vessel around the sea stack that nearly blocks entry to the small harbor. As the yacht comes into view, the boy gasps. *The Enforcer*?!, his mind says. While in captivity amongst the Splitter Nation, José heard tales about it, about its crew, and about the evil ship that accompanies it.

The men enslaving José threatened more than once to hand him over to the cannibals of the *Maji Wanga*. He can't believe *this* is the vessel they've commandeered. Sadie observes his shock and squeezes José's arm; looking at one another, they know that later, they too, will talk in greater detail.

On board the *Intrepid II*, Sadie introduces him as Captain Gutiérrez. While the little zodiac zooms back and forth with people, José, with pride, explains to the Deltas the procedures and usage of the pole tools he's designed.

As the last of the new arrivals reach the shore of their new home, the captured vessel comes into view. The crowd watches in silence as the boat struggles to circumvent the rocky stack and narrow entrance. It scrapes its port side, and a collective gasp escapes—but the yacht makes it. All cheer.

The entire group gathers on land and introductions are passed around, the mood becoming downright celebratory. The kids, cooped up from a long day at sea, are full of energy and explode with questions that Clara is delighted to answer. Her eyes twinkle, and she smiles with joy as she mingles with the youngsters.

"Yes...those are redwoods. No, the fog's a good thing...the trees can drink it. Yes, that boat's José's. He's the captain. I used to have chickens. Yes..."

"Kids...kids," Sadie interrupts, getting their attention, "slow down. You can't ask Grandma Clara questions all at the same time... okay?" She looks at the old woman and smiles lovingly.

"Okay boss," Caleb interjects, looking to Sadie, "do you want us to finish unloadin' or start settling people in?"

Before Sadie can respond, Clara speaks up. "Let's get everyone to the house. We've got a little surprise." She winks at Anna and José, who dash ahead to lead the group.

As they near the homestead, an old piece of tarp, decorated gloriously as a welcome banner, greets the new arrivals. It hangs between two poles at the head of a recently erected long table, where log rounds are used as chairs; it's set to accommodate everyone. There's just enough room to dine for a first meal together, and the food is plentiful. A huge pot of quail stew full of fresh garden vegetables, several loaves of bread, lemonade, and enough fruit for everyone to get his or her own apple or pear cover the table. Before they start, Clara asks everyone to join hands and offers a prayer.

"Lord, thank you for this wonderful day and for the food we are about to share with our new friends and family. Let it nourish our bodies...strengthen our souls...and bring us together in the joys of life... Amen." The old woman opens her eyes and begins by serving the kids.

Small talk buzzes amongst the crowd; and as the meal winds down, Sadie nods to Clara, José, and Anna, thanking them for their efforts. Standing, she addresses the group, reminding everyone that there's much to do. She begins delegating various duties and assigning temporary sleeping quarters.

Delta Force will stay aboard the *Intrepid II* and is responsible for unloading what remains on the *Enforcer* and guarding the harbor. She sends them with José, who's anxious to return and examine the hybrid engine on the captured yacht. He got a quick look at it earlier but wants to fully explore the functionality of its solar-charged electric system, and the efficiency of its fuel design.

The children, led by Clara, accompany the three teachers on their way to Anna's family campsite where they'll remain until other accommodations can be arranged. One of the colony's former animal tenders and a young garden hand help Anna get the goats and chickens situated, while Sadie escorts two middle-aged brothers, Cameron, and a couple expecting their first child, all around the homestead.

As dusk nears, Clara returns to join Sadie and Anna, so they can speak privately. A lot is happening and it's important for them to agree on what needs to be done. Sadie shares news of the recent Splitter activity: of their foul plan to create child soldiers, and of the importance of keeping the harbor diligently guarded. She tells them of the camaraderie and trust she's developed with the Delta guys. Overcome with emotion, Clara repeatedly gushes gratitude on Sadie for relocating the colony's orphans.

"I thought we'd divide their time between here and your place?" Sadie starts. "We could have the brothers build a bunkhouse...and a small school room up near your orchard."

Smiling, the old woman loves the idea.

Sadie turns to Anna. "How do you feel about it? Can the kids grow up around your family's campsite and home?"

Anna appreciates being part of the decision-making process; she nods, knowing whatever Sadie and Clara think is best.

"Okay, then, what about Sofia and Alberto?" Are you comfortable with them living in your place?"

The young girl nods again, thinking about a baby being born in her home and a family living there. She still struggles with the loss of her parents, but the excitement of new people, goats, and of course, the chickens—which she adores immensely—provide necessary distraction for the mourning child. Sadie and Clara reinforce the understanding that the homestead is, and always will be, Anna's, and that when she's ready, she'll live there again.

As for Rika, the garden hand, she'll return with Clara to help grow food. Trew and his long dreads will stay at Anna's, taking care of the animals and working to gradually increase their numbers to supply the island's growing population. The women talk in length about the brothers, whose background in construction made them an obvious choice for relocation; they'll move from site to site, building what's needed. The ladies discuss structures, building materials, and where to begin.

"What about...the...quiet lady?" Anna asks timidly. "Where will she stay?"

Clara is also curious about Sadie's choice. All the others seem very clear choices, but this woman's disposition doesn't quite fit.

"Her name's Cameron...she's survived years of Splitter brutality." Sadie shakes her head, saddened by what the woman's endured. "I offered her refuge...she'll live near the tail, keeping an eye-out, but...until then I'd like to station her at the helicopter clearing."

Without divulging specific details or breaking confidentiality, Sadie informs Anna and Clara of the deal she made with Cameron. She explains the role the newcomer took in ending the first Nation attack on the Yosemite colony. While they listen, Sadie also speaks of Adam, the captured Splitter being held at the colony, and all the information gained from him. Carefully leading them, Sadie's not sure whether they're ready to hear that she'll be leaving again, but before she gets to the news, the women are interrupted by a throaty sound. Looking up, they notice Caleb standing and smiling nearby.

"Back at it again, huh?" he asks. "It's nice to see the sisters reunited."

Clara gives him a big hug. "And it's nice to have you back." She breaks from their embrace and gives him a look that evokes curiosity.

"What?" he asks.

"Sadie tells us…you're the one…that named our island?" Clara hesitates, making Caleb feel maybe he overstepped his bounds, but then, her huge smile reappears. "Three Sisters is perfect. I love it," she says, giving him another warm hug.

"I like it, too," Anna chimes in.

"Well…" he starts, looking directly at Sadie, "everything's set for the night, so…" He stalls, wondering if Sadie has thought about his sleeping arrangements, hoping she wants him near. "Will you ladies… be…turnin' in soon?"

"We won't be too much longer," Sadie replies, anxious to return to the conversation he interrupted. "But there're a few things we still need to cover."

"Okay, then, I'll be…on the boat…with José." Caleb stares at the ladies. "See ya…in the morning."

They offer 'goodnights,' and as he walks away, Clara smiles sideways at Sadie, who ignores her look while attempting to get back to what she's intended for the evening. She starts by sharing additional details from Adam and the ghastly knowledge that, before the two Splitter yachts attacked the colony's Oceanside camp, they delivered a group of kids.

"We confiscated a detailed map of everywhere their boats explored. There's an island not too far south of here…the remnants of Big Sur, where they're settin' up…" Sadie halts, interrupted by a question.

"Big Sur? Was that a city?" Anna asks, unfamiliar with the name.

"At one time it was an absolutely…breathtaking scenic part of the California coast," Clara answers, with fond memories of her early days spent hiking and exploring the area with her husband.

Sadie continues. "Only a small part of it remains…south of the Bixby Bridge, its ruins, but…that's where the Splitters landed and took over. From what we know…they've captured or killed all the people livin' there and…took control of the local water source. They're planning to relocate their highest-ranking officers there…and…build an army of firsties. When the boats left, they were supposed to communicate any new discoveries, and continue…hunting for more… kids… but we stopped 'em…and right now, the Nation has no knowledge of it."

Clara looks at Sadie, connecting the dots. "And, so… what are your intentions?" she asks, not sure if she really wants to know.

"Well…I thought…for the next three nights, we'd meet…make sure everything's set…get the new folks settled…"

"Three nights?" Anna interrupts.

Sadie looks at Clara and reads the look in her eyes. "Because…" she begins, looking back at Anna, "after that…I'm taking the *Enforcer*… along with the Delta Team, and…we're gonna rescue those kids!"

Anna, stricken with fear, clasps Clara's hand. "No! You just got here! You can't leave us again!"

Clara nods in agreement, worried for Sadie's safety.

"I know I just got back, but…we can't leave the kids. We've captured two Splitter vessels and…I think we're meant to use them."

"But it's not safe," Anna begs. "And what happens if you don't make it back this time?"

Sadie wraps Anna in a hug. "Kiddo, I'll be back. It'll be okay, I promise."

"Sadie Mae Larkin," Clara says, almost scolding. "That's not a promise you can make and you know it. Anything can happen out there."

"You're right, but…we've got the advantage of surprise. They'll never expect an attack from one of their own vessels, and right now the base is mostly empty…there's only a few of them, but they're preparing for the arrival of more. If we don't act now, the kids will be lost forever, and…eventually more Splitters will come."

"I still don't like it," the matriarch declares.

"Me neither," adds Anna.

"I'm not overly fond of it, either, but…we're in a position to help, and…we should. Someone needs to stop 'em." Sadie grows quiet, knowing she's given them too much to contemplate.

They stand in silence for another minute before Clara suggests they return to the house. It's grown dark and there's a lot to do tomorrow.

As they walk, Sadie attempts to lighten the mood by shifting the conversation towards the new chickens and goats, but it doesn't have the effect she hopes for—worry about the rescue mission hangs heavy over them all.

SIX

Before sunup a blur of activity envelops the homestead and its surrounding property. Excited by a new day in a new place, people bustle about starting their morning chores and duties, preparing for the work that lies ahead. Sadie checks in on it all, moving from group to group while Clara and Anna prepare the morning meal. As Rika joins them to help with the food, the conversation shifts to gardening. The new arrival is anxious to learn the techniques the old woman employs—in particular, her homespun version of aquaponics that Sadie brags so much about. As their discussion deepens, Sadie leaves them to hike to the homestead's campsite.

"Saaaay-deee! Luna yells, running wildly.

She leaps into Sadie's arms, gets spun around and set back on the ground. The rest of the children gather, bouncing with energy and full of questions. When Auntie T and the other teachers join them, the entire group starts the hike down for breakfast. Luna never leaves Sadie's side, even during the morning meal, and only breaks away when it's time for the kids to return to camp for their lessons. With the children gone, Sadie reiterates the day's agenda to the adults before she meets briefly with Caleb and the Deltas.

"After lunch, I'll join you aboard the *Enforcer*, I want an update on weapons and ammo…plus a current status report. Make sure the damage from getting in here isn't serious, and start getting everything departure ready." Sadie motions to José, who sits nearby listening. "Join 'em and check everything out…thoroughly," she adds, knowing the boy hoped for the opportunity. "Make any needed repairs and fill me in later."

José nods. As they leave, he leads, feeling for the first time like one of the men.

Sitting off to the side and waiting patiently, Cameron finishes her drink and moves over to Sadie. "I'm ready whenever you are," she says, anxious to be back on her own.

"Grab the two boxes by the backdoor, get your gear, and meet me in twenty minutes…by the quad." Sadie looks to Anna as she cleans up from the meal. "Make that thirty."

As Cameron walks away, Sadie helps Anna carry the remaining items back to the house, where Clara has already begun preparations for the mid-day meal. The old woman smiles as they approach, grabs three mugs, and pours them each a cup of tea.

"It's so nice to have you home," Clara says, squeezing Sadie's hand as they sit together at the table.

Clara says no more. But the undercurrent of worry lingers from the previous evening's discussion regarding Sadie's plan to leave again. Tonight, they'll reconvene to talk further about the rescue mission, but for now the ladies stick with the day's plans and on which steps should be taken next. As they wrap up, Sadie leaves to find Cameron, who paces nervously while waiting.

They load the quad and within minutes are driving off the homestead toward the helicopter clearing. Along the way, Sadie points out features, making sure Cameron recognizes the route to Anna's family campsite and the cutover to the Memorial Campground. She instructs Cameron to explore the vicinity and shows her where to patrol while guarding the island's lone air-accessible location.

At the clearing, Sadie teaches Cameron how to gather water using the condensation collectors designated for the area. The independent woman is shown in detail how to use them before Sadie issues her one of the handguns stored on site. As Sadie hands over additional ammunition, she talks about protocol for a possible attack by air.

Finally noticing the look upon Cameron's face, Sadie stops mid-sentence. The woman's look hangs somewhere between utter disbelief, unprecedented sorrow, and a heightened sense of responsibility. Turning the gun over in her hands, Cameron realizes Sadie's stopped talking and is staring at her.

Cameron stares blankly at the gun before finding her voice. "No one's ever...given me a weapon..." She thinks of all the times she wished she had one.

"Well..." Sadie begins, realizing it's a rite of passage for Cameron, "as a member of Three Sisters and one of our first...guardians, we not only welcome you, but...put trust in you to protect our homes, our families, and our friends." Sadie shakes Cameron's hand. The gesture makes it all the more official, and finalizes the call to duty it invokes for the newcomer.

For the remaining part of morning, Sadie makes sure Cameron knows: what resources are available in the area, what animals can be hunted within the recently established limits, and how to care for her firearm. Before leaving, Sadie also shares her intentions to rescue the kidnapped children from the new Splitter base. Cameron listens, enrapt. Her anger boils with hatred of the Nation, and she finds herself offering to help with the mission.

"No, but thank you," Sadie replies, again validated by bringing Cameron to Three Sisters. "We need you here, to keep watch, or...as back-up at the harbor." Sadie stands tall and bold. "Three Sisters... will never fall to the Nation." Her words resonate between them. Nothing more needs to be said.

Sadie departs the clearing on the quad. As its noise fades away, leaving only the sounds of nature, Cameron opens the box that Sadie left. She examines the supplies rationed for her. There's more food than she expected, a set of new clothes that includes a jacket, one solar-powered inflatable light, and a box of matches. Her eyes grow huge. *No way! Tampons and toilet paper!* She's surprised to be gifted commodities of such rare existence. Reorganizing the box's contents with care, she finds a short, handwritten note attached to the back flap:

Dear Cameron,

We didn't get the chance to speak in person and I want to welcome you to our growing family.

Until recently, I lived all alone in these woods and knew nothing of the changed world and the evils of the Splitter Nation. Knowing of them now, and finding people who have survived and endured against all odds reinforces my belief that there's a higher calling—and a journey that still lies ahead for all of us.

May your path, wherever it takes you, at times cross mine so we may grow to know one another, and one day, call each other friend.

My home is always open,

Clara

After the third reading, Cameron refolds the letter and places it snugly with her belongings. She sits quietly along the edge of the open space, under a grove of redwoods. The trees, stretching far overhead, add to Cameron's sense of calm security, which is a curious and new sensation. The ground, covered by decades of fallen duff and accentuated by huge deer ferns, patches of sorrel, and swaths of giant three-leafed trilliums, intensify the emotions of the experience. Surrounded in solitude, supplied, housed, given a means and a way to protect herself, Cameron lies back, staring into the forest's canopy, and smiles like she hasn't done in a very long time.

Sadie, too, ponders life's changes. Driving the quad toward the campsite to visit the children, she realizes she's embarking on an entirely new time of her life. The days of hiding her existence and surviving solo are long gone, replaced with new responsibilities and greater consequences. Her home, the island of Three Sisters, and her life, suddenly have meaning and purpose. *Is this my destiny?*

Sadie can't help but think of her father, realizing none of this would be possible without him. His insistent planning, preparations, and intuition not only provided enough for her to survive over a decade alone, but also supplied a foundation of support that's already making a difference in the lives of others. Pulling into the campsite atop the cliff, Sadie wishes her dad were here to see it and help them along. Within seconds, kids—curious as to what's in the giant box being unloaded—surround her.

"Your teachers will show you when it's time," Sadie says, trying to placate the children and give the three women in charge of the youngsters better leverage. "As for now...shouldn't all of you be in your lessons?" Sadie looks to the two ladies still sitting from where the children had run. "Go on now, back to school," she prompts as Auntie T approaches from the other direction.

"I didn't expect you yet," Auntie T says, giving Sadie a hand. "Everything okay?"

Sadie smiles yes, and they work together to move the box.

"I have additional supplies...back at my place, but these should help until I can retrieve them," Sadie says, opening the top flap for Auntie T to look in.

Without any warning, the aged teacher wraps Sadie in a giant hug and just as quickly, releases her and begins examining the box's contents.

Sadie talks only briefly with her before wandering over to where the two brothers have begun working. Though middle-aged, the men are strong and labor as if in their prime, grinding away on their tasks. Veins bulge from muscular forearms and biceps thick from years of hard manual labor, throbbing as they supply blood for exertion. Seeing Sadie approach, the men wave in greeting.

"Hey, boss," the oldest says, adapting the lingo he overheard from Caleb. "Yer just in time...we got a couple questions for ya."

Looking at his brother, Lucas smiles at hearing him call a woman boss. Before the Tri-nami, the two of them ran one of the largest contracting businesses in the Bay Area—a group dominated by machismo. Red, his big brother, had been the most aggressive of all, the only one ever called "boss." The humility of survival and the opportunity to relocate have both men genuinely appreciating and trusting Sadie.

The growing sense of community and the importance of the role they're playing also reinforce their new outlook. Sadie clarifies why they need to build so many extra sleeping platforms for the kids so quickly. She transitions to telling them of the mission to save the firsties, and the need for the brothers to guard the harbor in Delta Force's absence.

"Whatever you need, boss," says Red as he motions to Lucas. "You can count on us."

Driving away in the quad and returning to the homestead, Sadie quickly checks back with Clara and Anna before leaving for the harbor. There, José reports findings, voices concerns, and asks for directions on how to proceed with the confiscated yacht. Sadie appreciates his professionalism; she is once again proud of the growing maturity and well-roundedness of the young man.

Since her trip to the Yosemite colony, José has taken on an even greater role at Three Sisters, and the responsibility suits him well. Sadie could swear he's also taller and, with regular meals and manual labor, José has definitely begun to thicken up. He's no longer the scrawny, beaten kid she first met, but a young man who is confident, capable, and a valuable resource.

With Caleb and the Deltas joining them, José shows Sadie the damage along the port side where the *Enforcer* scraped against the sea stack when navigating the tricky harbor entrance. The damage is formidable but only cosmetic and does nothing to weaken the integrity of the vessel. After a thorough dialogue about the errors they made and the steps to prevent them from occurring again, they sit to discuss the mission.

Weapons is first on the agenda. They talk about which guns will be designated for the harbor and homestead security and which will accompany them to the Isle of Big Sur, where they expect to encounter a small faction of Splitters. Sadie shares all the pertinent intel gained during her sessions with Adam—whose fate depends on their success—and outlines possible scenarios they may encounter. José learns that, once again, he'll be staying behind. He's assigned, with the brothers, to protect the harbor and keep the *Intrepid II* ready—in case things fail and he has to mount a rescue.

"You're gettin' us out of the harbor, though," Sadie says, knowing José had hoped to be on the front lines. "Once safely out, we'll drop you off with the zodiac. Until then, keep monitoring the tides and get this vessel sea-ready."

He nods, confirming his orders.

"Start with these." Sadie hands him two boxes, watches him depart, and turns to address the Delta Team and Caleb.

Sadie explains the radio charade that she and José pulled off when they first met, how they managed to stage a radio malfunction to trick the Nation that they were one of their ranks. A similar strategy will be needed for this voyage, and a discussion ensues on their approach being noticed. More than likely, the guards at the watchtower will make radio contact because of the boat's unscheduled arrival. If, by some chance, they go unnoticed on approach, then the plan is to sneak ashore, paddling the zodiac. Either way, carefully scripted radio dialogues and actions will reduce risk.

As the afternoon lengthens and minds grow weary, Sadie ends the session, reminding the men that they have one more day to finalize plans. She reiterates what they've accomplished so far, and everyone leaves for the evening meal with clear images of what they may encounter on the mission.

Yet, Caleb's doubts build as he walks alongside Sadie. She hasn't fully recovered from her previous injuries and the chance of worse harm lay ahead. As they near the homestead, he pulls her aside.

"You guys go ahead," Caleb says, when the others halt, "we'll catch up."

The men move ahead, eager for a meal. Following Caleb, Sadie thinks she knows what's coming. Tucked around a redwood tree, he stops and, remaining still, says nothing while attempting to control his heartbeat and breathing. Sadie defends their plan, her involvement, and the worthiness of risk.

Caleb can listen no longer. He moves toward her and pulls her to him with strong arms. He kisses her open lips with his before nibbling her neck. He returns his mouth to hers, his lips and his heart hungry. Sadie's fire ignites, her body responding with heat and desire. She devours his lips as he pins her against the tree.

"If something happens to you," he says with heavy breath, "I couldn't live with myself."

"Caaaay...leeeb," she manages between gasps.

Hearing his name enflames the man as he begins another onslaught of biting and kissing. Sadie is breathless, wanting, but she summons the strength to place a hand on his chest and push him away.

"Cay-leb."

He leans his forehead to hers. "Yesssss," he stammers, before returning his lips to her neck.

"Please..." she begs, newly distracted, "pleeeeeeeease...stop." His mouth breaks away momentarily, but when he sees Sadie's flushed skin, he leans in again. She places her hand in front of his mouth, and as he kisses her palm, Sadie regains control of the situation.

"Caleb," she says, fighting the sensations traveling her spine and burning between her legs, "this isn't...an appropriate time."

"You wanna wait until later?"

"No, that's not what I mean," Sadie says, fixing her clothes and straightening her hair.

"What then?" he asks, seeing Sadie regaining her normal, controlled state.

"There's too much going on. We can't afford any...distractions."

"Huh?" is all he manages, at a loss by her sudden change.

"The rescue mission. We're already taking too many risks and I...I mean...we...we need to stay focused."

"Ohhh...I'm focused all right." He moves closer.

"I mean it, Caleb!"

Sadie's tone and body language warn him not to push.

Discombobulated but still aroused, Caleb wants another attempt at changing her mind. But he reconsiders. *At least she didn't downright reject me...she felt something too.* Still, he can't help himself.

"Are you sure?" he asks, finally, taking her hand to lightly bite between her thumb and index finger.

"Yeeesss," she says, barely in control and pulling her hand away from the enticing tingle. "Come on...let's get to dinner."

"That's not what I'm hungry for." His eyes penetrate hers.

"Caleb," Sadie states plainly.

"Oh, alright," he mutters, knowing she's not going to budge. "But I'm gonna be thinkin' 'bout you...all night."

Sadie suppresses the effect of Caleb's sincerity and passion as she leads them back to the others. Together, they join the group at the table, where most have already begun eating. Caleb sits next to Sadie. She feels his presence and tries to conceal it with small talk directed at others. At the end of the meal, when just about everyone is gone, Caleb leans over to pick up Sadie's dishes and hesitates, hovering close.

"If you change your mind," he whispers near her ear, "you know where to find me."

Clara's eyes sparkle, and Sadie knows the old woman would love to talk with her about what she, alone, just witnessed—but not giving her the chance, Sadie stands, finishes cleaning up for the evening, and retreats to the house. When both Clara and Anna join her, they sit for their evening discussion.

"There's lots to cover, so let's get right to it," Sadie begins, looking straight at Clara, making sure the old woman gets the message.

Clara's eyes yearn for a story, but she understands the importance of what faces them and drops it, for now. Sadie, growing into her role as leader, gives directives and sets timelines. But she finds a certain, creeping nervousness set in. She takes a deep breath, then begins with worst-case scenarios.

SEVEN

"There, that's it!" Sadie points at the remains of what was once the iconic bridge of the Big Sur coast.

The concrete arches and spans of the Bixby Bridge lie in ruins beneath the ocean. Only the landmass to the south exists, where two protruding sections of the structure sit just above sea level. Using her binoculars, she scans the small watchtower. *Exactly where Adam said it would be.* The timing of their arrival with the setting sun was designed to put a glare in the eyes of any lookouts on shore, but the hazy, overcast sky doesn't do the trick; the boat's radio crackles to life.

"This is Split post IBS...you're entering protected waters. Identify yourself."

A long pause ensues as the crew waits for Sadie's command. At her signal, a single, extended static response is transmitted.

"Incoming vessel, this is Split post IBS, identify yourself...I repeat...identity yourself."

Sadie orders her crew to respond with broken segments of static. They slow their speed, coming into a position to anchor near a smaller boat already moored.

"Splitter post Isle of Big Sur..." The voice trails off as a better view of the vessel comes into sight, offering the speaker recognition. "Splitter post IBS, hailing the *Enforcer*...Is that you Cap'in?"

Sadie nods, and on request, the *Enforcer's* radio emits more static, followed by a few, broken, and carefully selected words that hint at radio malfunction.

"Repeat, *Enforcer*. You're breakin' up. Repeat...you're breakin' up."

Continuing the same static-based reply, Sadie and her crew eye each other nervously. They don't know if they'll be boarded or ordered ashore. Sadie closes her eyes and silently offers a prayer.

"Split post IBS to *Enforcer*, we're not receiving your radio transmissions. Sound horn once if you hear us."

Sadie responds with the vessel's foghorn.

"Alright, *Enforcer*, send over your zodi, we'll debrief here. Split post IBS out."

Going ashore isn't the option they hoped for, but at least they've maintained an element of surprise; so far, the Splitters have no idea what's coming. Sadie nods to Caleb and Dominic who take up their positions on the small craft. According to their intel, they expect anywhere from two to five men to be stationed at the post's tower. Maneuvering the zodiac, Sadie hopes their Splitter disguises prolong the deception as long as possible. As they near the massive concrete chunks of the former bridge, riddled with rusted and twisted rebar, a single guard greets them at the roughly constructed dock.

"Where's da Cap?" he yells. "And where the fuck is the *Maji Wanga*? You two break up or sumpin'?" Laughing at his own joke, he catches the rope Dominic tosses him.

As he secures the small craft to the dock, Dom leaps up and over the zodiac's side. He thrusts the tip of his knife into the man's side while simultaneously confiscating the guard's firearm. Still holding the length of rope, Dom turns the man to a position that limits the view from the post tower, elevated nearly thirty yards away.

"What...the fuck!" the Splitter groans loudly, blood dripping from his side.

Dominic presses harder with the knife. "You make any more noise and I'll bury this blade, understand?"

Sadie takes over, speaking in a deeper voice than her own to match her male disguise. She nods, gesturing to the watch post. "How many more men are in there?"

"Fuck you."

"That's not an answer we appreciate." Dom repositions his weapon against the man's crotch, the blade cutting through his pants and making contact with flesh.

"Okay! Okay! There's only two of us," the Splitter squeals, rising to his tiptoes, attempting to gain a little distance between the knife and his 'delicates.'

"You sure?" Dominic asks, not releasing any of the pressure he's applying.

"Yeeessss."

"Where's your radio?" Sadie asks. "Why aren't you carrying one?"

"Broken. I dropped it."

"So, what's protocol if you can't radio?" Sadie looks back at the tower before returning her icy glare.

"I'm supposed to bring ya up."

"You sure?" Dominic presses harder. "No all-clear signal?"

"Noooaaahhh," he responds in a rising pitch.

"Alright then," Sadie says. "Let's move."

Sadie and Caleb turn around, senses alert while walking side by side. At their heels follows Dom, controlling the nervous Splitter, who keeps looking to the tower, debating if he should yell. As if reading his mind, Dom's knife—pressed out of sight behind the man's lower back—draws blood, and the Splitter's concerns return to his well-being as they trudge up the incline near the watch post's structure.

At the base, a pile of stacked rubble elevates the view and creates a foundation for the lookout up top. Chunks of concrete debris serve as steps; the first piece they climb, though chipped and cracked, still reads '1932' to commemorate the year the bridge was completed.

Before they reach the top, a second Splitter appears. Caleb responds double time up the remaining few steps. He tackles the guard to the ground just inside the doorway. Sadie follows in case another man lurks inside. Finding the room empty of more Splitters, Sadie turns her attention toward Caleb's struggle—only to find he's ended the battle.

The captive Splitter, still under Dom's control, can't fathom what he's just witnessed. Lying on the floor in a pool of his own blood is the friend he was joking with just moments ago. The color drains from his face.

"Here," Sadie grunts, opening a small bag slung over her shoulder, "use that chair."

The prisoner lands with a thud on the seat. Caleb and Dominic use a roll of duct tape to secure him. Fearing for his life, the man knows he'll say anything to escape death.

Sadie addresses Caleb, maintaining her deepened voice. "Get the rest of our gear and signal the others." Turning to Dominic: "Check the bunker...expect it manned."

Before leaving with their orders, both men check to confirm it's clear. Using the lengthening dusk for cover, Caleb and Dominic depart, allowing Sadie to begin her interrogation. Dressed as a man with hair sheared short and—knowing the Splitter before her played a direct role in child abduction and abuse—Sadie's male persona rears its ugly head. Pacing back and forth, her rage intensifies. She addresses the captive with such force that he nearly falls over in the chair.

"The kids," she growls through a fierce glare. "Where are they!?"

Uncertain whether answering will change what seems an ill-fated outcome, the bound Splitter looks for help. His hesitation infuriates Sadie further. She reacts and thrusts the blade between his legs, cutting through his pants just deep enough to scratch the skin below.

"Okay! Okay! They're locked up."

"Where?"

"Inland from the old lighthouse."

Sadie's glare doesn't soften.

"Follow the path," he stammers, "just over a mile or so."

Caleb returns, signaling his presence before entering. He hands Sadie her bow and moves outside to cover them. She digs in her bag, deepening the captive's worries. To his relief, it's a notebook and pen she withdraws. Flipping to the first page, Sadie moves closer to him. Displaying an accurate map of the area and the Splitter holdings, Sadie demands details about the locals.

He looks at his dead friend. "Urrrrrrr jus gonna kill me anyways...after I tell ya what ya want...aren't ya?"

"What's to become of you," Sadie spits, yanking a handful of his hair to stare directly into his eyes, "is still to be decided. But...it's gonna start with you...answerin'...me."

He swallows in thought before speaking softly. "Yeah, a couple of 'em are still alive."

"How many?" Sadie holds out the map of the island. "And where are they being held?"

Holding Caleb at gunpoint, three men storm in! Their firearms versus her blade isn't a fight Sadie can win and she knows it. On demand, she drops the knife. Pushing panic away, she focuses on details, and the individual nuances of each man she must defeat.

"We heard the foghorn and thought we'd come a little early," one of the men says while guarding Sadie.

"En good thing cuz...we found this fucker lurkin' about," his buddy says, shoving Caleb to the ground.

"There's another! He left for the bunker!" screams the Splitter duct taped to the chair. "Get me out ah here, already! And someone go check!"

One of the men runs down the steps while another unties his buddy. The guard hovering over Caleb keeps his eye on Sadie as he mentions communicating with command. While the man is distracted, Caleb lunges for the radio and smashes it against the floor. Pieces of it scatter as he, too, falls to the floor after a blow to the head leaves him unconscious.

"Fucking shit!" yells the man as Sadie strikes.

She knocks the weapon from his hands. But before Sadie can reach the gun, another is pressed into the back of her head.

"I don't think so, asshole!" accompanies a kick to Sadie's leg that knocks her down.

Sadie scrambles to a standing position just as the gun's barrel is pressed into her temple.

"Put that fucker in this chair," yells the Splitter as he uses his hands to yank off the remaining duct tape from around his ankles. Standing up, he coldcocks Sadie just above the jaw. "Now it's my turn to ask the questions."

Sadie falls to the floor, fighting to remain conscious. Explosions of white flash in her vision and her hearing fades in and out.

"Get 'im in the chair!" the freed Splitter commands as the other two drag Sadie over and toss her into it.

Landing hard, Sadie's head rolls to one side; it takes her full effort to remain cognizant. Slumping further into the chair, she succumbs, the urge to vomit suddenly overtaking her. She tucks her feet around the chair's legs while tensing all her muscles and inhaling deeply as she leans forward while they bind her to the chair.

"Look at dat fucker," jokes one of the others, "you knocked 'im silly. Look," he lifts Sadie's chin as her eyes roll about, "Hell-lo-o." He lets go, and her chin drops.

All three of the militants laugh as Sadie attempts to focus her eyes and keep her head lifted—but the pain radiating from her jaw and piercing the forefront of her brain make it difficult. Leaning back into the chair, Sadie assesses her circumstance. Bound to a chair, Caleb lying unconscious, and with no sign of Dom, Sadie knows things are bad.

"Go see what's taking so long at the bunker," says the Splitter who punched Sadie. "I'll work on this one," he adds with sinister glee, fingering the knife she threatened him with earlier.

As one of the men leaves, the Splitter holding the knife drags the blade across Sadie's thigh. He stops the blade and hesitates with it between her legs.

"Should we...get the Commander?" asks his cohort.

"No, not yet...let's wait for the others to return. Besides, I got a score to settle." He laughs, scratches his chin, and returns his attention back to Sadie.

Her pain intensifies as he grabs a handful of hair, forcing her head back so he can place his blade along her neck.

"Tell me," the knife tracing from one side to the other, "how did such a young, little runt like you...end up here and in charge?"

Sadie's eyes roll into the back of her head.

"You hear me!" he shouts, her lack of reaction disgusting him. He shoves Sadie's head forward, sending another bout of flashing lights. He repeatedly snaps his fingers in front of her face; then, he slaps her with the back of his hand, drawing blood at her lip.

Sadie remains unresponsive, her eyes close.

"Wake the fuck up!" he screams, smacking her again with his other hand.

Sadie's head falls over her opposite shoulder, but her eyes remain closed.

EIGHT

"Go fill these!" the angered Splitter hollers, pacing about the watch-tower and kicking at two buckets stacked in the corner.

His comrade looks to the buckets and begins to move, but is hesitant to leave.

"Hurry the fuck up!"

The Splitter jumps to, picks up the buckets and walks out to fill them—leaving Sadie one less ignorant militant asshole to deal with. Tracking his movements with focused, intentional listening, she keeps her head motionless while manipulating a hidden implement sewn into her sleeve's cuff. She'd stealthily tucked the shirt's material into the palm of her left hand while they were being duct taped together behind her back.

Her minute manipulations go unnoticed. Making progress, sloshing water signals the return of the other man. A face full of cold water quickly follows; the salty sea liquid stings her bloody lip and the broken skin above her jaw line.

"If this bastard doesn't wake up, I'm just gonna kill 'im!"

More water explodes on Sadie's face, and she can't hold from moving her head slightly. It's enough to catch the Splitter's attention and, sitting upon the overturned bucket, the irate one faces Sadie.

He snaps his fingers repeatedly. "Wake up!" Sadie opens and closes her eyes.

"You better keep them eyes open!" He stands, placing the knife's blade edge along her neckline. "Youuuuuuu hear me! Open yer eyes!"

Sadie blinks several times, and staring blankly, opens them part-way. With an evil smile, he returns to his overturned bucket while watching his captive's eyes roll.

"Go keep watch," he says, without taking his focus off Sadie. "I got this one." Then, he gets to business. "I'm asking questions…and you better make damn sure to answer." He scoots the bucket closer, toying with the blade in his hand, then taps it against Sadie's nose. "Let's start with the *Enforcer*, and how *you*…managed gettin' it?"

Sadie blinks several times and rolls her head to one side.

"I said," he kicks her bound leg, "how'd you get that boat!"

Attempting to clear her throat and reclaim a masculine voice, Sadie mutters a few undecipherable syllables. He kicks again.

"Ayeeeee...twooooooooook...it," she stammers with difficulty.

He laughs. "Listen, you little pussy...there's no way a little runt fuck like you could take that vessel...let alone the men aboard, 'specially da Cap."

"Weeellll...I did," Sadie reiterates, straining to glare with unfocused eyes. "And ain't no...mo'," she blinks a couple of times, "of you...bastards comin' here, cuzzz...I stopped da *En-forc-er.*" A slight smile escapes from the corners of her mouth.

"Oh...you think you stopped this. You think you made a difference." He stands, raising his voice, "You smug little piece of shit." He strikes Sadie with the back of his hand, re-bloodying her lip. "You haven't stopped shit. More are comin'. We 'spect new arrivals any day."

Sadie moves her tongue around her bottom lip as the metallic tinge of blood fills her mouth.

"Not smiling anymore, are ya?" He retrieves her notebook, returns to his seat, and places the tip of the blade into Sadie's thigh. "So, what 'bout this?" he says, waving the pages in front of her face.

Her eyes move slowly from the papers to his face where they hover in study. He reads easily. Looking at what's being held, she sits up straighter, adjusting her legs to do so.

"It's a map, genius."

"I know it's a map, asshole!" he yells, and hits her with the notebook. "I wanna know how you got it...en what yer plan is!"

Sadie feeds his rage. "I'm takin' over...and savin' the kids."

"Oh, you think so!" He stands, leaning close to her face. "You're not doing shit tied to that chair. You think you know everythin', you smug little fuck!"

He strikes her again. As Sadie spits out a mouthful of blood, he laughs, proud of the result.

"You better give me sum details...like how'd all this was su'pose to happen?"

Sadie stalls, spitting more blood. Straightening up further, she adjusts her body and answers. "Easy...wipe out...you guards here... hit the barracks, finish off the Commander and...release the kids."

"Easy, huh? You couldn't even get the first part." He laughs at the audacity of the plan. "En you think you could take on almost half a platoon...and the Commander...even if you did make it past us, you wouldn't stand a chance against the Mighty 9...her pack of killers would tear you up in a second."

"Well...I'mmmmmm...not...done," Sadie says, her eyes focused.

The man takes Sadie's bait. "You'll be lucky to survive the night. I've got all the way til sun up wit you." He reinserts the tip of his blade into her opposite thigh. "So, you'd better wipe...that look off yer face."

Sadie squirms, adjusting the newly inflicted leg as his smile grows.

"That's wha' I thought," he says, feeling confident and in control, "So...where were we?" The blade moves from Sadie's leg, alternating between his hands as he toys with it. "I think you were gonna tell me 'bout this." He motions to the notebook.

"I already told you, I'm takin' over," Sadie snaps in a deep, aggressive voice.

His anger builds. "The fuck you are!"

He swipes the blade several times across Sadie's chest and abdomen, cutting through several layers of clothing. Yanking away some of the shredded mess reveals a bottom layer of material tightly wrapped around Sadie's torso, used to hide her female curves.

"Wha' the fuck! You're nutin' but ah...bitch!"

"Finally figured that one out, did ya?" Sadie says, mockingly, in her normal voice.

He lunges at her in a full-blown rage, but Sadie ducks sideways. She pulls a razor blade from her cuff and forcefully drives her arms forward and up, slicing his jugular. Blood sprays everywhere. She cuts the tape around her ankles. Escaping the chair, she grabs the blade he dropped and finishes the job by burying it hilt deep into the man's chest.

With her immediate threat eliminated, Sadie's focus turns to the Splitter somewhere outside on guard. She crouches, ready to pounce, but nothing moves. When no one enters, Sadie slides over to Caleb, still laying where he fell.

"Caleb...Caleb," she whispers, shaking his torso while keeping her eyes on the door.

Blood, seeping from a gash on the side of his head, in its initial stage of coagulation, draws Sadie's attention. After checking the wound, she grabs the duffle bag, rummages through it, and quickly cleans the site before hastily bandaging Caleb. He's still unresponsive.

Think. Come on…think! she commands herself.

Sadie grabs the duct tape. She wraps the tattered layers back around her torso. Standing at the door's side, she orchestrates a commotion and within seconds, the unsuspecting militant on watch rushes in where he, too, falls to the floor, bleeding profusely from the neck. Tricked into death.

Though it's too dark to see much beyond the soft glow of a few old solar-powered garden lights, Sadie checks each direction. Listening to the silence, her mind works on a plan. She returns to Caleb's side and tries once more to wake him. Failing, she curses, realizing the challenges ahead.

Sadie grabs her duffle bag and crossbow and runs down the stairs, returning just as fast, but empty handed. With Caleb partially lifted, she secures his body by standing behind him, and with both her arms under his armpits she begins moving him. Backing down the stairs, she tucks him behind the tower, out of view, and runs back up the steps.

Breathing heavily and sweating, she removes the shirt from one of the dead Splitters and puts it on, covering the shredded mess concealing her torso. She drags each of the bodies out of the watchtower and tucks them behind a patch of sagebrush. Back at Caleb's side, she makes another attempt at waking him.

"Come on Caleb! Wake up already!" she encourages.

He doesn't respond. Sadie shoulders her bow, tucks the knife into the top of her boot, and places a confiscated gun into the back of her waistband. Taking a deep breath, she moves out, then pauses near the pier to signal the other Delta guys anchored offshore. Devon and Derrick climb onto the small raft and paddle through choppy waves. As they approach, Sadie scans the area, uncertain about the two Splitters who haven't returned after being sent to check the bunker. What's particularly worrisome is Dom's failure to return, and although Sadie's eager to check on him, she can't stomach the idea of Caleb being left unprotected.

"We're not clear," she says to Devon and Derrick as they tie off the raft, "but the tower's empty."

Sadie points out features of the area's landscape while telling them to retrieve Caleb. When they return, she stashes the duffle bag in a better location and stations Devon in the watchtower. She sends Derrick back to the *Enforcer*, where he's instructed to keep watch while monitoring Caleb. As they take their positions, Sadie leaves in the opposite direction, creeping towards the bunker and the unknown.

Climbing the trail, Sadie can barely see through the darkness—each passing moment intensifying the fear crawling up her spine, a fear that threatens to take over. Nearing the bunker with her crossbow loaded, Sadie controls the flow of air through her nose and mouth.

A muffled sound halts her progress. Sadie strains to listen, attempting to locate and distinguish the noise; but movement from behind her changes her focus. Sadie grasps the knife. Tracking the disturbance, it grows closer. She tucks back against a giant stone. Taking a breath, she peers out one last time. She exhales. It's Dom.

"Glad to see ya," she whispers stepping out from behind the boulder.

"Sadie," he stammers, stunned by her appearance. "I cleared the bunker, but two more Splitters showed up."

"I know...that's why I'm here. Replacements came early." She stops talking as muffled voices travel towards them.

Dominic whispers even more softly. "One's injured...the second got the drop. I barely escaped." He quiets as the Splitters' voices become audible.

Sadie communicates via hand signals. Dom signals back and begins moving to attract the pursuers and set them up for ambush. The Splitters see the movement and begin tracking it. Forced to cross Sadie, she takes aim, and through the darkness, dispatches the trailing Splinter with an arrow through the neck. The Splitter in lead turns at the sound of his comrade falling. It's too late for him. Sadie's second arrow pierces his heart.

He succumbs, crumbling to a knee before falling over as Sadie pounces and kicks away his weapon. Dom runs to her. Together, they drag away the bodies before confiscating their belongings and clothes and regrouping at the watchtower. Along the way, Sadie reclaims her bag and updates her teammate back on the boat with a quick round of flashing signals.

Hesitantly, they approach the structure. Sadie whistles, then waits for the correct response. Finally hearing it, they leave the shadows and enter the tower, joined by Derrick—and Caleb, awakened and refusing to stay behind. He sees Sadie's swollen face; his concern is matched by hers.

"What happened?" Caleb asks.

Sadie checks his eyes. "The interrogation got a bit…heated. But I got more intel." Sadie breaks away from Caleb, opens the bag, and flips open the notebook. "Here's where we stand."

Caleb and the Delta guys comprehend the urgency of this gathering and don't waste time asking more, but it's obvious she took a beating and, she's wearing a different shirt.

"They've increased in numbers…to half a platoon, which could mean upwards of twenty." Sadie lets the number hang in the air before continuing. "The next shift arrives here at day break and since the two groups we just eliminated were three-man crews, we should assume that teams of four or five will return with the sun."

Sadie places the notebook on the tower's rough table surface and the men hover closely around it, watching her and the map as she shares more.

"Past the barracks," Sadie points to a hill where remnants of a ranch house exist, "there's some, elite, hit squad…nine of 'em guarding the appointed Commander of this place…" She looks at the Deltas and Caleb. "A woman."

The men look up, surprised.

"Where, exactly?" questions Devon.

"That, unfortunately, we don't know. I'm thinking…further down the old Pacific Coast Highway…beyond the point and possibly near here." Sadie's finger pauses at the former Little Sur river shed. "But they could be south of the water source and closer to the lighthouse… maybe even near here," she points further inland, "where the kids are kept. Some of the locals are still alive, too, but…I don't know how many or where they're being held. Also…" she trails off, lifts her head, and then continues, "we should expect more company…soon. Possibly another boat or two."

Sadie looks at Caleb, who knows what she's thinking.

"No, I'm alright," he demands. "We stick with the plan. Really… I'm good to go."

There's a long, heavy pause before Sadie responds: "Alright." She turns to Derrick. "Keep watch here. Station yourself outside with a vantage of both the boat and the tower door. But, first," she grabs the shirts from the confiscated goods, "everyone needs to change into these." She tosses one to Caleb and Devon. "I'll be right back."

Sadie returns carrying shirts for Dom and Derrick, but they're covered with blood. Picking up the buckets, she leaves again. Even with a quick scrub and rinse, the shirts don't come fully clean, but they'll suffice. They have to.

The wet material clings to the men's frames. Dressed in the uniform of the local Splitter regiment, they head out—hoping to go unnoticed and be out by first light.

NINE

The old coastal highway was easy enough to follow for a while, but its destruction and overgrown vegetation now leave only a narrow path winding right to where the Splitter platoon is stationed. The former ranch lay in ruin, but the Splitters have begun repairs, and a corner of the home's structure, still intact, houses at least one of the militants. A single fire burns in a rusted metal drum near the property's entrance; it illuminates the horse stables, which are in use. Beyond the converted stables, a repaired stretch of driveway curves back to reconnect with the highway. In order to continue with their mission, Sadie and her team must pass near the fire's light. They move slow and silent until their progress is halted by the appearance of a man.

They watch as he walks to the fire and tosses in another piece of wood before sitting upon one of the upturned rounds that are positioned for seats around the barrel. Nearby movement draws Sadie's attention. Another hostile emerges from the shadows and zips up his pants, moving closer to Devon. Sadie signals, draws her bow, and with minimal head movement, initiates action.

Devon sneaks up from behind the oblivious Splitter. He grabs him and covers the man's mouth while slitting his throat. As his victim falls, so does the other, by silent arrow. Both bodies get dragged into hiding as Sadie uses a small brush branch to sweep away the evidence of their doings. They settle back into cover before moving through the fire's light and past the horse stalls, currently used as barracks. Looking into one of the open-aired windows while passing, Sadie's met with a set of eyes peering back. On instinct, she lets loose an arrow. The proximity of her target combined with the force of the bow sends the arrow nearly through the man's skull.

As the body falls, his bunkmate jumps from the top bed, forcing Sadie to react quickly. Leaping into the small space, she strikes heel first into the side of his knee. It buckles with an audible pop, and Sadie finishes the job, striking twice through his chest with the knife from her boot. Their inability to go unnoticed has turned into an unintended attack. From the attached room next door, two more men stir. Dominic does his part and stops them cold. But the noise dominoes the next stall awake. Sadie and Dom move to take it together; the first Splitter is met by an arrow, the second by Dominic's blade as the man jumps mid-leap from bed. As Sadie moves to the next space, a lone Splitter stirs. He doesn't even make it out of bed, same with the one above, who meets his end while snoring.

A light coming from the next room forces them to kneel at the door's sides and wait. Sadie cringes with how things are developing. Watching red goo drip from her hands, droplets fall as everything goes slow motion: A head appears in the doorway, the man's eyes widening as blood spurts from his neck. The spray covers Sadie. As the body falls, Dominic turns to take on the next one charging in after his fallen comrade. They fall to the floor in hand-to-hand combat as Sadie snaps back into action, moving into the adjoining room. Another Splitter appears in her sights.

"I surrender! I surrender!" the man yells, with his hands held high.

Sadie makes sure he's unarmed and glances past him to the next room.

"Don't shoot!" the man begs. "It's just me, the rest are empty! Please...I can help."

Sadie motions and he moves to stand in front of her. "Turn around," she commands in her macho male voice.

When he does, they move forward, one step at a time, into the adjacent sleeping quarters. Finding it empty, Sadie makes him sit on the bottom bunk as Dom returns to her side, breathing heavily.

"Check the next room," Sadie says without taking her eyes off the man.

"There's three more...but they're all empty," hastily replies Sadie's hostage.

When he returns, Dominic confirms he's telling the truth.

"How many men are here in the barracks?" Sadie says, still keeping aim with her crossbow.

"There's eighteen here...well...some are on watch...at the tower and aahhh...there's another two guarding the house."

Sadie turns to Dom as she tallies the number of men they've already eliminated. "We've missed one," she says. "Spread the word, tell the others to hold their positions, then return." Dominic leaves, and Sadie's full attention turns to the man sitting on the bunk's edge. "Tell me about the platoon leader and the two up at the house."

He shares so much that Sadie has to refocus his output of information. She learns about the rotation of the two house guards, and details and specific tendencies of the platoon's leader, including his personal quarters, the ranch's reconstruction, and the awaited arrival of the highest-ranking Splitter in the Nation, President X, who'll relocate once the site approaches completion. By the time Dominic rejoins them, Sadie, astounded by so many details, feels her gut respond. In the dim light that filters between them, Sadie stares at the man, who has grown quiet.

"What's your name?" she asks, her voice deep.

"Antonio Leonardo Brazil, but here...just Leon."

Sadie tilts her head. "Tell me...Antonio Leonardo Brazil...besides wanting to save your life, why are you helping us?"

"Simple...I'm not one of *them*. Never was...never will be."

The two hold eye contact, but approaching footsteps break their thoughts. Recognizing who approaches, Sadie's apprehension takes hold first.

"What's wrong?" Sadie says to Caleb, making sure to stay in character.

Caleb steps closer before answering. "Nothing. Everything's good, I switched with Dom to return instead." He pauses, agonized that she is covered in blood. When Sadie turns away, he follows to face the Splitter informer, who carefully watches their interaction.

Sadie peers around the space. "Where's your roommate," she blurts, realizing he may be the man still unaccounted for.

"I'm...not sure," Leon says quickly. "He wasn't here when I woke up."

"Well..." Sadie hesitates. "Where would he be?"

"I think...maybe...up at the house. I've been suspicious of him and...the platoon lead. Somethin's goin' on. This isn't the first time he's disappeared during the night." The informant looks back and forth between Sadie and Caleb.

Sadie turns to Caleb. "Keep watch, I need a few more minutes." Without pause, she returns to questioning Leon. "I need details about the river's watershed area, the Commander's location...along with the M9s, and...where the kids are being held."

"You're here for them!" Leon says as he stands.

Sadie reacts hastily, raising her bow. "Sit back down."

"Sorry," he says, returning to his previous position. "I just...I'm... well...I wanna help. What's goin' on here is wrong and...it needs to be stopped."

"And why haven't you done anything before?" Sadie's anger begins to return. "You've been a part of this...and even helped?!"

"No...that's not..." He tries to decipher everything for himself. "I'm supposed to be here, but not...with these assholes. I think...I'm here 'cause...we're supposed to meet."

His words alert Sadie's gut instinct. "Tell me what we need to know to stop this."

Leon provides the details Sadie wants, leaving nothing out. "Oh my god!" he says, standing again as he gets to talking about the captured firsties. "You should hurry, there's another midnight march... tonight...it'd be easy to intercept 'em."

Allowing him to stay on his feet, Sadie asks for clarification.

"They march the children for hours...part of a sleep-deprivation tactic. They take 'em to the ruins...of the old lighthouse, they say it's haunted...probably to psych out the kids in fear." He sits back down, heavy hearted by the reality of such a horrible truth.

"Show me," Sadie says, maneuvering to open her notebook, "where."

He leans closer to the carefully crafted portrayal of the isle, noticing that beyond their current location the details diminish. "Okay, here's the bridge I spoke about earlier," he says, pointing slightly inland of the river's watershed. "Beyond it, just a bit...about here... is the Commander's place, and the kids are kept...here..." He pauses with a finger still on the paper. "From there, they'll loop south," he traces the route while talking, "then they'll march along the coast and use the switchbacks to climb up to the ruins."

Sadie adds the details to the map and takes a long silent look into the eyes of Leon. "There isn't time now, but...when there is... you're gonna tell me your story. Until then...I hope all you've said is accurate..."

She whistles softly and is quickly joined by Caleb. "We're keepin' this one with us," she says, motioning toward Leon.

They leave the room and rejoin the others still stationed on watch outside. As Sadie updates and directs the group, they split into two units and take opposite routes around the property's main living quarters. The ranch house is the last obstacle to circumvent, and the two guards are stationed exactly where expected. The Delta duo moves in on one of the Splitters as Sadie takes the second in her sights. One by arrow and another by blade, the bodies fall, only to be quickly dragged off and hidden.

With just two in the platoon unaccounted for, the teams maneuver through the ranch house's layout, closing in on the repaired section of the home. If they can eliminate these last two Splitters, then they're back to operating undetected—but if one or both are absent, then their chances of being discovered increase tremendously, a liability they can't afford. The construction site provides cover, and they near an area draped with tarps. Sadie detains Leon, placing him under the watch of Devon, who repositions himself to supply better coverage.

Deeper into the space, a hallway forms at its end. Muffled sounds behind a closed door hint at what's taking place. Sadie takes the lead and, carefully turning the knob, finds it locked. With an ear against the door and a flickering light emanating beneath, Sadie transitions to all fours and cautiously lowers her eyes to peer under. There's just enough space and light to confirm that two men are on the other side.

Both bodies, naked, collapse belly-down on their own accord. The one on the bottom turns to face Sadie's line of vision. She jerks her head away, making sure she's not seen. Returning to a crouch, she confirms they've found the unaccounted Splitters.

For a moment, all is quiet, before movement can be heard once again. Peering under a second time, Sadie has just enough time to react as the lock turns and the door opens, surprising them all into action. Caleb, from the left of the door, strikes high, as Dom, from the right, drops low.

The first man falls. Sadie takes aim at the second, who reaches for a nearby gun. Her arrow pierces his side and punctures a lung, jerking him violently just as his fingers grasp the weapon. The gun fires and before the injured, still naked man can turn, Dom's blade makes quick work of him.

With these last two Splitters eliminated, they stand, stunned, and worried that the shot's sound traveled too far and has given away their presence and advantage.

They quickly confiscate what's easy to carry, stash the bodies, and move to rejoin the rest of their team, also concerned about the gunshot.

Reunited, they depart, moving along the ranch property, reconnecting to a cleared stretch of road before heading south toward the watershed and the next set of obstacles. Within sight of the first structure, the group halts, fans out, and passes by without incident. Reaching the bridge, they are forced to stop and hide as two men appear and cross the narrow structure spanning the deep chasm.

Leon, who stands at Sadie's side, whispers, confirming it's two of the M9s who must have heard the shot. Debating their options, Sadie is forced to make a hasty decision and quickly provides a cover story before sending Leon out to greet the beastly men.

He moves closer. The men raise their weapons.

"Who's there?" demands one of the M9s.

Sadie tracks every move in the hairs of her crossbow. Her stomach churns, allowing doubt about this decision to creep about.

"It's me. Leon."

"Pee-on? Whacha doin' out here?"

Leon, who hates the nickname and their constant, idiotic demands, responds, "I was told to report…on the shot. They figured a couple of you'd come checking."

"Well…then?" the other M9 asks.

"It was a raccoon," Leon says.

"Ohh…the Commander luvs a little coon stew. Where is it?"

"It got away…they missed," Leon says, trying to stay calm while keeping eye contact.

"Tha' figures…bunch ah pussies can't hit shit. Come on," the grunt says, turning to his companion and already walking back. "Let's go."

As they disappear into the darkness, Caleb questions Sadie's decision to let them depart. They could have easily been dispatched like the platoon Splitters. Though Sadie agrees, she reminds the group that if those two didn't return, their unit would know something is wrong.

For now, Sadie's team remains undetected — and if it can stay that way as they cross the bridge, then they should be able to circumvent the M9s and the Commander completely, and head directly to the kids. Satisfied and allowing enough time to pass for the two M9s to return, the group moves to cross the bridge. Safely to the other side and past two small structures, Sadie's team speeds up, staying clear of the Commander's location with intel from Leon.

The sound of crashing waves grows as the route draws nearer the cliff's edge. It then veers inland and begins to open around the low-lying land surrounding the former state park grounds. Sadie's surprised that the area isn't completely consumed by the ocean, and with the low tide, the route is squishy, but accessible.

They reach a fork in the road and halt. Worrying that they missed their opportunity, Sadie splits them up and stations the Delta duo at the intersection as she, Caleb, and Leon race onwards. A hundred yards ahead, they see the light of three torches—confirming they missed their opportunity to ambush the men marching the kids. The discovery forces Sadie to change strategies as she hustles them ahead to catch up.

The tedious hike, accompanied by exhaustion, near starvation, and being roped together, slows the firsties pace to a near crawl on the way up the headland. By the final stretch, Sadie is within striking distance of the rear guard—who remains unaware of her presence.

Approaching the ruins of the former Point Sur Lighthouse, the group of kids is halted. The lead guard, followed by a few kids, enters what remains of the lighthouse. Sadie shoots from a knee and takes out the Splitter at the rear. Moving simultaneously, Caleb rushes up the side and tackles the guard. As his blade finds its mark, Sadie yells, commanding the kids to duck and close their eyes. The commotion draws the remaining Splitter out from the ruins. An arrow speeds through the darkness and strikes his chest. Leon jumps into action to free the kids, but the first child flinches, covering his head in fear.

"It's okay…it's okay," Sadie says calmly, in her natural voice. "Look…we're not Splitters." She removes her hat and kneels. "We're here to save you."

In their tormented, sleep-deprived state, the firsties are unable to process what's going on. Not sure if it's another trick or if it's even real, the kids watch trancelike through sunken eyes as the bindings are cut away from their wrists. Deep rope burns and layers of broken skin lay below their bonds.

Finally free, they do no more than sit; it's all their thin frames can muster. Sadie's heart breaks with each child she unties. Moving down the line, she offers each of them a drink from her canteen before dispersing what food she's brought along. The five-mile hike back is going to be a lot tougher than she thought, and the chance of not making it before sunrise increases with each passing minute. Staying crouched at the kids' level, Sadie hopes to motivate them.

"We have to get to where it's safe," she says. "Can you stand?"

The kids look around at each other, unsure and scared.

"Come on," Sadie encourages, helping up a little girl.

Slowly, they rise to their feet, some on their own, some with help. Sadie gives each another drink, hoping it will help get them moving. In total, eleven children slowly begin the long walk back the way they have just come. It's a slow, painstaking pace. As the night lengthens, they finally rejoin Devon and Dom who have nothing to report. Taking a brief break to give the kids more water, they pause to talk strategy but get interrupted by one of the boys.

"Are ya gonna git my brudder?" he asks, standing among them.

Sadie takes a knee to be at his level. "Where is he?"

"In da hole," he replies, pointing down the road that leads to where the firsties were held.

"The hole?" Sadie says. She asks if there are others.

The little boy nods yes. "Da utter big kid...dey both got put in da hole."

"There should be another guard there, too," adds Leon.

After finding out what they can from the kids, Dom offers to go. He departs at a jog, heading inland, as the rest of the group continues north, racing against sunrise.

TEN

Hiking in the early A.M. hours, not long before daybreak, Sadie and Devon put one foot in front of the other as each piggyback a small child. The youngsters had stopped walking, leaving them no choice but to carry the extra weight. After a while, Caleb and Leon offer to bear the load and take the kids upon their shoulders.

They walk another half mile before Sadie halts the group, allowing the kids to rest while she scouts ahead to make sure they can still pass unnoticed. When she returns, they split the children among them and move in smaller groups. She takes a position near the bridge and Caleb covers the opposite side, as the initial batch of firsties makes the trek. With all of them safely over, Sadie scurries across last.

"Almost there," she encourages, keeping them moving while hiding her concern at their slow progress. She turns to Devon. "Stay here, keep watch...don't let anyone pass."

Devon nods and retreats to the other side.

With the last mile within reach, the sky lightens, hinting at the awaiting day. Caleb, returning from a quick scout, gives the all-clear signal, and Sadie hustles the kids, allowing them to stop briefly when they finally pass the barracks. From her vantage point the ocean comes clearly into view; her stomach drops as waves pound and boom with thundering power.

"Shit," Sadie murmurs under her breath.

First light reveals their luck has run thin. A swell hits the island with force, eliminating the safe transport of the kids out to the boat. Sadie checks with Derrick at the watchtower; he managed pulling the zodiac to safety, but lost the small raft. Feverishly, Sadie retreats at a near sprint back to the barracks. After a quick cleanup from the bloodshed, she calls for the kids to be nestled into the bunks.

"I'll stay," Leon interjects adamantly, overhearing the conversation between Caleb and Sadie. "Go. I'll protect 'em."

Sadie looks into Leon's eyes. She then nods before running back to the bridge with Caleb to join Devon and check on the status of Dom and the missing kids. As the bridge comes into sight, so does the rising sun as it crests the ridgeline. Joining forces, the three creep around one of the nearby structures, but, hearing voices, they're forced to hide inside. The building—old, decrepit, and worn—teeters near the edge of a steep drop to the gorge below. It serves as the isle's pump house and vital supplier of water. The structure's insides are an odd mix of work shed and living space, cluttered with mounds of old, faded plastics, sorted by size. Bottles, originally manufactured for long extinct beverage and water companies, along with an assortment of caps, dingy and faded with age, sit scuffed and scratched, but organized neatly for repurposing.

The space doesn't offer much in terms of hiding places. As the voices draw nearer, Sadie and the men respond with readied weapons—but no one enters. Instead, the voices' chatter fades, giving Sadie a chance to peek through a partially boarded and broken window. Three fierce-looking men are visible, casually strolling toward another structure, where they stop.

Taking a turn watching the men, Devon whispers. "Too bad these," he motions to his and Caleb's guns, "aren't silent like your bow."

Silent. Devon's word sparks an idea as Sadie's eyes spot several pieces of steel wool from a collection of cleaning materials arranged along a rough-cut shelf. Picking out three plastic bottles, she cuts a hole in their bottoms, removes the screen hanging from a corner of the broken window, and cuts it into sections. Rolling up the pieces skinny enough to fit inside the bottles, Sadie fills the remaining spaces with the steel wool. Starting with Devon, she requests his firearm. Using the duct tape from the duffel bag she still carries, Sadie attaches the homemade silencer to the gun's barrel. She does the same for Caleb, and then for the gun tucked in her waistband.

"How do you know this?" Caleb asks.

Sadie glances at Caleb but doesn't respond. Peering out at the men, she worries as they disappear inside the small shack they've been standing near. Caleb knows he'll have to settle for finding out about the silencers another time; her focus is elsewhere.

"They're comin' back...and bringing two men...in chains," Sadie says softly before signaling her team into different positions.

As the voices draw near, she, too, moves. The door opens, and two bodies, crumpled together, stumble inside, caught off guard by a cruel kick to their backsides by one of the M9s. They fall, accompanied by the hearty laughter of arrogance from their captors, and land squarely on the floor near Sadie. One makes instant eye contact with her as she places a finger in front of her lips in the universal sign of silence. The men do nothing to get up.

"Get the fuck up en get to work!"

Still not moving, the command is followed by two lumbering brutes, who—entering the building with misdirected focus—proceed blindly. It's a costly error, one enforced simultaneously by blade and arrow, brutally and silently ending their lives. The third of their trio ducks for cover while raising his firearm. A bullet, quickly followed by a second, stops him.

"Holy shit!" Caleb says, impressed, watching smoke escape from his homemade silencer. "It worked."

"Drag him in," Sadie snaps, getting Caleb's attention away from the drifting smoke.

She searches the body at her feet as Devon does the same near his. They confiscate what weapons the M9s carried and search for a key to unlock the prisoners, who stare in shock with gaping eyes.

Sadie addresses the two guys still on the floor. "Are more comin'?"

She's been thoughtful in maintaining her male persona in the midst of these two men and finds it curious, especially in regard to how naturally she dropped it when rescuing the children. Unsure of what to make of what they've just witnessed and unsettled by the presence of three more men, dressed as Splitters, yet, seemingly aiding them, the two glance at each other, but neither speaks. Sadie, ending her search, turns her full attention to the M9s' prisoners, who have twisted around to take a seated position next to one another.

"Guys," she grumbles, motioning to their shackles, "where's the key to unlock these?"

One of them shrugs his shoulders and manages a bewildered head tilt. Sadie takes it as a good start and, studying their faces, tries another approach at gaining information.

"We're not Splitters," she states, straight-faced. "We're here to stop them."

There's no doubt in the truth of her words. The chained men perk up.

"They've got kids, not far from here," the eldest of the two states.

Sadie nods. "We've already rescued them."

"All of 'em?" the same man interjects, distraught.

"Two of the older boys are missing," Sadie answers, witnessing genuine concern in their faces.

Interrupted by Caleb, who enters and searches the body he's dragged in, Sadie moves Devon to lookout, peers outside, and then returns to the men.

"We sent someone to find them but expected them back by now," she says, pointing at them for emphasis. "And I think we're gonna need your help." She looks each man in the eye. "Will any more of these M9 killers come out here?"

"No, only these three," answers the eldest.

"They start together, but only one stays," his partner adds. "Every few hours they rotate."

The two men switch off sharing details about the schedule they're forced to keep and everything they've learned about the Splitters who enslave them. Mentioning the daily water delivery to the barracks, Sadie interrupts.

"No one there is expecting water," she states, hardened and cold. "Only the Commander, what's left of her M9s, and possibly a guard stationed where the kids remain." Sadie's eyes grow distant. "The rest have been taken care of."

A silence settles in the small shack, broken only when Sadie starts moving again. She rolls up her pant leg, exposing a patch of duct tape circling her upper ankle. Tearing it away exposes a small collection of miniature tools and picks. Sadie re-examines the locks binding the captive men, selects two pieces and goes to work. The first lock opens easily, but the second takes several attempts before it releases. With the shackles removed, the men stand and stretch their legs, unaccustomed to the freedom of movement.

Before they can express gratitude, a whistle from outside draws everyone's attention. Sadie peers through the broken window and replies softly. Watching Dom scurry from one tree to the next, she meets him part way to provide additional cover while he gets the two boys safely into the pump house.

"Dad!" exclaims one of the boys, running into his father's arms.

The second boy also gets pulled into the embrace. For a moment it's quiet, before a stream of questions erupts.

The dad scans their faces. "You okay? What happened? Where's your brother?"

The two teenage boys, though smiling at the reunion, show obvious signs of abuse and starvation. They stammer in their exhausted states, making little sense at first; but with a little encouragement and redirection, they unfold the tale of a horrid ordeal. Separated from the other kids and made examples of for attempting to defend the younger ones, they endured brutal beatings before being thrown in separate holes, where they'd lain trapped in pitch black for the past few days. The young men grow distant, distraught feelings of helplessness intensifying when their story ends.

Sadie is encouraged by their acts of bravery and praises their actions. "You two did good…looked out for the kids…" She shakes each of their hands. "I'm honored to continue to stand with you," she says, turning to address the rest of them. "Now…we're gonna need to work together as a team."

The dialogue continues with Dom reporting on his firstie camp findings and confirming there was only a single guard, who is "no longer of concern." With only the Commander and six of her goon squad remaining, the odds are still slim, but now seem more favorable. However, the extremist mercenaries that remain kill not only professionally, but for sport. Sadie and her team were lucky when the first three walked blindly into an ambush. The others won't be as easy—and could make this rescue mission very costly.

The plan turns to getting ahead of the Commander in her daily trip to the firstie camp. As morning lengthens, Sadie worries. *It's only a matter of time before they know we're here.* She turns to the rescued boys and men who provide all the intel they can before the group splits up. Leaving Devon and the freed foursome to guard the area, Sadie scuttles out, followed closely by Caleb and Dominic.

Dom remembers a good location to set an ambush and takes the lead. They run double time and crouch behind a massive chunk of stone debris. Opportunity soon presents itself; a man walks right into Sadie's crosshairs. Another trails.

"Only two," she whispers to herself. "I got this." An arrow flies silently. Then another. Two bodies fall, and her men scramble from their perch to search them.

"It's not the Commander," Dom communicates. "But they're dead."

Sadie acknowledges and, as her men hide the evidence, she relocates to scan the perimeter and ensure they don't get snuck up on.

"Four...and the Commander," Dom remarks, keeping tally of who remains and feeling confident.

Sadie nods, reiterates the necessity for caution, and moves while watching for any of the remaining M9s. If they can keep them confined around the Commander's headquarters and strike opportunistically, they may yet be able to get out alive.

Stationing Devon and Dom in position to watch for M9s that may leave their headquarters, Sadie and Caleb cautiously return to the pump house, making sure all is still okay. Finding it secure and those inside safe, Sadie outlines the updated strategy.

"There's another way...an old trail," pipes up the father, looking at his eldest son, who nods. "Around the back of the place. It'll get ya even closer."

Sadie asks for more.

The son answers: "We were on it...way up...when..." He drifts off.

"We were all up there," adds his dad, "when..." He shakes his head from side to side.

Slowly, his voice returns and he provides details of their survival and the fated trip that took them into higher elevations with nothing but backpacks and sparse supplies. Their hike had started from their backyard, now Splitter territory, where they took off into the Big Sur woods unprepared for what lay on the horizon.

Initially excited by finding a ledge with an expansive view from the Bixby Bridge to the north all the way to the Point Sur lighthouse to the south, they camped—not knowing what lay ahead would forever be seared into their minds. From their vantage point, they watched in horror as the ocean sucked out and the first wave of the Tri-nami hit the Pacific coast, obliterating both the iconic bridge and the lighthouse in a massive wall of water.

"The whole ground shuddered," whispers the second teenager.

"We stayed up there watchin'...not able to do nuttin'," says the second man.

The group grows silent. It's the father who finishes their tale of survival, of how they salvaged what they could from their flooded home and the neighboring ranch until the next catastrophe hit. When he mentions the thunderous earthquake and their scramble to get out in the open, clear of the falling trees, Sadie's focus wavers—the image of her husband's twitching leg surfaces, filling her mind.

"When the shaking finally stopped, the destruction was overwhelming, but…the land…actually rose. What remained of the lighthouse resurfaced from beneath the ocean, along with the grounds around it…even our land somehow drained. We worked hard…made it work for a while…until…"

When he stops talking, it takes Sadie a long moment to realize that he is not going to continue. Looking at him squarely, she finds new resolve. "Show me this trail."

ELEVEN

It's a good thing he's leading, Sadie thinks, watching the man in front of her slipping under one tree and over another. The path isn't much of a trail—more like an overgrown and feral wilderness over some dirt, but they're making progress and closing in on the property, just like they said. Halting just within sight of his commandeered home, the man points out key features and answers more of Sadie's questions. Then he quickly leaves to rejoin his son and keep watch at the water station with the other freed local.

Within seconds of his departure, Caleb and Sadie look at each other and split up to double their coverage. But a disturbance from inside the home draws their attention.

A thick-armed man covered in tattoos steps onto the back porch, letting the door bang shut behind him. He yanks a handcrafted ladder from along the side of the house and drops it with a thud where the roof and wall meet. Muttering to himself, he climbs up, and reaches for the antenna.

"How's it lookin'?" says another man, similarly built, gazing up from the porch, as the door slams shut again.

"Give me a minute already!" he yells, turning back. The man fuddles with the antenna. "Looks good...no prob here."

Caleb moves from his knee to his belly, worried that the mound of debris he's hiding behind isn't enough cover. Sadie feels her pulse quicken when the man stops descending the ladder and peers directly toward Caleb. He climbs back up another rung and stares long enough to draw his cohort's attention.

"Whacha lookin' at?" the man below asks.

"Thought I saw sumpin' move."

The M9 on the ground raises his weapon while nearing the trash mound. Sadie's gut tells her to act. Unable to keep both targets in her sights, she moves forward, hoping neither of the men will turn and look in her direction. She silently closes the gap in four seconds and, as the first grunt touches his feet back to the ground, the second returns to view. Sadie's first arrow pierces the head of the man from the ladder. Her second drops the other as he was almost on top of Caleb, who leaps from his cover, striking with his knife.

Sadie, exposed in the open, drops her crossbow, rolls sideways toward the house, and strikes, using her blade on another brute as he exits the house. From a crouched position, her first thrust penetrates the man's inner thigh, followed instantly with a stab between his upper ribs and ending with a slash across his neck. Each strike is acute, coordinated, and lethal. Caleb stands still, mesmerized by Sadie's deadly agility. He's not sure what to think.

The spell breaks when he realizes Sadie's signaling him to move into position opposite her at the door.

"Sadie, you okay?" he whispers, seeing a strange look upon her face.

Shaking her head side to side with a heart-stopping glare, Caleb realizes he's broken protocol by using her real, female name. She's barely recognizable: the short hair, Splitter attire, phony voice, and blood-covered, swollen, and bruised face. But it's more than just her appearance. It's her eyes.

Their fierceness refocuses Caleb of the threat at hand. Each threat they face increases the odds of death. Yet, Sadie doesn't waiver. She inches forward, pulls open the door and slips inside; then, with slow, deliberate, and cautious movement, she creeps ahead. Caleb follows. He lets go of the door and it slams shut behind them. Terror seeps in.

"Took you long enough!" a gruff voice yells from the interior. "Radio still ain't workin'…is it the antenna?"

As they creep closer the voice yells again. "Well, was it!?"

Finding it unwise to respond verbally, they realize that there's no choice but to push forward and prepare to come face to face with the last M9 and the Commander.

But, as Sadie steps closer, another voice—this time female—comes from behind.

"I suggest…droppin' it." The Commander presses a gun into Caleb's temple and points another at Sadie. "Clear!" she announces in her bold, female voice, with eyes pierced at Sadie.

Appearing at Sadie's side with his weapon drawn, the remaining grunt takes her crossbow and throws it out the door; he kicks the back of her legs, demanding a kneeling position. Sadie lowers to the ground, never averting her gaze from the female warrior standing only a few feet away, and positions both hands at the back of her head as requested. She watches as Caleb gets dropped into the same position, searched, and quickly bound. Evident by her actions, her body language, and her dress, the Commander is not to be messed with.

Sadie studies her opponent, a woman who commands men. She knows that she and Caleb's situation is dire. Taken hostage, instead of being slaughtered, is a sure sign that what's to proceed won't be good.

From his crazy grin, the last of the Mighty 9s seems anxious to get started; nearly shaking with anticipation, he's snapped to attention, given precise instructions, and sent to check the backdoor.

Standing just over six feet with hair that mocks the beauty it sits atop, the Commander's half-shaven head is only partially visible. A wave of deep, dark red strands hides the full details of the ink beneath on her scalp. Other tattoos accentuate the rounded curves of her cleavage and her muscular arms and shoulders. Her body art isn't the only display of sheer extremes. The Commander's black leather pants, boots, and corset each hold an array of weapons—some apparent, some concealed. They tell of a life of fighting—and winning. *But… there's something more*, Sadie thinks with a vague sense of familiarity.

"Dead…all of 'em," reports the shocked M9 still at the back porch, staying cautiously out of sight in case someone else lurks in ambush.

Speaking more to Sadie than to her subordinate, the Commander responds. "Why am I not surprised?"

The two women look at each other. One dressed as a man, one who lives in a man's world. They form judgements of the other, filling in the details of their lives from a minute of observation, both curious in the manner and methods the other will employ.

"Interior lockdown," the Commander initiates, directed toward her comrade. "Start forward."

He nods and hustles off, followed by sounds of sliding doors and latches clicking into place. Caleb, bound and hogtied on the floor, attempts to turn his head toward Sadie, but is met by a sharp kick in his side that sends familiar waves of pain through his ribs.

"You take this one," the Commander orders, hovering over Caleb as her death squad of one returns. "Lock him up."

The brute drags Caleb awkwardly away, giving him a final chance to look at Sadie. He has fear in his eyes, but Sadie gives nothing. He struggles against his bindings in a futile attempt to escape, concerned for her safety. His effort is meet with another burst of pain when the M9 drives the heal of his boot into his torso. The man laughs, dragging him from the room.

The Commander speaks to Sadie. "Turn around," she says.

Sadie, beginning to get up, is instantly halted when a small throwing blade penetrates her quad.

"I didn't say stand!" the Commander yells, kicking away Sadie's hand as she removes the implement. The blade clatters across the floor.

In lieu of asking again, the Commander cocks a gun. Sadie makes sure to stay on her knees, blood saturating the material around the wound in her leg.

"You want me to take this one, too?" interrupts the M9 as he returns.

"No." The Commander forces Sadie further into the interior. "Finish lockdown and see what you can get from the other." She halts Sadie's progress, opens a door and commands her to enter.

Creeping along on her knees provides Sadie with an opportunity to scan the details of her surroundings and the modifications added to the home that secure the inner rooms. The layout suggests precise planning, accommodating its users with all the essentials needed to sustain life. The room she's being directed into looks to double as sleeping quarters, with bunks similar to those in the barracks on one side and water storage tanks on the other. At the back, another door, reinforced with locking metal bars, dominates the space—an eerie focal point. Sadie's respiration increases, and she fights the panic that threatens to dull her senses.

"You're just in time," the Commander jokes, opening the door. "I put the final touches in this morning."

Forced at gunpoint, Sadie enters the space. What once served as a closest has been transformed into a confinement chamber with a multitude of eyebolts and chains attached to all three of its walls and ceiling.

"Turn around," the Splitter leader directs. Sadie does so.

"Start with that one," the Commander says, motioning to the metal bracket dangling from a chain above. "Put it around your neck...and lock it."

Once Sadie has it in place, she's instructed to lock her ankles and right wrist into the other shackles. The Commander finishes the job by locking Sadie's left wrist, leaving her captive's arms spread wide and unable to move. Even the slack from above is pulled tight, decreasing mobility. Pleased with the design, the Commander grabs a chair tucked in the opposite corner of the main room, turns it around backwards, and sits, straddling it, to observe what she thinks is a man chained before her. Pushing aside a swath of bold red hair, the woman's eyes narrow while taking in the details of her prisoner.

The bruising and swelling around her captive's face are recent. The confiscated, ill-fitting platoon uniform, covered in splattered blood, along with the lack of radio responses from around the island, indicate that many—if not all—the other men, have been eliminated. Of all the signs she detects from Sadie, it's a lack of hopelessness that makes the Commander consider that this runt of a man may be more of a challenge than initially thought. Standing from the chair, she pulls a knife from the top of her boot and approaches Sadie.

"I think you and I have lots to discuss. But first," she begins cutting away the material from Sadie's shirt, "I bet you've got some hidden goodies."

Ripping away the fabric reveals layers of duct tape and clothes, until eventually, only a tightly-wound wrap, flattening Sadie's chest, remains. With it cut away, the Commander stares into Sadie's eyes without speaking, and then continues by removing Sadie's shoes and pants until she's left in only her tiny and revealing undergarments. The commander removes two patches of duct tape, one above Sadie's ankle and the other along her abdomen, and smiles at the tools they hid.

"Clever girl," she whispers. She yanks back Sadie's head by grabbing what remains of her hair. "What else you hiding, huh?" she asks, running her fingers through Sadie's hair and finding two bobby pins. She discards them with a smile, then traces the edge of Sadie's scalp and along the back of her neck. Feeling a bump at the base of her hairline, the Commander picks at the edges until it peels away. "Razor blade...how handy."

Slowly, using the blade almost teasingly, the warrior gently cuts away what little clothing remains on Sadie's body in pursuit of any last hidden items that may be concealed.

Stepping back, the Commander kicks away the pile of discarded items and returns to straddling the chair. She is intrigued by her find. She was prepared to handle a man, but the discovery of a female changes the game. Sadie, yet to speak, calmly watches as her captor's eyes follow the curves of her now naked body.

"Wow…you're really…fit," she finally states, admiringly.

"You still look good, too," Sadie remarks in her own voice. Her comment has the effect she hoped for, the Commander revealing a subtle grin through her stark exterior.

"Sorry…might be that terrible haircut or…all your bruises, but… have we…"

Sadie interrupts, slowly shaking her head. "No, Russo, we've never met."

The Commander hasn't heard that name in years. She stands up straight. The mysteriousness of this woman, along with the circumstances surrounding her, adds to an increasingly troublesome feeling for the Splitter Commander.

"Your hair's different…way sexier," Sadie adds, keeping her opponent off balance. "And you've gotten more ink, but you look…" Sadie trails off, looking over the female form standing before her. "Really… badass." She smiles, watching the Commander reel with uncertainty.

Russo takes a step closer. Sadie continues the flattery.

"You were incredible, a true champion. And…from the looks of things…you still are."

The Commander regains a little ground. "You used to watch me fight?"

"A few times," Sadie casually replies, watching the former UFC fighter grow quiet in contemplation.

A long pause settles between the two ladies as Sadie anticipates the direction her adversary may take.

"You know 'bout me, but…what about you?" the Commander asks, admiring Sadie's smooth, pale skin. "You don't get much sun. You must live somewhere out here…in these outer islands."

Russo's accurate observation and the intrusive feeling it elicits warns Sadie of her opponent's intellect. A strange dynamic is developing between them.

Sadie nods in confirmation. "What else can you tell?" she encourages.

The Commander leans in close. "There's much to you, and this… is gonna take some time." She abruptly gets up and shuts the confinement room's door.

Sadie's surprise and terror are magnified with each lock and sliding bar she hears from the other side of the door. The Commander, slightly rattled and intrigued by her physical response to her captive female, regains her composure and adopts a different strategy.

Making haste to the opposite side of the house, she opens another door, allowing an orchestra of pain to emit from within the room. Caleb, detained in a manner similar to Sadie, also hangs naked, but he drips blood. His face is a swollen gooey mess, matched in color by the M9s knuckles, who, interrupted by his superior, momentarily stalls Caleb's torture.

"He talkin'?" the Commander inquires, looking Caleb over.

"Haven't asked, yet," replies the brute.

"Dismissed, soldier."

Turning to leave, he pauses. "Should I go work the other one?"

"No, that one's mine," Russo states, making sure he gets the message. "Recheck the lockdown and keep post at the radio."

When the door shuts, the Commander slowly makes her way around the naked man hanging outstretched. His physique, though lean and muscular, doesn't have the effect on Russo like that of Sadie's.

"Her disguise didn't last," she says, testing him.

Caleb's head shoots up, looking the Commander straight in the face. His reaction encourages the domineering woman.

"She hangs...chained...just like you..." The female warrior circles tauntingly around her victim, lightly tracing her fingers around Caleb's torso. "Also, without clothes." Stopping in his line of vision, only inches from his face, she halts. "I was thinking...maybe my guy... the one who just left you...would like a turn with your...girlfriend."

Her comment hits its target. Caleb lurches forward with fire raging in his eyes. *This one*, she thinks, retreating a step, *is gonna be a breeze.*

Grabbing a chair and turning it around, she sits facing Caleb, wondering how much information she'll be able to squeeze from him.

"Tell you what...how 'bout...you answer a few questions and I make sure that little sexy thang over there...doesn't ever have to meet him. Deal?"

TWELVE

Approaching footsteps followed by the sound of locks being undone has Sadie looking up in her chains. She's not surprised that it's the Commander who greets her, but Sadie finds everything she carries curious. The chiseled warrior sets the items down near Sadie's feet, pulls over a chair and sits backwards in her casual yet dominating fashion. The redhead eyes the nakedness dangling before her.

"I gotta admit. My intentions were a bit different when…you were a guy, but…" She lustily looks up and down her captive's bare body.

Sadie remains quiet, figuring it's best to let Russo lead this round.

"Anyways…I think a little attention is due," the Commander says. Moving gracefully, she stands, spins the chair out of her way and, taking a knee closer to Sadie, looks up.

The Commander's eyes drift to Sadie's thighs. She pauses before regaining eye contact.

"Okay?" the warrior asks.

Sadie barely nods. Russo grabs a sponge from the bucket, squeezes out the excess water, and uses it to wash away the blood from the three separate knife wounds covering Sadie's upper legs. Two of them, inflicted during her encounter at the watchtower, are rather superficial and have already stopped bleeding, but the larger and deeper one caused by the Commander herself still seeps fluid and blood all the way to Sadie's toes.

"Good thing it was my tiny throwing blade…huh?" Russo says, squeezing water directly over the puncture.

Sadie doesn't respond. She watches as her captor meticulously pours a cap full of hydrogen peroxide from a brown bottle into her affliction. The liquid fizzes white and burns as it disinfects, but Sadie doesn't flinch. After the second capful, the Commander steps back, continuing to measure Sadie's body language. A long silence ensues, continuing even once she moves again. The Commander swings the chair so close that it brushes against Sadie's detained leg. The bucket of water, along with the sponge, is placed atop it. Once again, she stares long and hard at Sadie. "I'm going to loosen your left arm. Wash up."

The Commander leans in closer than necessary and speaks in a light, but huskier tone. "You're filthy."

Russo provides enough slack in the chain for Sadie to reach where she needs. She starts by washing her face and neck before squeezing two spongefuls over the top of her head. The cool water drips down her torso, sending shivers as it travels. Sadie feels the attention from her observer, especially while wiping down her breasts. When the bucket sits empty and Sadie stands in a swath of damp floor, the Commander returns Sadie's arm to an outstretched position.

"You smell...and look...much better," Russo whispers as she locks the chain into position.

She overturns the empty bucket to sit atop it and, once again, disinfects Sadie's leg wound. The Commander then grabs a bandage roll and wraps it around Sadie's thigh, moving deliberately while doing so. Chained naked, with her arms and legs spread in an X formation, Sadie contemplates the angles of the game they are playing.

Done with the bandage, the former fighter stands, and hovering inches above Sadie's head, closely examines her facial injuries.

"Looks like...ya know how to take a beatin'," she states, noting the signs of abuse and the telltale signatures it has left behind.

The Commander lingers in a silent moment. Sadie waits it out, curious to discover her opponent's ideal outcome while pondering the next move. When the daunting, red-haired warrior steps back, it's simply to retrieve more from the pile of objects she set down upon arrival.

"We're not the same size," Russo begins, unfolding a cloth, "but I thought, for now...this would work." She wraps Sadie's body in a short sarong, tucks in an end to secure it, and leans close. "I'll find something...that suits you better...once we can get you out of these restraints." The Commander steps back to look over her work.

The narrow material barely covers Sadie's essentials, but the purple hue suits her well. With the modest covering in place, the Commander returns to her position of choice, straddling the chair. She takes a mental inventory before proceeding.

"It seems I'm in need of replacements," Russo pauses, drawing out the silence. "And you seem...more than capable, but I wonder..." No words follow.

Getting an inkling of the game being played, Sadie keeps eye contact with her captor. She breaks the silence. "Join forces?" she asks.

A sly grin is all the reply she gets.

"Tell me...exactly what...do you have in mind?" Sadie says, playing along.

The Commander contemplates her words carefully before speaking. "We're gonna be together...for a while. There'll be plenty of time for specifics later. For now, I think the two of us should get better acquainted."

Sadie, undeterred, switches tactics. "Alright, you start. Tell me... how'd you come to be a Splitter Commander?"

The Commander chuckles. "Easy...survival. How'd you manage getting here?"

"Easy...by boat," Sadie replies, lighthearted and smiling, matching Russo's body language. "And you?"

"Also, by boat." A strand of dark red hair falls over one of the Commander's eyes. Casually brushing it aside, she blinks with enjoyment.

Sadie takes a risk. "May I sit...while we chat?"

Her captor's attention shifts, making Sadie worry about a miscalculation, but then the Commander rises, slides over the overturned bucket, and hovers over her. Russo slackens the neck chain, then, one at a time, adjusts each arm restraint. With Sadie seated, she returns to her perch around the back of her chair. The women sit nearly at eye level, but the casual ease between them has gone. "Thank you," Sadie offers, letting the muscles in her legs and feet relax while taking a deep breath and slowly exhaling. "I'm not accustomed...to...standing still...for so long." She gazes imploringly at the woman across from her but doesn't say more.

"So..." the Commander starts, "tell me...exactly why'd you come here?"

"The kids. And you?" Sadie answers, keeping it short, and hoping to learn more than she divulges.

The warrior goddess stares, unsure of the dialogue's direction. Intrigued, she finally answers. "Me too."

Sadie doesn't respond verbally, but the Commander gets all the reaction she needs.

"You think differently?" Russo inquires.

Unsure if it's wise to answer, Sadie doesn't.

The Commander sees an advantage. "Without 'em, there's no future. If they don't survive…humankind becomes extinct."

Sadie dares to respond. "So…you're helping to…save 'em?"

"Of course," the Commander snaps back adamantly. "They have to learn to be strong…to fight…to survive…to not fall prey."

As Russo's eyes go distant, Sadie wonders what circumstances have shaped the woman seated before her. With chin rested upon her hands atop the back of the chair she straddles, the Commander's demeanor softens. When she glances back up, their eyes meet, and in the silence both women ponder the complexities of one another.

"Do you believe…takin' kids from their homes…from their families…actually helps?" Sadie inquires softly.

Her captor's eyes regain their edge. "Homes? Families? What world you livin' in? There's nothing but starvation and terror waiting for 'em. With me…they'll be fed, housed, trained, clothed. They'll learn to defend themselves…and eventually…they'll be the ones in charge. I'm giving 'em *opportunity*."

"At what cost?" Sadie questions. "And what happens when President X arrives and makes this his home? Does he feel the same? You sure they're not just…disposable resources to be used as needed?"

With the mention of the Nation's president, the Commander's attention returns to her adversary. Sadie can tell that her knowledge of his impending arrival was something Russo didn't expect; it's changed the redhead's demeanor once again.

"Interesting," Russo states, Sadie now worrying that she should have kept that bit of information to herself. "It seems…you're quite capable and…knowledgeable."

"Obviously not capable enough." Sadie lets her head drop. "I'm here, chained in this closet…" she glances up, "at your total mercy."

Sadie's words calm the fire growing in the Commander's eyes. Their soothing effect is what Sadie hoped for, but the savage doesn't fall for it completely. Instead, she gets up from her seat and pushes the chair aside.

"You're right, beautiful…you're at my mercy. I hope you haven't failed to notice how…nice I've been treatin' you." The Commander moves closer.

Playing out the current scenario, Sadie agrees with a slight head bob. "And I hope it only gets better."

The comment strikes perfectly—a mixture of excitement, unease, and uncertainty washes over the Commander.

Quickly regaining her footing, the warrior allows a smile. "You, my dear...are a hard nut to crack, but...I think I'm gonna enjoy..." she looks over Sadie's naked legs, "the two of us gettin' to know each other better. Like I said...we've got plenty of time."

"Exactly how long...will I be stayin' like this?" Sadie asks, indicating the restraints.

A hearty laugh escapes and echoes around the small confinement chamber. "Oh, Sadie...yer too cute."

Sadie's heart skips at the mention of her name. *Caleb talked!?* This insight forces the assumption that all he knows the Commander now knows. It changes Sadie's game completely. Watching the realization creep across her captive's face, the Commander takes delight in the moment.

"Caleb's rather protective of you and seemingly faithful...like no man I know. I think he'd do anything for you. But I'm curious...will you do the same for him?"

The Commander let's her question float in the air. Sensing an advantage, she quickly stands and shuts the door without another word. As the lock bolts on the other side of the door, Sadie pulls at her chains.

THIRTEEN

Sitting on the overturned bucket, Sadie's head jerks violently, awakening her from an uncomfortable slumber. Unsure of how long she's slept or for how long she's even been locked up, her legs tingle from loss of circulation and both shoulders ache from maintaining their outstretched position. The urge to stand along with the necessity to relieve herself create a dilemma. There's just enough slack in her restraints to allow a standing posture, and by manipulating her feet and toes, after several attempts, Sadie rights the bucket and uses it as a toilet.

Although she's relieved, a new problem develops as an unpleasant odor begins to fill the small space, assaulting Sadie's senses and choking her with stale air.

Shimmying the sarong loose, Sadie works to slide it lower until it falls, covering the bucket and reducing the foul smell. She pushes the bucket as far forward as her leg can reach, placing it in a position where she won't accidentally knock it over.

With the distraction moved aside, her focus returns solely to the confinement space. In the darkness, Sadie strains her neck and rotates it in circles. She moves each leg up and down, testing their range of motion. The familiar sound of the Commander's approach and the unlocking of the prison cell interrupt her exercises and she stands still.

"Ohhh...is this for my sake?" the muscled beauty asks, excited, eyeing the naked flesh once again spread before her. Any arousal, though, is quelled by the lingering smell. She looks to the sarong-covered bucket.

"Had to...use the facilities," shrugs Sadie. "Sorry."

The Commander uses the side of her boot to slide the bucket outside and then shuts the door. Not hearing the locks slide into place, Sadie perks up, but the woman reappears almost as quickly as she departed. In her hands hangs the sarong, but she makes no comment about it. The redhead turns her chair around and takes a seat while examining her captive's every detail. Sadie watches the woman's eyes slowly trace her curves before locking stares with her. They eye one another for a long time, both women hoping to gain secret knowledge of the other.

It's the Commander who finally speaks. "Would you like this again?" she says, holding up the sarong.

Sadie nods yes, but when the Commander stands, it's without the cloth. She takes a step closer and carefully tightens the restraint around Sadie's neck, removing all slack from when she was allowed to sit. The same is done with each of Sadie's legs, along with adjustments to her arms.

Smart, Sadie thinks, understanding the wisdom of such caution.

Once again outstretched in an X without any room to maneuver, Sadie's completely at the will of the Commander. Russo, enjoying herself, wraps the sarong around Sadie's torso, only to immediately remove the covering to redo it. This time it's taut, and as the end of the material gets tucked into place, Sadie softly offers thanks. The Commander doesn't respond and returns to straddling her chair. Sadie has an idea and a direction she'd like their impending conversation to go. But so does the Commander.

"Alright, Sadie. I'd prefer...if this didn't drag out, but..." Russo pauses to emphasize her seriousness, "it could." She raises an eyebrow. "If I need it to."

Sadie hears both truth and a pathway in the Commander's words. She waits for her captor's next line of inquiry. It starts precisely as Sadie hoped.

"Caleb's asked to see you...repeatedly." The Commander carefully watches Sadie's response.

Sadie makes sure to show no reaction. She knew this was coming; she expected he'd be used as leverage.

"I think...you'd like to see him, too," the Commander says. Content with how things are going, she leans into her chair. She's learned much from her male prisoner and is curious to discover what Sadie will reveal and validate.

"What is it...you'd like to know?" Sadie asks, straight-faced.

Weary of Sadie's compliance, the Commander ponders what angle her captive may be playing: "When should I expect your men?"

Sadie deciphers the question and calculates a response. She debates two things—either the Commander has full knowledge of all that's happened or she's bluffing, fishing for additional information.

Sadie hopes Caleb hasn't divulged too much, but thinks it wise to assume he has. "Not sure," she answers. "How long would the M9s take to save *you*?"

"That's different, and anyways...let's stick to me askin' the questions."

"Different? How so?"

The Commander isn't happy being ignored, but she doesn't allow it to faze her. "I'm prepared for your men, but...if things go poorly... Caleb will be the first to suffer the consequences."

Sadie doesn't flinch with the revelation; she'd assumed as much. She watches the confident woman in front of her, wondering how far she can push her.

"Going poorly? Hasn't that already happened? You're holed-up, with the last of your grunts...outnumbered, and...you've lost the island. Maybe you should consider joinin' *me*." Sadie watches Russo before adding a final touch. "I mean...you do seem...more than capable."

The Commander smiles at hearing her words echoed by Sadie. "You're awfully confident, chained as you are...but what makes you think I'd leave the Nation?"

Sadie grins. "Easy, champ. Survival. Adapting is what's gotten you this far." She tilts her head as far to the side as the restraint will allow. "Unless...you actually like...being under a man's control."

Sadie keeps pushing. "I mean...when President X arrives and takes this post, then what? You've lost the firsties...plus the platoon...Even your elite death squad...the Mighty 9 have been eliminated..."

The Commander finds herself agitated and frustrated at losing the upper hand. She stands, but then sits right back down. Sadie's a worthy advisory, but *she's* the one in chains, and it serves as a reminder of who has the edge.

"Tell me," the red-haired warrior begins, intrigued, "what exactly are you suggesting?"

"Go rogue. Leave the Splitters...don't let 'em have this island."

The Commander laughs, genuinely entertained by the audacity of Sadie's suggestion. "And how shall I go about that?"

"Simple, use the isle as bait. Keep up the charade of your firstie army...then, eliminate them one by one as they arrive...the arrogant bastards will never expect it. When President X finally makes the transition, he, too…can be removed from office."

The Commander, no longer laughing, listens as Sadie continues.

"The Nation's scattered. Once the alpha's down, they'll fracture further."

Sadie likes the direction things have gone and watches as Russo digests all she's hearing.

"And what about you?" the Commander asks, wondering what role Sadie envisions for herself.

"Me? I'd help. The Isle of Big Sur is too great an asset. They don't deserve it."

"Interesting…seems you've put some thought into this."

"Not like I got much else to do," Sadie jokes, attempting to ease any tension.

The Commander stands and stretches her arms overhead. The muscles along her upper body alternate between flexing and relaxing as they elongate with her movements. She pushes back a wave of hair that covers her eye and returns the chair to where it normally rests.

Sadie, sensing the end of their interaction and the Commander's impending departure, wants to end it on her note.

"Commander," Sadie says boldly. The domineering leader turns to face her as she speaks. "We could do it."

Sadie's resolve captures the Commander's attention. She plays variables against each other in her mind, making an audible reply impossible.

"And Russo," Sadie whispers, "you were right." She hesitates, letting the woman's confusion lengthen. "I would like to see Caleb."

Her admission gives Russo a moment to regroup, just as Sadie intended. Giving the Commander reason to leave feeling validated will give Sadie leverage down the line. The Splitter moves to close the door to the chamber, but Sadie attempts another foothold.

"Can I…get that bucket again?" Sadie asks, meekly.

Looking at Sadie through her dark ruby tendrils, Russo shuts the door, but the locks aren't engaged. Seconds later it reopens, revealing that her request didn't go unheeded. Besides the bucket, there's also a full bottle of water and a single potato. Repositioning the cleaned-out receptacle to its upside-down position, both items are placed on top. Without speaking, the Commander loosens one of Sadie's arm restraints and positions it so she can reach the water and food. Sadie takes the bottle and slowly drinks.

"Thank you," she offers, setting it down and reaching for the spud. The potato, though raw, at least provides some nourishment—and she's grateful, which is the Commander's purpose. While she chews, Sadie's neck restraint is also loosened to provide enough slack for her to sit. Another gift. This time, though, when the door shuts, the locks slide into position, leaving Sadie to wonder how long it'll be before the next check-in.

Sadie, carefully chewing on only one side of her mouth, swallows some potato. Feeling for the bucket, she sets down her food, and from the opposite side of her mouth, she removes a small length of putty from her upper rear gums. Hidden beneath the pliable pale substance is a short bobby pin. Sadie sticks it in the back of her hair and returns to eating. When the potato's gone, she tests the range of motion her loosened restraints offer.

Darkness skews the passage of time. Sadie attempts to estimate how long she's been held. While drifting asleep seated on the bucket, a sound draws her attention. The room's outer door is opened and movement in and out can be heard. Straining with each sound, Sadie attempts to decipher everything she hears; but when the prison door opens, what's waiting for her isn't what she expected: A small table, set for two, sits within view just outside the door.

"Time to talk," the Commander says, nodding to the table. "It'll be better this way."

Using caution and precision, she transfers Sadie from the confinement chamber to a chair, modified with chains for this very purpose. They sit in silence across from one another for what feels like eternity. The tattooed fighter breaks eye contact to pour them each a glass of water.

"Has Caleb been given food and water?" Sadie asks, picking up her glass.

"He'll be joining us shortly."

Sadie nearly spills the water as it reaches her lips.

Her reaction delights the Commander. "But first, there's...details to work out."

Russo starts by reinforcing the soundness of Sadie's theory. The isle's location could be used to unexpectedly eradicate arriving

Splitters, along with President X. The Commander is in complete agreement; they'd never see it coming. The charade could be maintained.

"The problem," the Commander goes on, "unfortunately...is us. And learning to trust one another."

Sadie nods in agreement.

"I have a solution...or...at least a starting point," the Commander adds, before taking a drink.

She unravels a plan of partnership. When it transitions to self-preservation and gaining each other's trust, Sadie's confidence begins to waiver. The Commander finds the elimination of her last M9, along with Caleb, a necessity. By her logic, it removes any pre-existing loyalties that could get in the way and creates an entirely new dynamic. "I'll take care of 'em both," the Commander offers, out of respect for a worthy adversary and as a sign of loyalty to a future comrade.

She'll shelter Sadie from having to execute a friend, and she'll give her time to say goodbye before the deed is done—something of a rarity in these times. Shocked by the outpouring of information and the mind-scramble accompanying it, Sadie stares at the woman seated across from her. Before a response can take form, the Commander gets up, feeling confident, and proceeds.

The Commander retrieves an array of items set beside the door, an armload at a time, and places them on the table. The setting changes from two to three places. A meal is spread upon it with an aroma released as a lid is lifted.

"Thought the three of us could dine together," the Commander says, adding another chair. She hesitates, watching Sadie, then leaves.

Sadie, making haste with the opportunity, removes the bobby pin from her hair. She bites the rubber-coated tips off and bends one end. She palms the implement as the Commander returns with Caleb in tow. He enters chained, beaten, and wearing a pair of shorts that don't fit. As their eyes meet, emotions surge between them. He, too, gets chained at Sadie's left. When the Commander sits, she serves each of them a large portion of roasted potatoes and rabbit.

The surreal atmosphere and odd energy surrounding the threesome creates an inability to digest the strange turn of events. The obvious absence of knives and forks at the place settings also tarnishes any attempt at normality.

Caleb picks up a spoon and stares blankly at it; his gaze goes from the utensil to Sadie and then to the Commander before he loops through all three again. The silence is interrupted by the sound of metal scraping across a plate as the warrior eats. Noticing the other two aren't dining, she pauses, mid-bite.

"Just eat. You need calories, and the food," she trails off, chewing and swallowing, "is delicious."

Sadie takes a bite, and Caleb follows. They eat without talking, but occasionally exchange glances. Anything they say could provide their captor with insight they don't want to share, so neither take the chance. As their plates empty, the last of the food is divided, but the second serving is eaten much slower. Sadie drinks the last of her water. She finds comfort in not having so many chains clank about, and rests her hand beside the other in her lap.

"Thank you," she adds politely. "That was delicious."

Figuring the Commander has some prepared dialogue, Sadie watches the woman eat the last of her meal and then remove the dishes.

"I'll be back shortly," Russo says, talking directly to Sadie as she opens the door and leaves.

Sadie reacts swiftly. She's already broken the bobby pin into two pieces by repeatedly folding it back and forth. She's managed to free one hand and proceeds with haste. Freeing her other arm restraint, she reaches for Caleb's shackles and tries talking at the same time that he does. They both stop, then start, once again at the same time.

"You first," he offers.

"She's planning to kill you. I think…when you leave here," Sadie whispers quickly while her hands work fast. "The plan is for her and I to join forces, stop the Nation, and control the island."

"I heard 'em," he says, watching the door. "She sent that last bastard out, used a trapdoor or somethin'…she's alone."

Sadie rearranges his chains, but is forced to return to her seat as the door opens. They try acting nonchalant, but the Commander senses something's up. The fierce one decides it's best to simply remove Caleb—permanently.

Moving towards him, her focus stays with Sadie. A huge error. Caleb wraps the chains from his arms around her throat! The Commander kicks and thrashes about. She turns everything within reach upside down. The table and chairs are tossed. The redhead repeatedly slams Caleb against the side of a set of bunk beds. Straining to keep hold of her, he clings to her back. His only chance is to choke her out. As the redness in her face becomes purple, the warrior's strength fades.

"Stop!" shouts Sadie. "Caleb, stop! We need her!" Sadie grabs Caleb and a handful of his chains.

He looks at Sadie, trying to understand.

"Stop, we need her," she says again.

He releases his grip as Sadie takes away the chains. She quickly secures the Commander with the wrist and leg restraints. Reduced to near death, the warrior gasps for breath.

"Russo...Rene Russo," Sadie says, as the color begins to return to the woman's face.

Hearing her full name, she looks up, choking, with bloodshot and watery eyes. Not since her childhood has someone called her Rene, and its effect is—odd.

Sadie holds the collection of throwing blades and a telescopic impact baton she's just removed from the Commander's body. "I don't believe the two of us are done yet," she says. "Unless you'd rather it simply ended now."

Rene drops her head.

"Good," Sadie says with finality, "for now." She motions to the closet.

There's a moment within the Commander where she almost opts for quick death, but her survival instinct has her finally crawling forward. Once inside the confinement chamber, Sadie quickly attaches the neck restraint.

"Go keep watch," Sadie nearly growls to Caleb. "I'll join you later."

FOURTEEN

Anxiously awaiting Sadie's arrival, Caleb hovers near the trapdoor in case the last M9 returns the way he left. The rug that covered it sits pushed aside and bunched against the nearby wall, where he keeps watch. With each passing minute, his fear grows as he fights the urge to leave his post and check on Sadie. When she finally does appear, he jumps to his feet.

"You okay?" he asks, speaking loudly.

Sadie raises a finger to her lips, motioning toward the trapdoor.

"I'm gonna take a look around," she whispers, "and find something to wear. You okay a little longer?"

He shrugs his shoulders; he can't really say no, or that all he wants is for her to stay near him. She turns to leave. Caleb watches her walk away in the short sarong that barely covers her backside, then returns to his spot against the wall.

Sadie quickly inspects the home's remaining rooms, gleaning what she can. Finding Russo's personal quarters, she rummages through her belongings. Besides a change of clothes, she hopes to gain insight into the psyche of such a ruthless survivor. The room is an unusual mixture of sleeping chamber, private office, and fitness station. One of its walls houses an array of blades and throwing implements, another, military munitions and supplies.

With hasty precision, Sadie looks through the closet and dresser drawers where she finds a silk scarf tightly wrapped around something firm. Unraveling it reveals an old photo, framed in silver, of twin girls with long blond braids—childhood versions of Russo. Even then, determination burns in little Rene. Putting it back, Sadie returns to Caleb; bringing food, water, their shoes, additional clothing, and a few random items she carries in a small box.

"Look," she says, softly, holding out her bounty before passing him clothing and food.

Sadie and Caleb eat quickly and gulp down the water. When finished, Sadie uses hydrogen peroxide to clean Caleb's facial wounds. He took a nasty beating—obviously his captivity was a bit different than hers. As she works, he wonders when this nightmare will finally end, when they can be together in safety back on Three Sisters.

His thoughts, though, are interrupted. Movement beneath them draws their attention! The trapdoor lifts a cautious inch, then another. Caleb and Sadie sit unnoticed on the hinged side. As it rises further, Sadie's stance changes. With a blade commandeered from Russo's room, she's prepared to strike. The door hesitates again, then opens further. A body slowly emerges.

"Dom," Sadie says, relinquishing her blade at the discovery of a friendly face.

The Delta leader is relieved to find Caleb and Sadie alive.

"The Commander's locked up," Sadie says in a whisper, "but there's one M9 left. He went out..." Sadie notices Dom holding a pair of night-vision goggles that match the ones she found in the home.

"No," Dom says flatly. "The Commander's the only one left."

Dominic updates them, starting with the discovery of their absences, and the scare of finding Sadie's crossbow among the dead M9s left outside. Its presence clearly indicated trouble.

"It was luck," Dominic says, shaking his head. "I happened to be stationed right where that guy crawled out from."

"How long...have we...been here?" Caleb asks.

"Bout two and a half days," Dom replies.

Dominic's answer snaps Sadie into action. Taking charge, she inquires about the rescued locals, the boat's status, and the ocean conditions. Unable to answer all she asks, Dominic is told to find out what she needs to know, to check on the kids, and then return. Sadie instructs him to post Devon at the watchtower with Derrick; she also wants the rescued men and the two older boys to join her when he returns. Instead of having him leave the way he entered, they unlock the interior rooms and reopen the home.

Alone with Sadie and comforted knowing they're finally safe, Caleb moves to embrace her. She allows it, though her thoughts are centered elsewhere—specifically, on the woman she has chained up.

"Caleb," she starts, wrapped in his arms, but not wavering from her thoughts.

He pulls her in tighter. He's exhausted from the experience, and overwhelmed with fatigue and injury—both physical and mental.

"I need more time...to talk with Russo," Sadie says, pulling away.

"Why'd you even save her?" Caleb asks—lost, confused, and seemingly unsure of it all.

"More Splitters are comin' here, and...if we're gonna stop 'em, we're gonna need what she knows."

"And you think she can be trusted?"

"That's what I have to find out."

Caleb's mind struggles as he contemplates all that's taken place. Mental snapshots of what he just survived dash through his brain, but one scene elicits a strange insight.

"You called her...Rene...and it surprised her. She didn't tell you that, did she?" he asks.

Sadie confirms with a nod.

"So...you knew her?"

"No more than you." Her response adds to his confusion. Observing Caleb, Sadie explains who Rene Russo is, or—was. "That woman was an Olympian...in judo. She became an MMA fighter and UFC champ. A real badass. She was the first female to openly challenge men, and she beat 'em in two professional fights. It ruined their careers and, afterward...no other guys would risk it."

Caleb vaguely recalls some long-ago headlines, but he wasn't familiar with the sport.

"I think the M9s were also former MMA guys...I bet they trained at the same gym or something." A strange strategy begins taking form in Sadie's head. "I gotta find out more."

Caleb questions whether Russo should even be allowed to live and worries about the risk of having her among them. Sadie defends her position, frustrated when he doesn't stop questioning her plans.

"Well...if she's such a badass, then how'd we stop her," he snaps. "She didn't even attempt to fight you."

"There's a *reason*. And...I need to find it. If I'm not back in two hours," she says, turning to leave, "then come knock on the door."

Back in the room where Russo is being held, Sadie takes her time before unlocking and opening the confinement chamber's door. Rene stands naked, chained in an X just as Sadie had left her. Sadie grabs the chair and turns it backwards, part in mimic and part as a display of comfort. "I can see...the...enjoyment in this," Sadie says, slowly moving her gaze upward to the fighter's eyes—where it stays—neither woman looking away.

Maintaining eye contact, Sadie begins. "Tell me...why would you, a 'psychotically-competitive woman,'" she says, quoting a term coined long ago by sportscasters to describe Russo. "Let me win?" Sadie doesn't expect a response and none follows. "Physically, we both know you can take me, yet...I put you in chains and locked you away...without a fight, which must mean." She stalls, positioning both her elbows atop the chair's back. "That you allowed it."

A grin spreads across Rene's face.

Sadie's hands clasp together, her chin lowering to rest upon them. "So...this...is what you want?"

"What *I* want?" Rene questions. "Or...is this about...what *you* want?"

Sadie smiles in return. "No, this isn't about what either of us wants." She turns the chair around and leans back. "No more games," Sadie says plainly.

A drawn-out silence ensues before Sadie reclaims the lead. Laying out a modified version of what they've already discussed—without the necessity of eliminating Caleb—she talks of using the Isle of Big Sur as a chance to start fresh. Rene listens without interrupting.

"You're the only one left," Sadie says, making her point clear. "The Mighty 9s are no more. The last of them fell...when you sent him out."

Rene is having difficulty digesting all that's being relayed and suggested. But she believes Sadie that the last M9 is dead. Counting on his return as an unforeseen advantage, Russo realizes she's on her own.

Sadie continues, noting a change in her captive's eyes. "Your ferociousness has...provided for you...and taken you far, but...I know there's more to you." Getting up, she retrieves a box she tucked aside and kept hidden from view. "I think," she adds, removing the familiar sarong and wrapping it around the athletic figure, "your aggression has been a powerful tool...used to protect and carefully guard what you keep hidden." Returning her attention to the box, Sadie removes a water bottle and offers Russo a drink, which the woman takes. "This is your chance...to atone for any...and *all* past indiscretions. To use your skills and training...for good, to protect and defend others."

The Commander explicitly says how she's already protecting the firsties, from what this world takes. "With me, they'll learn how to defend themselves, grow up strong and...be able to take charge in any situation."

"Yeah, but at what cost? To be turned into a generation that knows only pain and suffering...and killing?" Sadie moves to grab one of the other chairs and motions with it towards Russo, who nods without hesitation.

The chair is placed behind the erect prisoner, and, one adjustment at a time, Sadie methodically changes each restraint until both women sit at eye level.

"Thank you," offers the red-haired beauty.

"You're welcome. I know it's not comfortable," Sadie adds, emphasizing her more than basic understanding of how Rene feels.

In silence, the women sit, letting the air settle. Much hangs between them.

"Before the Global Flood," Sadie says at last. "I lost my brothers... when they were young and...it changed me...forever." Sadie's words hit their mark. "I think about them all the time...especially, after they visit my dreams."

Rene leans forward, her eyes softening.

"Even though I know better, part of me always thinks I should've been able to protect them." Sadie, confident in her gut instinct, takes the final item from the box and, holding it up, pauses.

Rene knows what it is. An all too familiar sinking feeling surfaces in her stomach and in her current state of captivity, Russo struggles to control her emotions. Slowly, Sadie unwraps the scarf and stares into the eyes of the little girls in the picture.

"She was beautiful, wasn't she?" Sadie says without looking at Russo.

"And smart," Rene adds, fighting eyes that threaten to water.

Sadie looks up, leaves her seat to loosen one of her captive's restraints, and hands over the photograph. "When did you lose her?"

"A couple days after this picture was taken," Russo answers, her gaze on her twin. "I left her behind 'cuz...I was mad about being late," she pauses, starting to choke up, "she never made it to school... I looked everywhere for her." A lone tear breaks free. "I still..."

Witnessing the heartbreak, Sadie understands how an intense psyche could be shaped by years of relentless self-torment. Wondering if the warrior can truly be persuaded to aide them against the

Splitter Nation, she's casual in her next line of inquiry. "What was your sister's name?"

"Rachel," Russo answers, still staring at the picture.

"How old were you two?"

The captive looks up at Sadie and then back to the photo. "Almost ten."

Sadie allows a silence to settle before adding what she's been building to. "Same as most of the firsties…here on the isle."

The Commander's eyes dart to Sadie's.

"The way firsties were treated here…is that what you'd have wanted for her?" The question isn't designed to draw a verbal answer, but rather to elicit another emotional response.

A light knock at the door interrupts their interaction. Sadie's pleased with its timing.

"That's for me," she says, standing up from the chair. Sadie slides the familiar bucket into the confinement chamber, along with some tissue paper and more water. "I won't be back 'til morning." She looks at her captive like a caring friend before adding a final touch. "You okay 'til then?"

Blurry eyed, Rene manages to nod, her eyes unmoved from the picture.

FIFTEEN

Nearing the ranch house and navigating the dark with his night-vision goggles, Dominic hikes the incline. Devon follows, wearing his own pair. Both Deltas, feeling good about the success of their mission, notice two figures around a fire. Out of habit, they creep towards cover, hiding their approach. Leon sits near a fire barrel, adding more wood with one of the smaller kids. Dirty streaks run down the little girl's cheeks as he talks softly.

"It was a nightmare," he says, soothingly, handing the child a drink of water. "You're safe, there's no monsters, I promise. As long as I'm here...no one's gonna get ya." He drapes his jacket around her shoulders, then returns to sitting on his log. "You wanna hear a story about that house?" he asks, pointing towards the ranch.

The youngster nods yes, while pulling the jacket tighter around her torso.

"Well," Leon begins, "a long...long...time ago my great-granddad lived there. For almost a hundred years...this...was my family's home." He pauses, watching the child, then asks, "Do you know how many one hundred is?"

Still teary eyed, the little one shakes her head sideways.

"Ummm..." he stammers, thinking of a way to explain it. "Well...it's...how old are you?"

"Dis many winners," she says, holding up one hand and the index finger from the other.

"You're six winters old?" he confirms, keeping her distracted.

"Uh huh."

"Well, look," he says, opening up her remaining fingers so all ten can be counted, "this is ten, but..." He stands and using a stick, levels the loose dirt in front of them. "I need your help for this." He waves her over; cautiously, she slides off her seat. "Put your hands out, with all ten fingers."

She does.

"Now look." He takes a knee. "Press 'em down and make a print." He demonstrates with his own hands, then wipes away his marks.

She keeps her fingers spread wide and, palms down, presses them into the soft dusty ground. Leon counts each finger mark out loud. When he reaches ten, he tells her they're going to make a total of ten prints. Each time she presses her hands into the earth, they count together while moving in a semicircle around the fire's lighted edge.

"So that's ten fingers, ten times," he says, as she finishes the last set. "That equals one hundred. Can you count that high?"

She doesn't respond immediately, but finally does, saying no.

"Well, then, let's do it together...okay?"

She smiles, and Leon starts at the first handprint, counting the little finger first. She repeats each number he says. By the time one hundred is reached she's smiling with glee, having forgotten the terrible dream that tore her from slumber.

"Dat's a lodda finners," she says as they finish.

"It is...and...it's a lotta years. That's how long my family lived here. Look," he says, pulling a faded picture out from an inner pocket of his jacket that she still wears. "These were my parents and...the little boy...is me. I was jus' about as old as you."

The child looks carefully at the family standing in front of the ranch house. "Da house is...diffent...it's willy, willy big and...boo-tee-full."

Leon smiles. "It was, and one day...I'll make it so again."

The little girl rests her head against him. Seated close to each other, they stare into the old photo as the fire's flames flicker a soft orange glow. Beginning to drift off, the little one closes her eyes. Once asleep, Leon picks her up and starts to carry her back to the barracks.

Dom steps from the shadows, giving Leon a start. "This was your family's?" he asks, evaluating Leon's body language.

Leon nods confirmation, motions to the kid in his arms, and departs. He takes her inside and, returning alone, he joins the two Deltas at the fire where the conversation turns to Leon and how he came to be on the Isle of Big Sur.

"My parents inherited the ranch...we lived here for most of my childhood, but...I got sick and...everything changed. They sold the property to cover my medical bills and...moved us closer to Stanford, where I was being treated. I spent my teens...in and out of chemo and radiation treatments." He thinks of the hardships and years of sacrifices his parents had made for him. "Eventually, though, I went into remission."

"Ooh-kay," Devon leads. "So…how'd you end up back here and workin' for the Nation?"

Leon looks hard at Devon. "I didn't work for them…I used them… to get here."

"Explain," Dom commands.

Leon's look doesn't alter. "I was living on a houseboat at Lake Oroville when the floods hit. People flocked to the shores and camps sprung up everywhere. Then…*they* arrived." He shakes his head as images of the tragedy resurface and flash through his mind. "The Splitters took control of the area…claiming the water…I escaped getting killed only cuz they needed my skills."

Dom squints his eyes and tilts his head with a sideways glance. He doesn't have to ask for a further explanation.

"I'm talented…at carpentry. My custom-built houseboat drew their attention. It got…confiscated, along with all the others, so…I got assigned to work on the boats they wanted modified." Leon swallows and then continues. "If I refused…it was torture…or…tortured to death."

"So, how'd you end up here?" Dominic asks.

"The lake eventually dried up…forcing them to relocate, and… when they moved…I was taken along to Tahoe. There…I made myself valuable…got assigned to the fleet scouring the Pacific coast. When the Commander needed work on her vessel…I toiled away, perfecting everything she wanted while learning what I could. Pleased with my work…she made sure I got assigned to lead construction here…on the island. But none of 'em knew my history or connection to the ranch… they've just been usin' me. I've kept quiet…waiting for any opportunity…waiting for the right moment. I know I'm supposed to be here. And then… you guys arrived…"

They sit in silence for some time before Dominic turns to Devon, who nods in approval. Both Deltas, at ease with Leon's sincerity and their newly gained insights, find the uncertainties they harbored against him vanishing. Satisfied, they quickly update him with Sadie's orders before walking over to the reconstructed section of the ranch.

Leon heads straight to the radio and checks the dials. He shrugs his shoulders.

"It looks like everything's okay," he says, turning up the volume. "It's got power."

"Try it, then," Dom demands, eager to move forward with his orders.

Leon sits at the console and holds down the receiver. "IBS Ranch to Command Central, do you copy?" He waits for a response and tries again. After his third attempt, there is a crackled reply.

"Copy, IBS Ranch, this is Command Central."

The Deltas high five, recognizing Caleb's voice.

"IBS Ranch status report: all-clear. Repeat, all-clear. Over."

"Copy that, IBS Ranch. Command Central out."

Leon turns to face the Delta boys hovering nearby. Both men turn in unison before quickly departing, anxious to check on the last of their trio stationed alone at the watchtower. They head out, going north and on approach, they signal him.

When they hear the appropriate response, the Deltas move forward and into the watchtower. The pack is reunited. They present Derrick with his own pair of night-vision goggles, along with a small handheld radio. The team shares the latest updates before deciding on an evening rotation. Each will take a rotating shift on watch, allowing the group some rest.

Just before first light and with the ocean's swell beginning to taper, Dom takes off at a trot to make good time returning to Sadie. Along the way, he peeks in on the barracks and the sleeping kids before waking Leon, who moves to the radio. Following the A.M. radio check, he heads out, jogging in the soft glow of sunrise.

Dominic follows the path and reaches the small water station. The two local men and their two teenaged boys have finished filling the day's water quota. The work is joyous for them, knowing they're supplying rescued firsties and no longer under the vicious control of the Nation.

"Alright, guys," Dominic says, addressing the men. "Deliver the water to the barracks, then hustle back so we can meet at your place. Your input's necessary."

The two men get to work and disappear down the trail, encouraged by a new day's dawn. The father amongst them is eager to retrieve his youngest. Along the way, he's overwhelmed with gratitude; he knows he'll never be able to repay these strangers. Returning as a threesome, they regroup with the two older boys and gather at the house as requested. Sadie greets each of them with a firm handshake before getting straight to business.

"My name's Sadie," she states in her own voice. "We came here to rescue the kids, but...it seems more's gonna be required." She hesitates, gauging their various reactions. "The Splitters on this island... have been...terminated. But...we've spared the Commander."

The locals show confused looks, but Sadie doesn't deviate from her manner or tone.

"The Splitter Nation plans to occupy and control this island." She looks each of them, individually, in the eyes. "But I believe...with the Commander's help, we can prevent that from ever happening."

The home's true owner speaks up. "What makes you think she'll help...or can be trusted? That woman..."

The group's attention is stolen by sounds from the radio! Caleb hops up, worried about the unscheduled radio contact. He makes minor adjustments to improve the sound's clarity, and Sadie takes the seat next to him.

"Command Central, this is IBS Ranch, do you copy?

Caleb responds with a building unease. "Copy, IBS Ranch, this is Command Central."

"Incoming vessels have made contact. We confirmed radio failure at the watchtower and advised direct contact with Command Central. Over."

"Copy that, IBS Ranch." Caleb reads a quick note Sadie jots down. "Did you get an ETA?"

"Negative, advised radio contact directly with you in one hour."

"Copy that." Caleb reads Sadie's next note. "Further instruction after contact; Command Central out."

"Copy, IBS Ranch out."

Caleb swivels from the console to face the group. All faces show concern except one.

"Alright," Sadie says. "We knew this was comin'. They don't know we're here and that's just the way we're gonna keep it."

Her calm demeanor bestows confidence to her team. Sadie proceeds with precision. Each person, including all three kids, is assigned a specific task, giving Sadie a quick window of opportunity. Returning to the prisoner's room, she slides open each lock, but pauses with the last one for dramatic effect. Inside the confinement chamber sits a weary, emotionally drained ghost of the former warrior, blinking rapidly with the sudden light.

"Sorry for this," Sadie starts. "But I'm gonna need info. Fast. It seems the time is upon us and...either *this*...is gonna work. Or it's not."

Taking a deep breath, the fallen Commander attempts to regain her composure. Sadie loosens one arm restraint at a time, adjusting the captive's position to one of more comfort.

"Thanks," Rene offers meagerly, knowing her arms are being moved only because Sadie needs something from her.

"I assume you must already know why," Sadie says, taking a seat across from her.

Russo nods slightly.

"Okay, then," Sadie begins. "Two vessels are en route...how many should we expect?"

"Rest of the platoon, 'bout twenty...plus each ship's crew."

Sadie's gut tells her that Russo has begun to relinquish her commitment to the Nation. One way or another, affirmation of this will come soon enough; asking the Commander for specifics on the logistics of new arrivals and the communication protocols used, Sadie gauges Russo's every response for honesty or deception.

"Anything else we should know...or be prepared for?" Sadie asks as her final question.

Russo stalls for the first time while answering—initially Sadie believes it's because the woman is deep in thought, but it's something else entirely. Russo's eyes squint before an adjustment settles across them.

"Success. Now! That's how *this* works," Sadie says forcefully, hoping Russo will divulge whatever it is she's contemplating.

Locked in eye contact, the captive knows she has to decide one way or the other. She knows Sadie's right. Any future depends on success—right here, right now.

Russo speaks. "If you want 'success, now'...we're gonna need a few things." A hint of a smile crosses her face before disappearing with such swiftness that Sadie questions whether it ever existed. "I got a little sumpin'," adds the Commander, "that could be a big help."

SIXTEEN

Returned and gathered, the group's eyes look to Sadie. She verifies completion of the assigned tasks and praises each of them when they respond affirmatively. Due to the impending arrival of more Splitters, she quickly jumps into outlining a strategy—making sure the group's in full support, especially the freed locals whose home now serves their cause. Talking directly to the patriarch, Sadie confirms that he's amenable to the arrangement.

"Okay, then..." Sadie begins, after receiving his confirmation. "We need to prep for the radio dialogue...and get ready." She delegates additional tasks for each person.

When the local men and boys have dispersed, Sadie pulls Dominic and Caleb aside to fill them in further, specifically with the details Russo just shared.

"You believe her?" Dom asks Sadie, who affirms. "Okay then, whacha wanna us to do?"

"Double time it to the barracks, grab Leon, and check Russo's boat." She turns to Caleb. "Sorry, but...you gotta go, too. I need you to man the radio and maintain IBS Ranch while Leon's gone. Immediately after the vessels make contact, I'll radio. Then I'll join ya as fast as I can."

Caleb thinks about arguing his assignment, but after a direct look from Dominic, does not. The two men grab their gear and head out on the urgent mission. As they depart, the two locals return, moving awkwardly, uncomfortable in their new clothes. Dressed in Splitter gear, they're hesitant about asking why it's been ordered.

Sadie notices. She compliments them on their disguises. "They're only for precaution," she adds. "Hopefully, we'll confront 'em at the coast." She points north. "The plan is to keep them off the island, but...if needed, we'll fall back to the barracks, and...as a last resort, come back here to your home. This will be our stronghold." She turns to the father. "You should be the one to stay here, with your boys, and operate the radio." She turns her attention to the man's best friend. "We're gonna need you to leave with me. You'll replace Caleb at the ranch's radio, and...if needed... retreat with the kids back here."

Both men accept their responsibilities and transition to the radio console, where Sadie runs them through procedures and protocols, making sure they use, and understand, proper lingo. Sadie fills in additional details about Splitter communication patterns she gathered from Russo; anxious to deduce the accuracy of her intel, she moves the dials to match the corresponding channel. The men rehearse their calls.

Static crackle emits from the equipment. Nodding to the father as an indicator of his status as radio operator, he reaches his hand to adjust the knob.

"Cchhhhh...ccchhhhh...Co...mand Central...Repeat. This is inbound Split Vessels *Argo* and *Beta*, hailing IBS Command Central. Do you copy? I repeat...do you copy?"

"Copy, inbound. This is IBS Command Central. Been advised you're en route. Please provide ETA." The man's hand trembles.

"ETA, six hours."

"Copy that. Be advised...radio is still down at Split post IBS. Once anchored, prepare for boarding and inspection. After inspections are complete, your orders will be delivered. IBS Command Center out."

"Copy. Over and out."

The father takes what feels like his first breath in minutes, the pounding in his chest eases and his heart rate slows.

"Perfect," Sadie says, clasping him on the shoulder. "You did good. Keep post, maintain the scheduled radio checks, and wait for word."

He looks to the young boys, who stand near. He swallows, straightens his shoulders, and with a mixture of pride and determination, responds, "Yes ma'am."

"Gentleman," Sadie begins, shaking each of the youngster's hands. "Being brave doesn't mean you're not scared...it just means... that, even when you are scared, you still do something about it."

With her words, the two older boys stand a bit taller. As for the youngest, his eyes travel to his father's, and then to the radio dials.

Kneeling, Sadie speaks to the small boy. "You should learn all about that radio, too." She glances at the father before continuing. "Because, one day...workin' it...might be your job."

With an atmosphere set for departure, Sadie motions to the father's best friend standing nearby to follow her. She slings a bag across her back, and they depart. Quickly realizing her companion can't keep up with her pace, Sadie waits until they reach the water station before going on ahead. She takes off at a brisk run, the knife wounds in her quads aching with each stride. Sadie reaches the ranch and slows only a few steps away from Caleb—who jumps at her approach.

"Just you?" he asks, worried, while looking past her.

"No, he's behind…twenty minutes or so." Sadie talks while controlling her breathing and recovering from the run. "We got about… five hours."

Dropping her bag, she rips open the zipper, takes out several items, and begins removing her shirt. Once again needing the security and machismo of her alter ego, she unfastens an elastic bandage roll and tightly wraps her torso.

Alarmed by the risks they're taking, Caleb jumps to help, and Sadie lets him. Before dressing with additional layers of clothing, she tears off several pieces of duct tape. Under each strip, Sadie hides small implements to her forearms and around both ankles, adding to her mysterious abilities and Caleb's sense of curiosity. She tucks bobby pins into various locales, including within her short hair, smudges her chin and jawline with soot, and finishes her disguise with an old tattered hat taken from one of the dead M9s.

"Sadie…" Caleb begins, met by her icy glare. He doesn't continue, partially in disbelief of the transition he just witnessed and partially because he knows that, once again, she won't be using her real name and Sadie's not happy that he just did.

Sadie pulls another item from the bag. Caleb can't help himself. "Is that…silly putty?"

"Ah huh," she mutters, wedging a piece of it deep into the back of her gum line, using it to conceal a final small bobby pin.

"How do you…know…all this?" Caleb asks.

A cold, distant look answers him. Then Sadie grunts, "Not now," before taking off for a perimeter check.

As she returns, so does the local man they've been waiting on. He can't hide his shock at her changed appearance, but without hesitation they head inside and radio Command Central. With the call completed, she nods to Caleb, and the two of them head out. He can barely keep up with the pace Sadie's set, but he doesn't complain or slow. As she pulls ahead, the watchtower comes into sight, its presence a welcomed relief. *At least the running's over,* Caleb thinks, catching up to where Sadie stopped.

In low tones and gestures, she splits from him so they can circumnavigate the area until reaching their designated locations. Sadie whistles to the watchtower, and when an appropriate response is returned, she, alone, approaches. Ducking into the small structure for a brief two minutes, she asks for an update.

"Dom and Leon are still out there," replies Derrick, pointing to the sailboat.

With binoculars to her eyes, Sadie scans the Commander's boat. Observing no indication of movement on the vessel, she hands them over to Devon to keep watch. He soon sights Dom and Leon and yells to the rest of the team—who have moved outside to prepare for contact with the *Argo's* and *Beta's* scheduled arrival. They've been stacking concrete debris that lie scattered about from the bridge's destruction into small mounds for cover. Dropping their last chunks, they hustle towards the zodiac as it zooms to shore.

"We found it!" Dom exclaims on approach.

Unloading the crate on the dock, the small group stares in astonishment as it's opened.

"Anyone ever use one of these?" asks one of the Delta guys, staring with huge eyes.

Each of them responds no. All eyes fall on Sadie. She cautiously lifts the weapon, but sets it aside when she sees a manual beneath it. Flipping through the pages, the group learns the proper way to hold, load, and fire.

Deciding the best location for its use, Sadie outlines possible scenarios. Quickly, they come to consensus. Sadie divides them into three teams of two and makes sure that each group understands their roles. Two teams will simultaneously motor out when the *Beta* and *Argo* arrive. Under the guise of IBS Splitters, they will gather intel and inspect the boats before returning to shore to report.

Sadie and Caleb, who'll stay on land, move the long weapon behind one of the newly-erected concrete piles. They have just enough time to prep it before Devon signals. They scramble back to the tower.

The two Splitter vessels come into view, and all of them take position. The two teams, waiting on the isle's makeshift dock, steady their nerves. When both boats anchor, the teams leave the dock and approach in the zodiacs, adding to Sadie's discomfort with their risk. She keeps a visual on them, observing one member from each team scratch their heads in the practiced sign of 'so far so good' from aboard their assigned vessels. But her concern doesn't ease, especially when they disappear below deck on the Splitter boats.

She breaths heavily. *It's taking too long*, she thinks. When they finally resurface, a sigh of relief escapes her lungs. As they return to shore, the men scramble up to the watchtower to share the details of what they've seen and heard.

Sadie's surprised to hear that the *Beta* holds all the platoon passengers, while the *Argo* carries all their cargo. "Well, that's not very smart," she comments with a plan brewing.

Her comment confuses the men. But before offering further explanation, Sadie scans over the two enemy boats with the binoculars. "Okay, our timing's going to have to be perfect, but…I think we're gonna end up better than we thought." She outlines their next moves.

The group is confident with Sadie's directions and anxious to secure the island and everyone's safety. As the two teams shuttle back out to the boats with specific directives—for themselves and for each of the ships—a new sense of discomfort enfolds: they know killing will soon commence.

Tied to the *Argo*, Dom and Leon climb aboard to tell its crew their cargo vessel will be moved closer to shore for unloading—but first, what few supplies the *Beta* carries will be moved ashore. At the same time, Devon and Derrick, aboard the *Beta*, instruct its crew to fill their lifeboats with what items need to be unloaded.

From the security of the tower, Sadie watches her plan unfold. The Deltas, back on their zodiac—loaded with goods—approach the dock, followed by the other small lifeboats from the *Beta*.

Sadie nods to Caleb, who leaves her and heads off in the opposite direction. When the last of the small crafts dock, Sadie moves into position. She removes her hat, the signal for attack! From behind the pile of concrete, Caleb shoulders the rocket launcher, mumbles a quick prayer, and takes aim at the passenger boat carrying half a platoon of Splitters. The target lined up in his crosshairs, he fires on the *Beta*, surprised at the ease of using such a destructive weapon.

A thundering explosion follows. The boat bursts into pieces. The sole remnants of its crew stand at the docks frozen in shock. The distraction provides Sadie, Devon, and Derrick an opportunity to attack and eliminate them with blades and arrows.

Hoping the other team, still aboard the *Argo*, was just as successful during the explosion's distraction, they hastily jump into the zodiac and zoom out. Sadie, Caleb, and Derrick climb aboard the *Argo*, searching the vessel while Devon checks the water and the flaming wreckage for any survivors that might need to be dispatched.

At the *Argo's* helm Sadie finds Leon positioned among three dead bodies; below, she finds more dead Splitters sprawled about, one is still alive and held at gunpoint by Dom. Reunited with their team and growing more confident, they leave Dom with his hostage and move deeper into the vessel, this time with better intentions. They reach the men chained in the cargo hold, who stare in utter disbelief at being freed. Sadie, in a deep voice, asks questions. The Splitter uniforms worn by their rescuers add to the captives' confusion, but rubbing their wrists and ankles as Sadie picks each restraint free, they begin to respond.

"No, dey's two mo," responds one of the skinny, dirty slaves through several missing teeth.

"Da cooks," his companion, in similar shape, adds. "Check da storage in back of da galley…dats where dey keep 'em."

"Alright," Sadie starts, looking toward Leon. "Go check and," she turns to the rescued slaves, "get these guys some food. We'll be up shortly."

Tattered, beaten, and starved, the rescued men limp away as Sadie returns to where Dom holds his Splitter prisoner.

"Bring him below," Sadie orders, gruffly, as Caleb aides Dom in physically forcing the man to move. "Lock his right arm first." They wrestle with him, shackling his arm.

"Fuck you! You fucking deserters!" the man yells, under the impression they're members of the Nation. He fights and kicks, attempting to get free.

Caleb manages to secure the wrist restraint, but as he moves to grab a leg, he's met with a knee to the groin that stops all his progress. At the same moment, Dom slips, giving the angry Splitter the chance he wanted. The man pulls a hidden blade from beneath his jacket and lunges, barely missing Dom. Chained, the Splitter doesn't have the range to reach any of them, but that doesn't halt his threats or the explosion of foul profanities that spew from his mouth. When he finally pauses, more to catch his breath than to stop his filthy barrage, Sadie starts to ask a question—but the man interrupts.

"You think I'm gonna talk! You dumb mother fuckers! Ain't nutin' ya can do to git me talkin'." He lunges forward, swinging madly with his blade.

As he slows, Sadie tries again, this time with some added pressure from Caleb and Dom and their weapons.

"Sheee-it, you think that scares me? Go 'head, shoot! I'll never betray the Nation! Not like you bastards." His knife hovers over his chained arm.

Deranged, he starts another rant, yelling how no torture could ever break him. In a fit of rage, and to prove his point, he begins cutting his own flesh, attempting to free his arm. As blood drips and splatters about, he keeps hacking away while exploding with an unsettling hatred.

Back to back shots ring out and his noise and horror are silenced. His body collapses to the ground. Both Dom and Caleb turn in shock to Sadie, who stands holding the smoking gun.

"He was of no use to us," she says, coldly, before leaving to check on the people they just rescued.

SEVENTEEN

"It's gonna hav'ta be you," Leon says, motioning towards the back door, as the freed slaves sit to eat.

Sadie approaches the space. Peering through the small diamond-shaped window, she ducks instinctively as a skillet thuds against it. Checking again, another item strikes the door. Sadie stares back through the window at her aggressor and softens in her demeanor. She removes her hat, grabs a rag, and undoes the lock. As she opens the door, a large pot followed by two cans of food take to the air and crash to the ground. After a brief hesitation, Sadie slides a small stool into the space. It, too, gets hit by a flying kitchen object.

Sadie moves to sit upon the stool while dodging one last projectile. Instead of talking, she wipes away the soot from her face, while keeping eye contact with the elderly woman fiercely guarding the younger female behind her.

"Ma'am, no one's here to hurt you," Sadie says, in her normal voice. "Or you either," she adds, trying to make eye contact with the lady cowering behind the elderly one. "I promise."

Suspecting only lies after years of abuse, the ragged woman doesn't falter and stands her ground. Sadie smiles at such bravery, but it quickly fades as the images before her sink in. Both women, clothed in rags, are dirty and bruised. Broken skin covers both their ankles and wrists. Sadie's breath catches.

"How 'bout...we start by getting rid of the chains?" Sadie says, without moving from her perch. "Look." She raises her pant leg to expose a duct-taped ankle. "And I've got two more patches here," she says, pointing to her forearms.

The women don't know what they're being shown, or why, and aren't sure of anything.

"I've hidden tools, underneath...some...for pickin' locks." Sadie pauses. "I'll show ya."

Undoing her top layer's buttons creates a noticeable discomfort in both captives. With the shirt removed and another long sleeve to go, Sadie talks softly, removing her arms from the sleeves in an attempt to ease their fears.

"See," she says, holding out an arm before tearing the tape away from her flesh.

The elderly one steps slightly closer.

"It's okay...my name's Sadie. I'm not a Splitter...there's no more of them left." She peels back the strip on her other arm and examines what's hidden beneath. "These should work," she announces, pulling three implements from the sticky surface. "But...I'll have to move over to you."

Both women's eyes widen when she stands. Sadie continues talking softly while gingerly moving forward. She stops two steps away and holds the tools for the women to view. Even the one still hiding behind the other tilts her head to peek.

Sadie motions to the metal clasps hanging from each of their extremities. "Which one...do you want gone first?"

"Vis un," the old woman finally answers through a mouthful of missing teeth.

Sadie takes a knee to examine the woman's ankle and the apparatus chaining its captive to the wall. The damage around each of her appendages reveals a lengthy time spent in shackles. The skin is scarred, calloused and, in some spots, seeps from layers of infliction.

Sadie frees the chain from the old woman's leg and inspects the shackle still attached around her ankle. Its design, identical to the others worn by both females, will require different equipment to be completely removed, but after Sadie frees the chain from her opposite wrist, at least the elder isn't restrained. Stepping aside, the grandmotherly figure motions to her companion, to whom Sadie turns.

"It's okay," Sadie encourages, waiting for the woman to respond.

When she limps forward, Sadie works on the chains in the same order, until both of the second woman's limbs are freed.

"I'll get these off too," Sadie says, tapping the metal clasps still around the younger woman's wrists. "But...I'm gonna need better tools."

The older woman wraps her arms around the younger female as they embrace in a bewildered stupor. Sadie gives them a moment before gently asking for their names.

"Mee-Maw," says the older one. "En vis is Rowin, buth...she von' palk."

The younger woman offers a hesitant nod while briefly braving eye contact. Sadie isn't exactly sure what Mee-Maw just said, but she explains what they've recently accomplished on the isle, including the eradication of the Splitters, along with how many men are helping her. Sadie encourages them as they move from their tight quarters and join the others. When Mee-Maw sees the freed slaves devouring old food scraps, she rapidly signs to Rowin, who jumps to collect what's asked. Together they bustle about making a decent meal, while Sadie scavenges for tools. Returning with a hammer, chisel, and tin snips, along with an armload of clothes, she removes the metal clasps from their ankles and wrists before offering the rescued women and men a fresh set of clothes.

"Why don't you heat plenty of water and take a proper bath," Sadie suggests as they look through the items.

As the women depart, happy at the chance to bathe and change, the two freed men sit with their rescuers. They, too, get updated on what's occurred on the island, along with the plans to keep the Isle of Big Sur free from Splitter control. Then they're asked if they're willing to help.

"Ya kiddin' us? Of course, we'll help. Ain't no way we're ever gonna forget whacha dun fer us? Besides...we ain't got nowhere else to go, so..." He pauses, looking at his friend who confirms with a thumbs up. "Ya got a deal. We'll help fight those sum ah bitches... fer as long as it takes."

Their willingness gives Sadie the go-ahead on another one of her information quests. Multiple questions follow. After sharing what they know, the men take a turn getting clean and changing. Sadie sends Leon back to shore to report on their success and to relieve his replacement at the ranch's radio.

There's much to inventory and move off the cargo vessel and once a plan is outlined and assignments are given, the rescued men and women move about—energized by freedom, cleanliness, and fresh clothes. Even though they're dressed in Splitter uniforms, they take pride in knowing it's a way to stand against the Nation and serve a greater good.

Until dark, it's a constant shuttling back and forth from the vessel to the shore, in an effort to offload as much as possible. Sadie, machine like, moves at full pace, pushing aside her body's need to rest. When they finish for the evening, she retreats to the cargo hold and makes an effort to calculate what it'll take to complete the job and where things should go. Scrambling to climb upon the top of several containers, Sadie halts only when she hears Caleb calling.

"Hey boss," he starts, also tired, sore, and fully fatigued. "Mee-Maw says everything's ready."

Sadie clambers down and joins the group in one last trip ashore—they carry everything prepared for feeding their growing numbers. Leaving the vessel for the night with the Delta Team on duty at the watchtower with their meal portions, they head to the barracks, where the kids are hungrily waiting. Mee-Maw and Rowin watch the youngsters quickly empty their soup bowls, feeling a growing sense of pride as they ladle out seconds. Feeding the kids creates fulfillment for the rescued women, a feeling of meaning and hope.

Once everyone has eaten and the kids have bunked for the night, Sadie makes sure the adults understand what's to be done. With everyone's confirmation, she leaves in the dark, followed by Caleb, who trots well behind her, with extreme difficulty. The eerie green glow and limited peripherals of his night-vision goggles add to his disorientation. Sadie slows as he falls further behind, but a race is running through her mind. They near their destination, and she waits for him so they can approach together. A quick signal from Sadie is all that's needed before the locals open their home.

"That was fast," the father says as they enter.

Sadie doesn't waste a second, quickly sharing details of what's transpired along with what potential outcomes they can expect.

"Okay then...you two should rest," the father's friend adds, when Sadie finishes talking. "You're gonna need some sleep and...we got ya covered. We got it all figured out...one of us keeps watch while the other sleeps near the radio."

"Yeah," the father butts in. "We moved in a cot, so...anything transmitting will wake us."

Caleb nods in gratitude, ready to collapse, and moves to crash for the night. When Sadie doesn't follow, he turns.

"They're right." He motions towards Sadie. "We need rest." He grabs her hand and lightly tugs. She steps closer, wanting nothing more than to sleep for days, but her mind isn't done for the night. She moves closer to Caleb and wraps him in an unexpected hug.

"I'll join ya in a bit," she whispers while they embrace.

He pulls her closer, kisses her forehead, and doesn't even ask what she intends. In his current state of exhaustion, he can barely stand; just knowing that she accepted curling up with him is enough. As she turns and departs, Caleb watches her long enough to see where she's headed. It doesn't surprise him.

"Sorry if I woke you," Sadie apologizes, opening the closet door as Russo blinks with the sudden light exposure. "But you and I have a few details to hash out."

"Should I take your presence and demeanor as a sign of...our first success?"

Unsurprised by Russo's observation, Sadie confirms her question and dives into what she's intended with the visit. The two women talk late into the night and by the time Sadie returns to Caleb's side, he's snoring and seems nearly dead to the world. It's only a few hours later, as the day begins to lighten, that he rolls over and realizes she's near. Moving closer to her, his movements snap Sadie from a disturbed slumber.

The abruptness of waking and the lack of rest leave her feeling queasy and unable to relax. With an elevated heart rate from bolting awake, Sadie stands. Her stomach is sick. She needs more sleep.

Caleb watches while she stretches, wondering if Sadie's anywhere near as sore as he feels. By the time he too gets to his feet, she's already moved to making tea and getting food ready for everyone. One by one, the locals appear, and Sadie greets each by name and with a handshake.

While they eat, talk is casual, but as soon as the meal ends, Sadie directs the conversation toward the former Commander and the room she occupies. Skillfully, she outlines what actions she thinks are needed, while giving each of the island inhabitants a chance to voice their thoughts and concerns. Even the youngest of the three boys speaks when asked his opinion.

"Okay then," Sadie says, standing. "How 'bout...in...twenty minutes?"

With the group's confirmation, she turns, dishes out what remains of breakfast, and heads to feed Russo before all of them will join her. Along the way, Sadie grabs a small bag she prepared before going to bed the night before. After unlocking the first door and knocking on the second, she exposes the woman locked inside.

"You got less than twenty," Sadie begins, while grabbing the items she set aside. "Eat quickly and change." She unlocks several of Russo's chains and hands over the bowl of food and the bag.

Russo eats as Sadie moves about the small room, rearranging the sparse furniture.

"Really?" Rene asks, questioning Sadie's choice of clothes for her.

"Jus' hurry up," Sadie responds, ready to move forward.

Reluctantly, Russo puts on the outfit. "I forgot I even had this shit," she murmurs, and then louder: "You went through everythin' I got...didn't yah?"

"Yep," says Sadie, sticking her head back into the confinement closet to check on the captive's progress.

Russo has everything but one arm inside a rather plain and conservative-looking outfit. To finish dressing, her last restrained wrist needs to be unlocked.

Sadie motions to the arm. "You ready?"

A long pause ensues, as the question hangs between them. Locked in silence, Rene swallows, then finally nods before Sadie moves to free her limb. Fully clothed in a simple white blouse and grey slacks, Russo exits the confinement chamber and moves to the chair where, again, restraints are used. A knock on the outside door announces it's time; when Sadie opens it, the freed local men and boys enter, followed by Caleb. The boys are nervous and uncomfortable despite their preparation for this interaction. The group stands in a semicircle around the imprisoned woman. The silence lengthens.

Finally, the father of the group clears his throat. "I'm speakin' on behalf of all the Isle of Big Sur inhabitants...those lost...and the few present. But...as a father." He looks at his two young sons, standing nearby, and the third boy who became a part of his family a long time ago. "It's hard to forgive what you did to my sons," he says, his emotions strengthening. "And well...you got a lot to prove...before I'm ever gonna be able to forgive you...let alone trust you."

Russo doesn't speak as a rising heat flushes her cheeks, a growing sense of unease strengthening. Facing those she's harmed is a difficult challenge to accept. It's more painful, somehow, than any fight she's experienced.

As the father's anger grows so does his volume. "You may have helped to eliminate the recent arrivals, but...yer gonna hav'ta do way more than that to gain anythin' from us! You should be ashamed! How can you sleep at night? You've got a mighty debt to pay...if we allow it." He regains his control, breathing deeply. "So...here's your first chance. Wha d'yah have to say for yourself?"

The once dominant Commander—who looks and feels nothing like her former self—looks him squarely in the eye before moving her gaze to each of the others. Thinking of her twin sister with a heavy sadness, the last of her fierceness fades and she speaks honestly.

"You're right...I don't deserve forgiveness. What I've done...if it was my family..." Russo pauses, overwhelmed with shame. "I'm sorry, and...whatever remains of my time, I want to make amends... if you'll allow it."

A long silence follows her words, leaving Russo uncertain of her future. Sadie gives no clear indication either, as she returns the captive to her cell and chains. With her secure and locked away, the group leaves to reconvene in privacy and discuss their next steps. An agreement on how to proceed is formed, and they get to work dividing up various tasks. As they move forward, a constant onslaught of noise erupts from the room just beyond the confinement chamber where Rene is locked.

For hours, the fallen Splitter listens, wondering what's going on. As the day draws to an end, her door finally opens. Sadie brings more food, water, and some news. The exterior room has been modified with old chain link fencing and posts, creating a prison cell. The water storage tanks and door are no longer accessible from the space, but are separated into their own area.

"This isn't humane," Sadie says, unlocking Rene and moving her to the new quarters. "So, from now on...this will be your place. You'll continue serving in whatever capacity is needed to keep this island free of Splitter control and...help these folks here."

Russo looks around, noticing that some of her belongings have been placed inside. Sadie attaches a shackle and chain to her ankle and another to her wrist. Out of habit, Rene can't help but observe the new structure's integrity and what potential weaknesses may exist.

"The men...will bring you food and water," Sadie says, closely watching her as she attaches the opposite ends of the restraints into the back wall. She motions to the newly installed gate. "When they deliver your rations…it'll be through the access slot."

Rene moves to examine the area and discovers there's just enough slack in her chains to reach the gate, but not enough for her to exit. She paces about the small area, checking her range and wondering how long this room will be home. It's an improvement from the closet, but it's still a prison, and a small one at that. She sits upon the bunk that, at this point, seems a luxury, and she goes through what belongings have been returned to her.

"So…you're leaving me?" Russo says, looking up.

"Your actions will determine your future," Sadie responds. "So, don't do anything that'll get you shot. I hope…that when I check next…you're still here and those you've harmed feel…you've been worth the effort."

EIGHTEEN

"Goodbye, my friends," Sadie says, shaking hands with each of the men and boys, as Caleb follows, doing the same. "Thank you for your service...for sharing your home, and for taking on the responsibilities of Command Central."

Caleb's not exactly thrilled with heading out this late, especially after such a heavy day of work, but he realizes the closer they get to leaving the isle, the better he'll feel. Sadie feels so too, and looks forward to running off the day's emotional stress. Disposing the M9s' remains was a harsh necessity, and the torment of the task won't fade easily from either of their minds. Haunting visuals linger with the stench of burning hair and flesh. Caleb would have preferred to spend the whole day inside, working with the others on the holding cell's modifications, but Sadie asked for his help and he couldn't leave her to it alone.

They skirt what remains of the funeral pyre and its fading embers as Sadie begins a slow jog. Caleb exhales, exhausted by the constant hustle and reluctantly follows behind. As Sadie's muscles warm, her pace quickens, creating a steady rhythm for her moving meditation. Before realizing it, Sadie nears the ranch house and barracks far ahead of Caleb. A fire burns at the site. Joining two men standing in horror at the side of the burn pile, Sadie slows and greets them.

"Dis...is da las' of it," one of the recently-freed men says, disgusted by the task but grateful to be of service. Sadie places her hand upon his shoulder. "Thank you. We didn't have the resources or time to bury 'em, and...honestly...I don't think many of 'em would've deserved the effort. Even so...may their souls be judged appropriately."

They stare at the flames in silence until the sound of approaching footsteps and heavy breathing snaps Sadie's attention away. When Caleb nears, the two of them head inside to check on Leon. They find him toiling away, happily engaged in working on the ranch house.

"You look...like you're home," Sadie begins, convinced of Leon's character.

There hasn't been an appropriate time for him to tell Sadie his whole story, but what she does know speaks well.

Leon sets asides his tools and grins. "This place was spectacular, and...one day...it'll be so again."

Noticing the small child balled-up in the corner, Sadie motions questioningly towards her.

"She gets night terrors...been through too much," Leon says, shaking his head in disgust. "Here, with me...she does better...even with all the construction noise."

He smiles lovingly, touched by such a little angel. Since their fireside night when he taught her to count, they've been nearly inseparable.

"I'd like to adopt her," he blurts, surprising Sadie and Caleb. "I know it's not the plan, but please, hear me out. Taking all the kids to Three Sisters...stresses your resources...you've said so yourself. We've got plenty here now...and...there's kids stayin'...just down the road. I'll protect her. If something happens, we'll fall back with them at Command Central, as planned...and hole-up there." He takes a deep breath. "Her parents are gone and...I'm pretty sure she witnessed their murders. She's got no one but me, and...I don't want to abandon her."

Leon walks over to where the child sleeps and gingerly pulls the covers over her shoulder. Sleeping soundly, the little girl doesn't stir.

"She asked if she could stay," Leon says, returning to Sadie's side.

Sadie doesn't respond.

"We did exactly as you instructed," Leon begins, a bit defensive. "We told the kids about Three Sisters...and prepped them for leaving." His voice catches as the memory surfaces of the little girl clasped to his leg and crying. "Please Sadie, she begged to stay with me, and...I want it too."

Who am I to not allow it? Sadie thinks, watching him.

She okays the arrangement, and Leon thanks her profusely. When the two men from outside—along with Mee-Maw and Rowin—enter, no time is wasted. Sadie carefully covers details on maintaining the isle's charade of Splitter control: complete with timelines, radio consistencies, and defense preparations. Each member of their growing team understands their responsibilities, the importance of depending on one another, and what dangers lie ahead.

As the group begins to disperse for the night, Sadie pulls the two women aside to talk privately and confirm that they feel both safe and comfortable. They answer, each in their own way, but Mee-Maw, adding more, stops mid-sentence—suddenly aware of Sadie closely watching her mouth as she strains to understand what the elderly woman is saying. Her lack of front teeth, top and bottom, make pronunciation a challenge.

"So's I...cubben...bith...bown," the old woman sheepishly offers, talking slowly after a lengthy pause.

Embarrassed, Sadie is first ashamed of staring, but then anger overtakes her as Mee-Maw tells of fighting back against her abusers only to face greater suffering. When the Splitters captured Rowin, Mee-Maw deflected whatever she could away from the young woman, giving herself up instead. The old woman even told her friend to be complacent, as it kept beatings to a minimum, preventing the younger woman's teeth from getting smashed out as well.

Sadie wraps the elder in a hug and clasps the hand of the younger. "Never again ladies." She steps back. "And..." She pauses, moving to unwrap two items from inside a canvas sack slung over her shoulder. "Do you know how to use these?"

Both women shake their heads with uncertainty.

"Well...when you learn how to use them, and...how to take care of them, they're yours."

Mee-Maw and Rowin stare at the weapons, hesitant with fear and shock at being given guns.

"I hope you never need 'em, but..." Reading their reactions, Sadie rewraps the guns. "Learning to shoot isn't just important for protecting yourself...it'll also help protect the rest of us...'specially the kids."

Easing their concerns, Sadie prepares the ladies for what to expect in their training in the upcoming months. They'd feel better if she was staying on the island, but they understand her need to return home, and even more importantly, what's at stake. Leaving Sadie's presence, the two women walk arm in arm, contemplating the turn of events in their lives.

As they disappear into the night, Sadie moves inside the ranch house to find Caleb asleep upon a pile of cloth tarps. Instead of resting alongside him, or waking him to join her, she heads out and hustles towards the watchtower. Hearing the proper response when she signals, Sadie approaches the small structure, surprising the one Delta awake.

"Everything okay?" Devon asks softly, making sure not to wake Dom, asleep inside as he greets Sadie at the bottom of the steps.

"Yeah, who's patrolling?" she whispers.

"Derrick, but we're switching soon."

"Perfect. What about the radio?"

"Moved in and ready...should be good for the mornin' check-in."

"And the other supplies?"

"There's still more to move ashore, but everything you wanted is ready and packed. The *Enforcer's* ready for departure."

Feeling exhaustion setting in, Sadie sits upon the rough stone steps while waiting for Derrick's return. When he arrives, they wake Dom for the shift change, allowing Sadie the opportunity to speak with the entire Delta Force.

"I don't know what I'd do without you guys," she starts, appreciative of the bond they've developed. "And...I want to thank you...for everything. None of this would have been possible without you."

She hugs each in turn, and the men—feeling the same gratefulness—experience a sense of sadness, knowing soon they'll part company. They've not only grown extremely fond of Sadie, but the security of her presence and the leadership she provides will be missed when the team stays on the island, protecting its inhabitants and keeping it free of Splitter control.

Sadie switches gears by surprising the men as she hands each of them a cigar. "Not sure...at this very moment...if the time's right and...Caleb should be here with us, but...I thought we should at least recognize...and celebrate our success here." Sadie bites off the end of the cigar she's holding. "How 'bout...we share this one...and you boys keep yours for another occasion."

Still shocked, the men nod without speaking.

Sadie lights the stogie, takes a few puffs, and passes it. "To successfully saving the kids, reclaiming this island...and of course...to stoppin' the Nation."

The cigar passes among them as Sadie talks out various scenarios the men could encounter in her absence. The Delta guys listen, add what they can, and ask for clarification when needed. Satisfied with all the particulars and with their celebratory smoke finished, Sadie departs, ready for some much-needed sleep before all the early morning activities begin. The short distance back to the ranch house proves more difficult than she expected, a heaviness in her legs slowing the pace.

Inside, she finds Caleb, who hasn't even changed his position, and lies down near his side. It's only a couple of hours later when the rising sun pulls her from slumber. Getting up, and feeling queasy with another night of minimal sleep, she stretches, mentally preparing for the journey ahead.

"Did you sleep at all?" Caleb asks, sitting up and rubbing his eyes.

"A little," Sadie responds, before moving over to the radio where Leon has just begun receiving the morning's calls—including one from the re-established radio at the watchtower.

With everything in order, breakfast with the kids becomes the next priority. Although the children have begun to recover physically, it'll be a slow path to normalcy, fraught with years of turmoil. They're fed heartily, and as they begin to leave both Mee-Maw and Rowin follow, carrying additional food they've prepared for the youngsters' trip. Wishing them safe travels and a speedy return, the freed women shed a tear, happy to be a part of a team but saddened to see Sadie leave.

Once all the children are settled aboard the *Enforcer*, Caleb and Sadie pull anchor, leaving the Isle of Big Sur and heading north. The boat moves with ease in the calm ocean, making for a smooth trip, and a brief time of reflection. The swell remains minimal and, at one point, a lone gull flies alongside the boat's port side before flying away into the horizon. As the tail of Three Sisters becomes visible, the kids are gathered on deck to hear more about their new home, the people already living there, and how much longer the journey will take. Some of the little ones brave questions, but most remain silent, unsure and fearful.

Since learning of the Nation's radio coverage, Sadie no longer finds it safe to contact those waiting upon their return. So, they approach unannounced, traveling along the eastern side of the island. Skirting the numerous sea stacks, they proceed with caution, listening for any radio transmissions and keeping a careful watch. Nearing the northern side, they slow to a stop, anchor the *Enforcer*, and prepare the anxious children for going ashore. Sadie zooms away first in the zodiac; nearing the harbor's entrance, she's finally observed. Initially, her approach causes alarm, but as she begins waving at the brothers, they finally recognize her. Red runs to meet her while Lucas hustles to spread word of their return.

Sadie steers towards the anchored *Intrepid II*, and after a quick exchange, she pauses as all the others come running. Between the looks of surprise, joy, and confusion, Sadie knows there's much to share. But first, she wants to get the kids ashore. When José, in an overflowing rush of emotions, scrambles to join her, he nearly tips them over.

"We were so worried!" he exclaims, almost falling over as he lets go. "What took so long?" He looks at the wounds on her face. "And, what happened?"

"I'll explain everything, but first...let's get the kids and the boat in here."

Before they depart, the two brothers join them, and all together they zip back to the *Enforcer*. The men board the vessel to help move the kids and prepare for the careful re-entry into the harbor. Once the last of the youngsters makes it to safety, Sadie stands with them at the cliff's edge—introducing the adults while simultaneously getting bombarded by Clara and Anna, who cling to her in joy.

Watching as José steers the *Enforcer* around the massive sea stack that protects the tiny harbor, the group cheers when it passes safely and drops anchor.

When Caleb joins them, Clara's eyes moisten even further. She didn't like seeing the bruises on Sadie's face, nor the dark circles under her eyes, but it doesn't compare to the damage *he's* suffered. Sadie and Caleb both display the hardships they encountered on the rescue mission.

"Where are the Deltas?" Clara asks, concerned.

"It's okay, they're safe and helping the other survivors." Sadie doesn't get to add more before the old woman inquires further.

"And...what about you two? Doesn't look like it was all that safe."

"We're okay too," Sadie says, grabbing Caleb's hand. "I'll explain later...for now...let's get back to the homestead." She turns to the brothers. "Don't worry 'bout unloading now...just grab the boxes I mentioned. The rest we'll get in the morning."

Anna leads the kids. Nearing her home, they're joined by the other children and teachers who hiked down for the evening meal. At first, all the youngsters are shy, but soon a murmur of talk bubbles among them, reassuring Sadie about her decision to relocate the firsties. The outdoor table gets extended, additional seats moved in, and more food is brought to feed the growing population of Three Sisters.

Before it grows dark, the new children are issued bedding from the boxes carried ashore, and as the kids and teachers set off for the night, Sadie promises the chaperones she'll fill them in tomorrow. As for everyone else, they reconvene in Anna's home, anxious to hear what Sadie and Caleb have to share. The group remains quiet as the two of them take turns filling in the details of the mission. When the Commander and her M9s are mentioned, José stands.

"You fought 'em?!" he questions. "I've heard 'bout the Mighty 9 when..." he trails off, not wanting to think, let alone talk about the days he spent as a slave to the Nation. "I thought they were... unstoppable."

"Not anymore," Caleb states matter-of-factly. Then he grows quiet as flashes of his time in captivity and the abuse he suffered surface.

Sadie continues, explaining why they spared the former Commander, and she divulges some of the information she gained from the warrior.

"So that's why you didn't radio," Anna interjects. Then, worried, she asks, "You think the Splitters heard us before?"

Clara is also concerned about the brief radio contact they used when Sadie returned from the Yosemite colony and, suddenly, has a growing sense of unease.

"I don't think so, but if they did pick up our short Morse code, they still wouldn't know where it came from. From now on though... we have to be more careful. But...we're gonna set up communications around here...and with Big Sur."

"How's that supposed to keep us safe?" Red asks.

"We're gonna do it under the guise of additional watchtowers... on IBS. We've laid out a timeframe...and a ploy for the radio controllers...we'll keep the Nation thinkin' the island is still preparing for their big relocation. The cargo ship we took control of had plenty of communication equipment, and...we brought some of it here."

Sadie decides to share a bit more before wrapping up for the evening. "Our friends in Big Sur...falsely reported the safe arrival of the platoon reinforcements back to the Nation's headquarters...so they won't suspect anything. We also had them relay that their two boats suffered damage due to rough ocean conditions they encountered before arriving. With the next big swell, it'll be reported that one of the ships broke from anchor, crashed into the other, and sank." She pauses to make sure everyone is following. "The cargo ship will be deemed badly damaged...requiring extensive repairs, rendering it incapable of returning to headquarters...givin' us...more time."

Impressed by Sadie's plan, Red nods. "Okay boss, so...what's next?"

NINETEEN

As morning greets the homestead, work around its many sites is already well underway. The men, who slept aboard the *Intrepid II*, move efficiently while unloading the confiscated items brought back to Three Sisters from the captured cargo vessel. At the house, the young couple, who'll be taking on meal preparation, get breakfast ready while Anna, Clara, and Rika prepare to depart for Clara's home. When the men return, burdened with heavy loads, Trew and José shift duties and move on to the animals. They'll also be keeping watch and guarding the harbor, so—feeling a necessity to learn from one another—they begin establishing a routine. Nearing time for the morning meal, the kids and teachers appear. Only Sadie is absent. Caleb notices but his concern is quickly addressed by Clara.

"She's still sleeping," the old woman says, to his surprise. "Did she sleep at all while you two were gone?"

"A couple hours…here and there," he answers.

"Poor thing, she didn't even move when Anna and I got up." Clara moves to help set the table for breakfast.

After eating with the others, Caleb pulls aside the three ladies responsible for the children and fills them in, since Sadie still hasn't appeared. Before they depart to start the day's lessons, he divvies up the supplies designated for the campground and one at a time, each youngster is given the task of carrying an item back. He talks gently with each of the kids, making them feel secure, and that they are an important part of a growing team. Aware of what else Sadie wants moved, Caleb shares information on the next set of chores before heading back to the house to check on her.

Peeking into the bedroom, he stands quietly at the door watching Sadie sleep. The two of them went through a lot together on the Isle of Big Sur, and being away from her last night was not what he wanted—but with everything going on, he understands. There's still a mystery to Sadie. Ever since they reunited—when she saved his life—he's been continually surprised by her. Now that they're home, he hopes to find out how she knows so much, including her lethal tactics.

When Sadie rolls over, her eyes open to find Caleb standing nearby. Seeing the amount of light penetrating into the room, she's suddenly aware of how late it is and abruptly sits up.

"Don't worry, we got it," Caleb reassures her, seeing Sadie's concern. "The boat's unloaded, the teachers have been filled in and everything you wanted is either done or being worked on." He moves to her side, kicks off his shoes, and joins her in bed. "You needed the sleep. You can't keep pushin' so hard. It's not healthy...or safe... and..." There's a long pause as he moves closer, pulling her to him. "You're not alone anymore."

Sadie rests her head on his chest and closes her eyes. She did need the sleep and this quiet moment between them feels good. But it doesn't last long, as Anna opens the door.

"Ohh...sorry," she says, embarrassed. "I was just...bringin' you... some breakfast."

"It's okay. I'll be out in a sec," Sadie says, reassuring Anna.

Caleb gets up. He kisses Sadie's cheek and pats Anna on the head as he leaves. Sadie rolls over while stretching in bed and, feeling her body's soreness, slowly gets up. Her pack sits against the wall; she opens it up and dresses, happy to be free of Splitter attire and back in her own clothes.

She uncovers a small pouch tucked neatly away and stares at it, knowing what it holds. She picks up the velvety pouch and slowly opens it, revealing her old wedding ring. She holds it between her thumb and index finger, gently cradling the gold band. Hiding her identity meant leaving it behind, and much has happened while it was off. But for the first time since her husband's death, Sadie thinks she's ready to move on. Pressing the band to her lips, she whispers a final goodbye. A lone tear breaks free. *I'll always love you, Markus.* She returns the ring, and puts it away, back out of sight.

Heading to the kitchen, she's greeted with a lengthy, grandmotherly hug that is worth a million words.

"Feel better?" Clara finally asks, concerned about Sadie and the danger she puts herself in.

"Uh-huh. I didn't even hear when you two got up. You about ready?" Sadie asks, looking at both Clara and Anna.

They nod in reply as Sadie sits to eat her cold bowl of oats, washing it down with a cup of tea. Outside, Red, Lucas, and Rika, also packed for the trip, join them at once. Sadie double checks that they've got what's needed and confirms with the brothers. They're hauling goods to Clara's before leaving to meet Sadie and Caleb at the Memorial Camp. As they part ways, it's Anna who sheds a tear while saying goodbye.

Watching them leave, pride wells within Sadie. The world may be in ruins and over lorded by terrible people, but Three Sisters, her home, is a place of hope, love, and opportunity.

Heading outside and veering toward the harbor, she checks on the progress of its added security measures and spends time talking with José. She shares, in greater detail, the encounters she experienced with Russo and probes him for further information. The young man adds what he can about his time in captivity, then asks plenty of questions about the cargo ship left anchored at the Isle of Big Sur. He's particularly interested in how much stored fuel it possesses and thanks Sadie again for the barrels with which she returned.

From the harbor, she meanders back to the homestead and looks over the chickens, the goats, and the quail that were relocated from Clara's. Once their numbers increase, the island will have a sustainable protein source to help support its population. In her absence, a considerable amount of progress was also made in the garden space. Several raised beds, constructed of small logs, have been built, filled with dirt, and planted with late-season crops. Sophia and Alberto are working on the last couple of boxes, but seeing Sadie they pause, eager to share their news.

"Oooww. Put your hand aquí," Sophia says, holding the palm of her hand on her growing belly as she feels the baby kick.

Sadie does so and smiles with the sensation. "Ohhhh...this little one's gonna be full of energy."

"We can't thank you enuf," Alberto begins. "The chance to come 'ere en raise our niño, en safety..." His voice chokes. "It's ah blessin'. Muchas gracias."

"And thank you," Sadie adds, motioning around. "It looks wonderful."

With a light heart, Sadie continues her rounds and finds Caleb packing the four-wheeler. He stops as she approaches, caught by the seductive look in Sadie's eyes. When she gets closer, her actions are even more surprising. She leaves him breathless.

"Wow," he says, when she finally breaks her lips away, freeing his mouth to speak.

"Ready?" Sadie asks, with her arms still wrapped around him.

"I'm ready for anything you got in mind." The sensuality in his eyes and the deep tone of his voice make Sadie giggle.

"Not for that!" She backhands him playfully on the chest. "Ready to leave?"

"Ohh," he responds, deflated, but still playful. "Yeah, this is the last of it."

"Alright, I'll grab my things. Pick me up at the house."

When Caleb arrives a half-hour later, Sadie has her pack and crossbow. She tells him to drive the quad and she sits behind him, her arms wrapped tightly around his torso and her cheek resting against his back. Her touch feels so good that he drives slowly en route to the camp so the feeling can last longer. As they near the site, the sound of the engine draws the kids' attention. Luna comes running ahead of the pack, excited as always to see Sadie.

"I missed you at breakfis," the little one says.

Sadie picks her up and spins her around before touching her feet back to the earth. A new arrival about the same age as Luna stands shyly aside, watching their interaction.

"Dis my new fend," Luna says as she moves to the girl's side. "En we share ah bunk!"

Smiling, Sadie steps closer, drops to a knee, and shakes the little girl's hand. She talks a bit more with the children then says goodbye and goes to speak with the adults. The women gather around Sadie as Caleb announces to the kids he's brought lunch. The kids' meal provides Sadie with just enough time for a chat with the three teachers on how the children are holding up.

From the campsite, Sadie and Caleb travel deeper into the woods, heading for the small clearing accessible by air. As the wheeler slows, Sadie carefully scans the surroundings. Dismounting, they head towards the structure, curious as to how its guardian has been managing. The area's improvements are obvious, but Cameron is nowhere to be seen.

I know you're here, Sadie thinks, making another scan of the place and turning to Caleb. "Would you wait by the quad?"

Knowing the question was a request, he shrugs and heads back towards the machine and rests, lounging with a foot on the steering controls. Sadie calculates the locations of prime hiding positions. With a hint of movement detected as she surveys the area, her gaze narrows. She whistles softly. After a moment, Cameron replies and steps from behind a tree. Watching her approach without making a sound, Sadie knows that Cameron is the woman for the job.

Cameron halts a stride away, noticing the abuse Sadie's suffered. She shakes her outstretched hand and acknowledges her wounds. She waits for Sadie to begin the conversation and answers everything that's asked. Before shifting to the updates she's come to share, Sadie retreats from Cameron to the four-wheeler to collect the items designated for this location, including the food prepared for the journey. She speaks briefly with Caleb, still lounging, who moves to begin setting up for the night.

Sadie rejoins Cameron in the small shelter and talk shifts: to what Sadie's learned of the Splitter fleet scouting the expanded Pacific Ocean, which boats she's already helped to commandeer or sink, and the intel she's gained from Russo. Sadie shares how the Nation's gas-powered vessels have been exploring the vicinity closer to their Tahoe headquarters—where many are scheduled to return to report their findings and move goods—while the sailboats were sent out on further expeditions.

Despite her experience moving with the Splitter ground units, Cameron doesn't have much to add. All she can produce is a vague recollection and years of gossip about the M9s' ferocity and their brutal Commander. The conversation shifts again, towards the start of Cameron's final relocation. She listens intently.

"Who's gonna keep station here?" she asks when Sadie pauses for a drink.

"For now, it'll be unguarded."

She is taken aback, but doesn't have to wait long for Sadie's justification. The Splitter Nation, with their diminished air capabilities and lack of knowledge of the small clearing, reduces the risk of them finding the space. Mystified by Sadie's intel and plans, Cameron finds security knowing they're teammates and prepares for her duties around the southeastern tail area of the island—where she will live as previously discussed.

The ladies break from their conversation only to eat. Caleb joins them but feels awkward, intruding upon Cameron's comfort. After the quick meal, Sadie returns with Cameron to the shelter, leaving him alone. Sadie makes herself more comfortable by unrolling her bedding, and continues the dialogue where they left off. The women talk late into the evening until Sadie simply curls up and falls sleep.

Early in the morning, after a patrol of the area and breakfast, the three of them secure the site and head out on foot to the Memorial Campground. It's a quiet hike. Along the way, Caleb's mental anguish threatens to overtake his grasp on reality. The image of his buddy, chained and dragged, obscures what's actually in front of him and he nearly trips on a root.

"You all right?" Sadie asks repeatedly, until Caleb finally hears her.

Without answering, he nods with a blank expression, depicting anything but his being of sound mind. Sadie lets it go. At camp, there's work to be done but Caleb's visions intensify, especially as the cross erected for a memorial comes into view. Every time he's visited, its sight has always affected him deeply, but this time, accompanied with his weakened mental state, the cross looms over his guilty conscience. Tormented and ashamed, suddenly he can't escape the relentless begging for it to end. He keeps hearing his friend's voice, echoing between the trees, fleeting, teasing, whenever he tries to track it. His soul suffers further. It will not stop.

Caleb is in a stupor when Sadie returns. She cleans and cooks two quail she hunted by slingshot and rehydrates a package of freeze-dried peas and carrots. Sadie passes out the food as they sit around the fire, eating in near silence. The ladies finish their meal and wander off to set Cameron up in the place's hidden overlook, tucked above a thicket of redwood branches. From the giant, elbow-shaped arm that grows from a redwood older than all the others, she can see everything. An extended wooden platform adds enough room for the two women to sit and talk further about Cameron's responsibilities.

By the time Sadie climbs down and returns to Caleb, he still hasn't eaten much. He's transfixed, gazing upon the flames and the pulsing embers glowing in the campfire. Her presence does not break his daze. Unfurling her sleeping bag, Sadie sets up in the small shelter, expecting Caleb to join her. He doesn't. She eventually rolls over towards the fire.

"Caleb," she whispers, repeating his name a little louder when he doesn't respond.

By her third attempt, and with no noticeable change in his demeanor, Sadie's concern grows. The state he was in when she'd first found him, along with her discovery of the tortured remains of his friend, speaks of the torment they suffered at this location by the Splitters. Obviously, it's all coming back. Spinning her legs around, Sadie sits on the edge of the small raised platform, watching the fire's dying light illuminate the poor man a few feet away. Getting up, she adds more wood to the fire; moving to his side, she wraps his bedding around his shoulders and sits down. Caleb finally reacts, moving an arm and the blanket around her.

"Caleb...what is it?" Sadie asks.

The question hangs for so long that Sadie's not sure whether he's heard it or if he just doesn't want to answer. Eventually, his words find an escape—he falters, attempting to explain the guilt he carries. His first mumblings don't make any sense, but as Sadie waits, Caleb finds the strength to share his anguish. He describes gruesome details.

After several failed attempts at talking, he admits that he's the one who actually killed his friend; he'd begged Caleb to do it. For days, between bouts of torture that left him without fingers and toes, before they started removing features of his face, he begged Caleb to end his life.

Caleb's confession eases a heaviness that he's carried since it happened. As they continue talking, it's with the hope of beginning his healing process. They sit for hours deep in discussion, appreciative of one another and the privacy that permits them to talk freely. As night nears dawn, they slip into the sleeping shelter and curl up together, whispering softly while resting their eyes. What seems like only minutes later, the sound of an approaching engine startles them alert.

Sadie's out first, awakened by the brothers' arrival. But realizing it's later than she'd thought, she greets them happily. Red and Lucas are full of energy and excited to explore further. Now that they've visited Clara's unique canyon home, they're eager to see where Sadie lives. She and Caleb pack up for the trek into her section of the island while the brothers examine the campsite and hidden lookout. The more they see, the more excited they become, learning all that Three Sisters has to offer.

TWENTY

After a full day's hike, the group is relieved to finally stop for the evening—although the three who have never been here before look around, confused about the destination. There's no sign of a cave. The surroundings don't match any of the mental pictures they've formed. But it's been the same along the entire route they traveled. Whenever they neared other sites Sadie wanted to share, whether it was a cache location or the giant boulder she'd taken refuge in after discovering Caleb, she invited them to search it out for themselves. Everything she creates comes from and blends with nature.

The brothers slowly turn in a clockwise circle, examining the terrain. Cameron scrambles to climb a large fallen redwood. It makes Sadie smile at Caleb. He also enjoys watching the others trying to locate the cave, but it's the quiet woman who, jumping down from the log, discovers a space cleared away beneath a second fallen tree.

"I found it!" exclaims Cameron, caught up in the search like a child on an Easter egg hunt and yelling to the brothers while pointing to the location. She then climbs back up on the log and is quick to regain her normal, reserved manner.

Red and Lucas climb over the debris and inspect it for themselves. The space feels even smaller when all of them cram inside. Sadie shares the story of its creation and how vital a location it has been for her over the years. As she shares more, tales from her years of solo life leave the others stupefied. They listen, convinced they'd never be able to manage such a life without going crazy, let alone thrive like Sadie has.

Feeling hungry, Sadie grabs one of the cave's many food supply buckets and lets each of her guests select their choice of a freeze-dried meal. They dine with a carefree ease. Even Cameron, usually shy and peripheral, finds herself smiling and growing more comfortable among them. The brothers opt to sleep out under the stars and say goodnight as they exit the unique structure. Caleb moves to Sadie's side of the cave, but before he can unfurl his sleeping bag, she motions towards the door.

"I don't...wanna make Cameron feel...awkward," Sadie whispers, nearing him. "So...maybe you should join the men?"

Caleb stands, dumbstruck and motionless. Seeing his disappointment, Sadie kisses him lightly on the cheek before he exits. Outside, the night air is chilly for the men, but his reception is lighthearted and warm. The brothers poke fun at his presence and joke around as Caleb makes himself comfortable. Their camaraderie strengthens with each joke, and as the fun-making turns to more serious topics, Caleb divulges the story of his first experience in the cave.

He tells them about waking up, alone, in the darkness, thinking he was blind and bound, discovering that the rope around his wrist was there to help him find the door; how when he moved he learned the extent of his injuries; and how, as clarity returned, he finally discovered all the care that Sadie had provided.

"She dragged you...that whole way?" Lucas says, amazed after hiking the route she'd taken. "She saved yer sorry ass. You're gonna be doin' whatever she wants...forever."

Laughing, Red joins in. "Yeah, we thought you followed her like a lost little puppy cuz...she's so damn good lookin'. We didn't know... it's cuz you got a life debt."

As they continue joking, Caleb blushes—making the men laugh harder and prod more. Red literally rolls over, still chuckling, as he curls up to sleep. The eldest of the two brothers doesn't recall the last time things felt so jovial, and he drifts into slumber with a smile. As for Caleb, it takes him much longer to find sleep, his thoughts swirling around Sadie—in particular, her tight body and all the things he'd like to do to it.

Before first light, Sadie walks from the cave and finds Caleb among the men. Waking him softly, she whispers, asking if he'd like to join her for a quick patrol. Though she's fully aware of everything going on around the island—where everyone's located and the diminished threat of a Splitter invasion—some habits just don't fade. Besides, getting out gives her a chance to speak in private with Caleb.

As the sky grows lighter, they pause and he takes her hand. At first, he only holds it. Then he moves toward softly kissing it. He focuses specifically on her ring finger, where her wedding ring—to his delight—is nowhere in sight.

"So...now that we're home, 'the time's right.' Right?" he asks, kissing the spot one last time.

Although comfortable, Sadie fights a lingering sensation. "Caleb," she begins, taking her hand back and sitting upon a large rock. "I'll always love my husband and the time we shared, but...I...ahhh..." She hesitates, finding it difficult to express what she means. "Can we...ease into things? I'm still adjusting to...all these changes, and so many new people...let alone, sharing my home and the security it's provided."

He sits next to her. "Sadie, whatever speed you want is okay. I never thought I'd see you again...or get a second chance, but..." He takes her hand again. "I do believe...you findin' me wasn't a coincidence...we're destined to be together."

She's contemplated the same thing even though she didn't want at first to admit it. Fate, for whatever reason, has realigned their path.

The two get up and walk holding hands toward the cave where there's already a pot of hot tea prepared by the men. Breakfast closely follows. After eating, the group packs and heads out. They traverse the many slopes and ridges. Sadie points out various features and locations while talking about the hope of one day clearing a road with José's tractor work.

The group camps for the evening under the protection of several redwoods and is back on the trail with the rising sun. As they near Sadie's childhood home, nearly destroyed by the earthquakes, Sadie feels a familiar tug in her gut—the sense of loss that creeps in when remembering her mom, brothers, and her father. The family cabin sits old and splintered, partially crushed by fallen trees and covered in a mishmash of tarps, coverings, and years of debris. They skirt its edges and go around the backside until finally stopping at what the newcomers view as an even worse-off structure.

Unsure whether it's safe, they tentatively follow Sadie as she enters the nearly collapsed shed and opens the entrance to expose the hidden apartment. Just as Caleb had done when he'd first arrived, Sadie's guests ask all sorts of questions, becoming enthralled by the stories of her father, and all he accomplished. Informing the brothers that they'll be sleeping here, she reveals and unlocks the entrance to the rest of the bunker's interior. Their mouths drop. At first, they're unable to speak, but when the lights click on, expanding the view of the space, they turn to each other, chattering back and forth nonstop.

Giddy, they move about as Sadie gives them a quick tour of the common spaces. She leaves Red and Lucas, who can't believe their eyes or their ears with the stereo; they've regressed to teenagers as they explore her music collection and play song after song. Cameron and Caleb, though amused, leave to help prepare a meal to feed everyone. Sadie moves in and out among them, returning with various items and supplies, often providing instructions before disappearing again.

Retreating to her private sanctuary, Sadie rearranges a few things, while putting a couple of other items away. She takes a deep breath, contemplating the ensuing evening, and discovers a fluttering in her stomach. The sensation lasts throughout the meal as the rest of the group eats heartily, feeling celebratory.

After a long dinner, Sadie asks Caleb to settle the men in the apartment while she focuses on setting Cameron up on the futon in the living room. When Caleb returns, he finds Sadie sitting at the table, looking over several papers and making notes.

"I was hoping you'd help me with a few things," she says as he enters.

"Sure, whacha need?"

He follows Sadie to the storage section of the bunker and watches as she manipulates and opens the door. This time, however, she's prepared to show him the entirety of her supplies and the true extent of what the bunker holds. Opening and lighting the various areas, she steps aside, letting him take everything in.

"Sadie...what...how..." Unable to finish, Caleb slowly walks the nearest aisle of goods, scanning the well-organized shelves.

Sadie removes the clipboard hanging nearby and follows. After wandering among all the food stores, Caleb does the same through the clothing section; then, an area labeled personal goods; followed by many others, such as: medical, first aide, office items, and more.

"Really?" he says finally, stopping to turn and look at Sadie. "You've even got baby and kid supplies? How...did all this happen?"

Sadie sits on a box and scans her surroundings. "My dad did it all...for me. I didn't even know until...the end." An image of her father, bloody and dying, surfaces as Sadie remembers how hard he fought to live long enough to show her.

"But, how?" Caleb asks, interrupting Sadie's vision.

"I've thought about that...a lot, and...I think it all started when I first came home, after...the accident."

This time, Caleb has a mental image. It's of Sadie, heartbroken and distraught, when he cruelly abandoned her after most of her family died. Their deaths forced her to return home, and then to stay, so she could look after her father. He added to her pain without considering anything but himself. Caleb realizes, once again, what an ass he'd been all those years ago.

Sadie fails to notice his anguish, explaining further: "I was home and...in the background, the TV was on some random channel. I wasn't paying attention...I didn't think my dad was either, but... something caught his ear and sparked a discussion. It was something about winning a lifetime supply of chocolate, which...led him into talkin' about how someone could even calculate something like that. He thought the estimate would depend on the individual and...how much the person consumed. At first, I didn't give it much thought, but...I was happy he was finally talking, so...I played along and answered as he asked questions...tryin' to figure out what my lifetime supply would be."

"We went back and forth on types of chocolates, amounts... and what an average person's typical consumption would be. Since I didn't eat much chocolate...my supply would be small. Then...he wanted an example of something I used a lot...so we could calculate that equation. I think...from there he...studied what we used." She pauses, looking around. "Because he amassed lifetime's supplies of... everything...for both me and my husband, even..." her voice waivers, "future kids."

Caleb lets her emotions settle and truly feels the pain of her loss. Although the information makes sense, it doesn't answer everything.

"So..." he ventures, "I get how he figured it, but...this is a lot of stuff...this place is huge, it's way bigger than I thought. It had to cost..." he trails off, shaking his head, unable to calculate the expenses for building and stocking the bunker.

Sadie smiles sheepishly. "Umm...there's still more...to show you."

Caleb's eyes widen. *How many more surprises can this woman possibly have?*

"As for cost," Sadie continues, "I have no idea...musta been ridiculous. I know he sold many patents, and obviously...my dad made a lot more than he'd ever divulged cuz…well…you can see." Sadie motions around the room.

For the next couple of hours, the two of them continue talking while gathering the supplies from Sadie's lists. Each item gets subtracted from the appropriate inventory clipboard. As she checks off one last item, they transition to the kitchen where, organized into specific piles, is everything they moved.

Sadie heats tea water—stalling for what's ahead—knowing she needs to show Caleb her personal quarters and eventually go to bed. As if reading her mind, he moves closer, wondering what she has in store for his sleeping arrangements—hoping it includes being with her.

"So…are we…goin' to your room now?" he asks, accepting the mug she hands him.

Sadie battles with herself to find an appropriate response, trying not to feel forced into an answer. The few thoughts that dash across her brain aren't close to good enough, and she dismisses them as fast as they appear. Settling on simplicity, she gives a slow nod of yes while fighting the temptation to avert her eyes. Seeing Caleb's change, and feeling the effect it has on her, Sadie wavers. She breaks eye contact, lifts her tea, and takes a sip, trying not to shake as she does so.

Opening the door to her quarters, she quickly moves them past the bed and into the adjacent room. The small workspace there, complete with a desk, table, and chairs, opens to another area.

"No wonder you look so good!" he jokes, looking around.

The space, a personal gym of sorts, has everything that someone into fitness would require. Besides three different types of cardio equipment, there are also sets of dumbbells, kettle bells, medicine balls, weights, and balance trainers. A mat covers the farthest corner and, hanging from the walls, are a variety of punching bags, along with implements for martial arts training. Caleb moves about, acquiring some insight into Sadie's ability to defend herself, but there's still so much he wants to ask.

"Ummm…" he stammers, examining the wear on one particular training target and then on a speed bag. "I've wondered a lot, about how you know…the things you do…I mean, you're deadly accurate with your bow…and scary good with a knife, you…can pick locks, know how to hide things on your body…I'd never even think of using. You made us homemade silencers for god's sake. And your reactions, they're not typical...obviously you've had training. So...I guess what I'm askin' is...how do you know all this stuff?"

Sadie takes a long breath, knowing this conversation was inevitable.

"It all started after..." She remembers the pain he'd caused her. "Well...after you...left me. I was a mess. I barely kept it together after my mom and brothers died, and then...when you..." She can't speak aloud of finding him cheating on her.

Embarrassed by the reference to his past actions, Caleb feels the blood draining from his face as the unforgivable event surfaces between them.

"I was confused...hurt...and really angry," Sadie goes on. "I lost most of my family...my dad was becoming more and more obsessive with his behaviors and...I just...well...I needed an outlet. It started with joinin' a gym and taking kickboxing lessons, which...led to self-defense, then...to martial arts, and...it just kept evolving. The work-outs eased the pain and gave me some direction. After a while...I got invited to a weekend retreat on survival training and the instructor and I..." She smiles, thinking about Markus and their first few months together. "Eventually...we married."

Caleb feels a creeping jealousness at the smile on Sadie's face.

"He was incredible...former Special Forces, but...an explosion damaged his hearing...which made him ineligible for active duty. For a while he stayed with the military as an instructor, but...the money in the private sector was too good and too easy. So...he started his own business...running survival courses, hand-to-hand combat. He could teach any type of fighting skill you wanted to learn. I went to a lot of 'em...we even developed a series of classes specifically for women. It was really cool, and..."

As the night lengthens—and Sadie becomes exhausted from sharing so much—they grow quiet, just sitting together. In the comfort of silence, both begin to nod off. Sadie jerks awake as her arm falls asleep and a tingling sensation shoots through it. Forced to change positions, she gets up, and with Caleb in tow, moves toward the bed.

Before lying down, Sadie notices they've stayed up nearly all night; morning is already upon them. To Caleb's disappointment, Sadie doesn't join him in bed. She disappears into the room's bathing area and washes up, leaving him alone again.

TWENTY-ONE

It's only midway through the morning, and Sadie already feels the lack of sleep catching up with her. With the supplies relocated to the apartment side of the bunker and everything clearly labeled by destination, she decides it's time to move outside. The group exits the same way they entered, and Sadie gives them a tour of the property, ending at the barn area, which, like much of the forest, lay littered with fallen redwoods. During the earthquake, many of the tallest ones on Three Sisters had their tops violently snapped off—dropping sections the size of regular trees—but near the barn, several of the redwoods were completely uprooted.

They near the giant log along the front of the building, and Sadie begins to waiver. It affects her the same every time she sees it. Sending the group ahead, she tries hard to block out the image it induces. Passing the spot where the tree crushed her husband, she tries not to look, but her eyes—torn to the site—can't help but glance. Markus's twitching leg appears as her blood pressure plummets. Caleb, noticing Sadie's lagged behind, turns and sees the color drained from her face.

"Ya'll right?" he asks, taking a few steps closer.

His voice breaks the spell, freeing Sadie to look up. Shaking her head as if clearing away the image, she pushes forward, barely grunting a response, and moves ahead to the door with its sturdy frame. Its sight also affects her, but not as drastically. Inside the barn, she opens every door and window, airing out the place for the first time in years. The daylight penetrates every corner. The newcomers are further amazed at what the space holds as they help remove the covers and tarps that protect the equipment and vehicles.

The brothers call to each other every time they find something new. They go back and forth, amazed at the inventory and diversity of the barn's equipment. Cameron scans the area on her own, and once help is no longer needed, retreats outside. Sadie pulls out her lists and pauses when Caleb catches her eye.

"What?" she blurts.

"Nuttin'…it's just…now, I know."

Sadie's quizzical look makes him chuckle.

"I know...how come you always got somethin' to write with," he says, still smiling. "I thought you just had lots of paper, but...now I know...you actually got...a *lifetime* supply. And, for you...that's a lot more than chocolate." He smiles, and then laughs at his own joke.

Sadie does so too, barely, and goes back to what she's here to do. Between her and the men, they collect what's needed, placing things in various piles differentiated by their final destination.

With the task complete, she transitions into a lengthy discussion with Red and Lucas. They're well aware of the reason Sadie selected them to relocate to Three Sisters and the need for their skills. They'll be spending time between the Memorial Camp and the bunker's apartment while working out of the barn.

The chainsaws and Alaskan mill attachments, along with a few barrels of gas to power them, will allow the men to cut plenty of lumber. Even though the barn's supplied well, they'll run out of fuel before they ever run out of trees to mill. At least the task is a little easier since the materials are already on the ground and they won't need to fell any more trees. She passes the brothers each a new notebook so they can sketch a few designs, starting with a couple of bunkhouses for the campground, additions for around Anna's homestead and, eventually, Clara's.

"Sadie, we're gonna need more help," Red finally says, calculating the enormity of the jobs. "I mean...we're good, but...there's only two of us.

"Agreed," she responds immediately. "Start with movin' the supplies, then...start milling. When you got what's needed...move to Anna's. By the time you've got enough lumber to build there, we'll have more workers."

Her statement stuns the brothers and Caleb.

Sadie offers a sly smile. "I'll be returning to the Yosemite colony... a lot sooner than planned," she says while looking over some of the sketches. "But, first...I gotta get Cameron set. So tomorrow...when I head out first thing...I'm gonna need you men to start trekking goods. At least the quad's part way. That'll help," she adds as a parting gesture before heading out to check on the woman.

Cameron, sitting upon the very log that crushed Sadie's husband, notices her approaching and jumps off.

"Need anything else?" Cameron offers.

Sadie nods, but gets distracted by Caleb's approach. It's clear he wants to talk privately with Sadie, so Cameron leaves and returns to the barn.

"When were ya gonna let me know!?" he says upset, watching Sadie stare blankly. "Sadie...Sadie."

Sadie can't help the emotional turmoil bubbling through her. She's standing at the exact location where—she closes her eyes as her respiration quickens.

"Sadie? You alright?"

Caleb places a hand on her shoulder, and Sadie crumbles into his chest. It catches him off guard as he wraps both arms around her. He can tell she's crying. Not sure why, Caleb just lets her be.

"Sorry," she finally says, after regaining control and lifting her head. "I...ahhhh...struggle with...this spot."

Caleb looks around, trying to figure out what could be the problem, but nothing's obvious. When he moves to sit upon the fallen redwood, Sadie abruptly stops him. Even more confused, he inquires about it. Moving them away from the tree, she slowly begins her sorrowful tale. The pain she exudes breaks Caleb's heart and hurts him more than he ever imagined it could. Her voice cracks and tears stream down her cheeks when she gets to how hard she tried to rescue her husband and how long his leg kept twitching. By the end of her story, she's emotionally spent and exhausted.

Eventually, when Sadie's ready to move, they head back to check on the others. Red and Lucas are deep into the chainsaws, taking them apart for general maintenance and making sure they're functional.

"When's the last time these ran?" Lucas asks casually.

"Years," Sadie replies, trancelike.

Red turns the mill attachment over in his hands and inspects its bolts. The simple tool, along with the edger attachment, fits three of the four chainsaws. When Cameron finishes mixing the appropriate ratio of gas to oil, she hands over the can, glad to be done with the assigned task. Before they attempt starting the saws, Sadie motions to Cameron and tells the brothers to close up when they're done, then to return later for an early dinner.

Back in the bunker, Sadie retreats to the storage area before returning with several armloads of goods. She outfits Cameron with an array of new clothes, shoes, food rations, and supplies. Overwhelmed, the woman finally stops insisting it's too much and simply gives in to Sadie, who talks about their journey ahead and how they'll split the load. To complete what seems necessary, a new pack is also added to the mix and Cameron's left to stow her goods. When the brothers return, the same is done for them. They put up a stronger fight to the generosity, but they're no match for Sadie. By the end, they've taken everything she's set aside for their needs.

After everyone is given the chance to bathe, a luxury none of them takes for granted, they sit for one last meal together. Talk is light and even though Sadie joins in, Caleb can sense the penetrating sadness she masks. With dinner finished and things tidied, her guests retreat to their spaces in preparation of an early start, leaving her and Caleb alone.

He doesn't want to be intrusive, yet he can't help but ask, "You gonna be alright?"

She nods. "Yeah, I think...I jus' need some sleep."

Caleb's not certain what to do or say. "Where...do you want me... to sleep?" he finally asks.

Sadie hesitates long enough that Caleb grows self-conscious. Instead of answering, she stands and takes his hand. She leads him to her quarters, where they climb into bed together.

"Just sleeping, though, okay?" she murmurs, snuggling up against him.

Both of them jolt awake at the alarm's sound. *Morning already?* Neither moved from their original position, but, well rested, Sadie gets up to stretch while Caleb watches. Her quad wound—the deeper one, still of concern, especially after all the running and hiking that followed the injury—aches, and she's careful not to overdo it. Noting Caleb hasn't taken his eyes off her, she returns to the bed's side and gives him a quick kiss, but hastily retreats before he can pull her in for more.

"Thank you," she says, surprising Caleb. "That's the first time I've slept all night after...after seeing that damn tree. Usually, it keeps me awake or...I'm haunted by the same, terrible nightmare." She tilts her head, which Caleb finds quite cute. "I don't think...I even had...ah single dream. I was out...completely."

She goes back to her yoga, and mid downward dog, Caleb finds the view delightful. He'd like to drag her back under the covers.

The more he thinks about it, the more aroused he becomes, until, so affected, he has to keep hidden beneath the blanket—at least from the waist down. He forces his mind to another place and quickly realizes they've yet to talk about a return trip to Yosemite. He's still not happy with Sadie, especially since she didn't discuss any of it with him, but before he can verbalize anything, she addresses him.

"Sorry, I dropped goin' back to the colony on ya like that. I meant to talk about it with you last night, but…we never really got to it. You'll go with me, though…right?" Sadie turns, looking over her shoulder before grabbing a clean shirt. "You heard the guys…we need the help and so could the crew on IBS. Besides, with what we've confiscated from those bastards…we can help a lot more folks now."

Caleb listens but doesn't respond. He doesn't want to return yet. He'd like to finish recovering from their last ordeal and just spend time with Sadie. He's not fond of rushing off into more danger, but he'll follow her anywhere she wants to go, and Sadie knows it.

"Come on, already," Sadie urges." The sooner we get things done…the sooner…we'll be back together."

Caleb smiles, knowing her statement was meant to entice him. "I'll meet ya in a few," he says, rolling over.

When Sadie leaves, he gets up, uses the bathroom and, catching his reflection in the mirror, pauses to examine his own wounds. The discoloration of his facial features is still evident, along with numerous scabs, and his ribs ache in an all too familiar way. He returns to the bed and dresses while scanning her private sanctuary.

Noticing a picture flipped down, he turns it over and finds it's of Sadie and who he assumes to be her husband. The man appears about the same height as him, but clearly, the guy is jacked. His shirtless torso and defined musculature make Caleb feel a bit inadequate. And he can't keep his eyes off the way Sadie is looking at him, or how her hand rests upon his chiseled abs. Setting it back, Caleb retreats to the gym area to bust out a few sets with the dumbbells.

In the kitchen, Sadie makes a large pot of steel cut oats. Waiting for them to cook, she packs what supplies couldn't fit in Cameron's backpack. Her movement wakes the woman, who quickly grabs her gear, thinking she's overslept. Joining Sadie, she notices that none of the others are present and relaxes as a cup of tea is poured for her.

"What?" Sadie asks, noticing the look on Cameron's face.

Cameron shakes off the question while still displaying a hint of amusement.

"Oh, no...talk to me," Sadie says, waiting and expecting a response.

The woman stalls a little longer by sipping her hot tea. She has too much respect for Sadie to not answer, but feels a bit guilty for what she was thinking.

"Sorry," Cameron starts, "I was just...amusing myself."

"Uh-huh...with what, exactly?" Sadie says, maintaining eye contact.

"Well...you. Looks like...you...finally spent a night...actually sleeping."

Sadie blushes in response, knowing Cameron refers to her and Caleb. They haven't been sleeping much, but it's not for the reason she thinks. Before Sadie can comment—even though she's not quite sure how—Caleb walks in.

"Good morning, ladies," he says, interrupting their interaction. Cameron nods a reply.

"Would you get the brothers?" Sadie says as he kisses her on the cheek. "Breakfast is ready."

He heads over to the apartment side of the bunker and finds both men up and discussing strategies for moving the load of goods.

"Well...good mornin' Romeo," Red says, greeting Caleb. "You back to joinin' the bachelors?" He chuckles softly, joined by his brother.

Caleb smiles. "Breakfast is ready." Then, before leaving, he turns back. "And no, fellas...my bachelor days are over."

The group wolfs down the hearty oats, fills their water containers, and then everyone grabs their packs and loads. The men, setting out in one direction, say their farewells as the women head the opposite way. Caleb lags behind, hoping for some departure affection from Sadie—but she's already too far into what lies ahead to notice.

TWENTY-TWO

It's only the second night of their journey, but Sadie and Cameron have comfortably settled into a routine. They travel well together, matching pace and abilities, hiking long distances in near silence while studying the terrain and its subtle signs. Often, the only chatting comes when Sadie identifies specific areas and their resources or reveals one of her hidden sites. Cameron will set up when they reach the tail of the island, but she'll move about these other shelters, too—although, on this evening, the women plan to camp under the open night sky.

Since they're along the southern coast, they won't be building an evening fire. Its light would travel too far out to sea and with a scouting Splitter fleet about, there's just no logic in taking the risk. Looking toward Big Sur, Sadie wonders how things are going for the Delta guys and the island's other inhabitants. Establishing communications between the two sites is an asset she hopes to acquire, and this trip is, in part, being made to begin that process. *Tomorrow, though*, she thinks, fading into slumber.

Before sunrise they've already packed and started along the cliff's edge. As the day brightens, so does the pace, and it doesn't take long before they've neared the base of what Sadie calls the 'tail' of Three Sisters. Stowing their heavy gear and eating en route, they climb the ridgeline and begin traversing the narrow peninsula, which eventually transitions into two additional islands. The further they hike, the more wary Sadie becomes of a growing unease building in her gut. The looming sea stacks, protruding through the fog along the eastern side of the coast, add to the eeriness. Ever since her first visit here, something's elicited this sensation; investigating ahead, she's curious as to why.

"Should be somewhere past *here*." Sadie strides ahead, running toward a small divide and leaps across it—from mainland to the smaller second island of the tail.

Cameron doesn't hesitate and makes it across. Excited to be in new territory, yet alert, Sadie's senses amplify. As they hike, Sadie carefully scans for signs of the old cell tower that once loomed over these parts, praying it didn't completely tumble into the ocean below. Hopefully some segments of the giant antenna survived and lie hidden under years of growth. If just a section or two could be found and salvaged, then Three Sisters' radio coverage and reception could become that much closer to reality. As they hike, the marine layer just offshore dissipates, revealing a massive sea stack. Its appearance stops Sadie, who slowly observes the area before moving ahead. When she stops abruptly a second time, Cameron takes notice.

"Look," Sadie whispers.

Just beyond Sadie's pointed finger, Cameron sees it too. Although mostly hidden, its purpose is clear; and it signifies the presence of other people. Sadie removes the crossbow slung across her back and moves closer to examine the snare. Cameron follows suit by removing her gun from concealment. Further along, the ladies discover a second snare when movement is detected. A small rat, with one leg and its head caught in the wire trap, makes a last desperate attempt at escape. The final effort squeezes the last of its life out of the small rodent. By its side, the women stand in silence, deep in thought about how best to proceed.

"Should we...leave it?" Cameron finally asks, in a barely audible whisper.

"Wha d'yah think?" Sadie asks, just as softly—intrigued about Cameron's instincts.

"Not sure. It's not right to take it from someone, but...who's the someone?"

Sadie nods. "We can hole-up here, wait to see who comes checking, but...it might take 'till morning...or longer. Or...we keep goin' and find out for ourselves."

This time, Cameron asks Sadie what she thinks.

"Somethin' tells me to keep goin'...and leave the rat."

Cameron concurs. Working as a team, no longer communicating verbally, they stalk ahead. A large, half-shattered concrete pad emerges through the undergrowth, marking the location of the former tower. The concern about who's trapping animals and where those people are forego their search of the antenna for usable parts.

Nearing the last of the tail's islands, Sadie almost misses another telltale mark of human life. She freezes, with hand raised, signaling an immediate halt. She points to a trip line, nearly invisible among the undergrowth.

Following its length, they uncover the full booby trap. Its design and setup, vaguely familiar to Sadie, is simple but deadly. If sprung, the bamboo whip—with a pole full of sharp, footlong spikes—would penetrate at chest height.

"This ain't for huntin' game," whispers Sadie.

Cautiously circumventing the trap, the women halt again with their next discovery. In front of them lies the chasm separating the second from the third island. But even more curious is the metal bracket lying perpendicular to the gap, a similar one visible on the other side.

They examine the apparatus, which Sadie believes has been salvaged from the cell tower, and decide its function must be for crossing the divide. Besides a similar bracket on the opposite cliff's edge, there's also another metal length that appears to slide over and connect with the side she's on. The problem is, they have no way of reaching it.

"Must have been left by someone on the other side," observes Cameron.

Peering below to the ocean, Sadie watches as a large boil disrupts the water's surface and a small wave rolls through the gap. The space doesn't span too great a distance; it's just big enough for a boat to possibly fit through, but it's definitely too large to jump. Walking along the cliff's edge, scouting both directions, Sadie suddenly has an idea. She removes the small length of rope secured to her daypack and attaches one end to the middle of an arrow shaft. She stands upon the other end, taking careful aim before releasing her arrow.

The weight of the rope throws off the accuracy and power of the arrow's trajectory, and it sticks into a barren patch of dirt next to her intended target. Grabbing the length of rope from beneath her foot, Sadie tugs hard enough to pull the arrow out and sets up for a second try. This time it hits its mark. It penetrates through one of the gaps in the crisscrossed metal framework and plunks into the earth on the other side. Being careful with the amount of tension she exerts, Sadie yanks the rope to get the arrow to break free from the dirt; she quickly gives it slack so it'll fall to the ground without retracing its original route. By pulling slowly, the arrow swivels and catches between the metal sides it went through. Maneuvering back toward the bracket on their side, Sadie keeps the rope taut.

Cameron, who's been keeping watch for any movement from behind them and across to the other side, joins Sadie as she pulls the bridge across the gap. Its wheeled design slides easily and, once across, lines up perfectly. Although narrow, the metal looks secure and capable of holding their weight, but still, they proceed one at a time. Safely across, they use the mechanism's own rope to return it to where it originally sat. Then, as they had done on the opposite bank, they brush away the few footprints they left behind.

Moving barely at a crawl and examining every detail, the women assume that more booby traps lurk in their path. As the tail widens considerably, so does the growth upon it, making negotiating a safe route even more challenging for the two women. Each redwood tree, stone, and fern potentially hide dangers. When Cameron halts, so does Sadie. The area ahead, where two boulders leave a gap large enough to walk through side by side, seems a perfect setup. On both sides of the space, downed trees, a collection of massive boulders, and tangles of branches block an easy bypass. Cameron searches toward the left, while Sadie checks the right side. Her path is blocked clear to the cliff's edge, so Sadie returns to find what Cameron's discovered.

"Few spots we could climb over...but nuttin' obvious," Cameron reports.

"Same this way," Sadie nods in her direction. "Which means..." — they both look at the gap — "it's gotta be bad."

Staring at the boulders and the space between them, nothing is apparently obvious, but even so, neither of the ladies wants to risk closer examination. They head to one of the spots Cameron felt they could climb and examine the terrain. Partway up a mess of branches, it becomes apparent that it's not passable. The way is blocked by barbed wire wrapped among the trees and their downed limbs.

They find the exact same obstacle for the other potential routes, so returning to the boulders' gap, they hash out possible strategies. Deciding on a tactic, Sadie picks up a thick, weighty piece of a branch. It's only two to three feet in length, but it provides just enough weight. Cameron returns with a medium-sized stone and awaits Sadie's finger countdown. On three, she tosses the stone, while Sadie covers them both with her bow.

The rock lands before the gap and rolls toward the opening, but veering right, it strikes into the boulder and stops. Nothing happens. They switch positions. Sadie aligns her throwing motion with the target. She slowly swings her implement several times back and forth, gauging its feel and weight, before finally releasing. As soon as the branch leaves her hand, Sadie resumes her grip on her weapon. The branch penetrates the gap and lands ten feet past the space. Again nothing. Still not satisfied, the women reload for second attempts. Cameron's second rock lands directly in the space and disappears. So does Sadie's when she tosses another rock in the same location. After several more throws, they feel it's safe enough to take a closer look.

With slow and precise footsteps, Cameron approaches the now exposed pit for examination. Sadie keeps sight of the area through her bow's crosshairs. She doesn't move until Cameron waves her over. They peer into the hole below. It is dug about head high and full of sharpened wooden stakes. *What are we getting ourselves into?* both women think.

Along the right side of the pit there's just enough of a ledge to pass by single file. After further investigation, Sadie goes first, makes a thorough check of the other side, and then motions for Cameron to follow. Before leaving the area, they gather a couple of larger branches, along with several handfuls of duff and toss everything below. The debris covers the few stones they threw, which sit on the bottom of the pit. The large branches, sticking out, make it appear they're the culprits that sprung the trap.

Shrugging her shoulders, Sadie hopes it's a good enough cover to conceal their efforts. The women venture forward. Moments later, a discernable trail becomes apparent, making them stop. Debating on whether it's another trap or simply a pathway heavily used, they take cover opposite one another and wait. After a lengthy debate with herself, Sadie emerges and hesitantly scouts the area. She moves from cover to cover along the route while Cameron stealthily follows, filling each place that Sadie vacates. The ground becomes more and more worn in appearance—and when the trail splits into two, once again, they pause, contemplating their options.

"Split up?" Cameron asks, through a series of gestures.

Sadie nods, raises five fingers, and then points back to where the trail split. Understanding her meaning, Cameron picks the left fork, leaving Sadie to the right. After the allotted time and with nothing to report, they return to where they parted. Each shakes their heads negatively, then they decide on searching for a longer period of time.

Nearing the fifteen-minute mark, Sadie finds an opening along the cliff that is littered with feathers. Upon closer examination, the scattering appears to be the remnants of seagulls. Piles of bones, mostly wings and broken skulls, sit to the sides of several oddly shaped structures mounted atop posts. The box-shaped devices, slatted with numerous thin, wooden pieces, angle to a bottom corner, where a small piece of tubing drains any liquid into a camouflaged container sitting on the ground below.

"Fog," Sadie mutters to herself, as to the purpose of their function, impressed by the design.

She moves beyond the small clearing, where the trail turns inward. The cover of trees is welcoming. Sensing the presence of another human being, Sadie darts around a redwood with her crossbow readied. Controlling her breath as the sounds of movement near, she's convinced it's only a single person, but nonetheless, Sadie prepares for anything. When Cameron comes into view, Sadie, thankful, lowers her weapon, waves an arm, and steps out to a surprised reaction. Whispering in extreme proximity, they share their findings, surprised to discover that they describe the same thing.

"Fog...catch-ers?"

Cameron nods, thinking Sadie's guess could be accurate—but the sheer quantity of slaughtered birds at both sites leaves much to the mystery. Compelled by duty and curiosity, the women proceed even slower, refusing to succumb to their growing fear of the unknown. A single worn path leads them deeper into the tail's final section. Every step is scrutinized. Ahead, a medium-sized redwood, stripped of its lower branches, butts directly against the trail. Sadie stops before approaching, then, working with her teammate, they slowly circle around the spot, moving opposite one another.

From the backside of the redwood, more remnants of the old antenna, along with signs of its present use, become apparent. Someone's using the tree as a giant antenna—which means they have radio capability! Looking up at the apparatus, they see regularly spaced pegs on alternating sides that parallel its height. A length of wire weaves down the tree but disappears below ground. Its direction suggests that it follows the trail.

Beyond the antenna tree, the space opens considerably, and additional signs of wear and usage become noticeable. An outcropping of boulders causes them another pause. From their vantage points, Sadie and Cameron observe the feature's details, then move forward, stride by painstakingly-slow stride, each bypassing the mound with a wide berth. Besides her ever-present gut response, Sadie's instincts continue to warn of danger.

Once on the other side and tucked into the safety of a giant old growth, thick with low hanging branches, she catches a glimpse of something that draws her attention. Signaling Cameron to change positions, Sadie moves closer. A hint of material, whose appearance suggests it's manmade, peeks slightly above the top of one stone, but disappears behind another boulder. Scanning the varied surfaces, still from a distance, Sadie detects a potential way to reach the spot. The more she looks, the more it appears worn and regularly used in a couple of places. Carefully retracing her steps, she returns to cover and signals Cameron over.

Sadie nods toward the stones and then leans into Cameron. "Might be somethin' here."

Even though Sadie's lips press close to her ear, what's said is barely audible to Cameron. The extreme caution she uses alerts Cameron, who doesn't respond, sensing Sadie's working on a plan. Instead, she continues scanning the area, making sure no one approaches from where they've yet to search, along with where they've already come from. Sadie keeps watch too, and after several minutes, she whispers again. Separating, they move first to hide on opposing sides of the rocks. After waiting and watching for an hour, Cameron moves to search what remains of the island.

Sadie's stomach churns while questioning the decision to separate. Anxious for Cameron's return, time moves slowly for Sadie. When she detects a slight noise, it's with a prayer that she continues listening. She keeps her focus all around the area, fighting the urge to stare at the location designated for Cameron's return. She scans continuously, and when her friend appears a bit of the tension releases. Cameron gestures, sharing that there's nothing new to report and returns to the position across from Sadie.

After they've kept watch for another hour, Cameron rejoins Sadie, asking if they could have missed something. Sadie doesn't think so, but even as such, doubt creeps in. The day lengthens. A decision needs to be made. Sadie leans her head back, resting it upon the massive redwood trunk and turns her gaze skyward. While mentally debating options, suddenly, all her thoughts stop. She tilts her head, stands, and then changes her angle. Cameron follows Sadie's line of vision, curious as to what has drawn her attention. Then, she too notices. High out of reach, another series of climbing pegs have been hammered into the tree.

Wondering how to reach them and the nature of their purpose, Sadie works at solving the mystery. She moves about the base of the tree, examining its fine details. On the opposite side, a gnarly burl twists outwards. Feeling around its knobby protrusions, Sadie finds a solid grip and climbs upon it. From her new vantage point, she examines the thick, dense bark, finding another clue. Reaching into a gap in the bark, Sadie snaps down a metal peg from its upright and hidden location. It locks into position, perpendicular with the tree like the climbing rungs she'd seen above when she first gazed up the tree's trunk. Within reach, and angled at the next height, there's another, and so on, until she's spiraled around and reached where they meet the others, allowing their user to climb straight up.

Nodding to Cameron, Sadie continues climbing. She is careful not to grab any of the thick branches that she knows, by nature's design, snap off easily under pressure. Focusing only on the next peg, Sadie makes sure not to look down, especially as the height increases.

Pausing when the pegs' angles change, she peers up and finally locates their end point. She climbs on. When she's only a few rungs from the structure's bottom, Sadie examines the tabs drilled into the tree that anchor the platform. The pegs lead directly to an entry point; and cautiously, she creeps forward. Just before she gets her eyes above for an initial peek, the cold chill of steel presses firmly into her forehead!

TWENTY-THREE

Stuck, completely trapped, and cursing her decision to climb, Sadie knows there's no way to physically defend herself. Motionless—wondering whose mercy she's under—Sadie debates whether or not to speak. Deciding against it, she waits for instructions, since, so far, she hasn't been shot.

"Up," a gruff, male voice finally commands.

Only half above the platform, she's halted.

"Stop. Raise yer right arm," the voice instructs.

The rifle's barrel never leaves contact just above Sadie's eyes. A second implement is used to manipulate the removal of her bow. The strap is lifted from across Sadie's back, over her shoulder, and then off of her raised hand.

"Sit," is the order that follows its removal.

Atop the perch, Sadie takes a cross-legged position while peering up for the first time. A lone man stands before her. With eye contact, Sadie gasps!

"Sir...it's me...Sadie," she states softly.

The rifle breaks contact from her forehead but remains pointed in her direction.

"Sadie...Sadie Larkin," she reiterates calmly.

The man remains quiet for some time. Sadie begins to fear he doesn't recognize or remember her.

"Sure, it ain't...Zaid?" he finally asks, leaning closer.

Sadie—relieved that old Ned remembers her—hopes he's operating within some level of stability. The last time she saw him, he wasn't, when her father was killed at the hands of the Splitters—and for the first time Sadie turned into her male persona to kill as 'Zaid.'

"Yeah, looks like Zaid's been busy...huh?" Ned remarks, still gauging the depths of the woman across from him.

Sadie simply nods yes and waits to see what'll happen next. He sets the rifle against the tree and grabs the hooked pole he used to remove her crossbow. Several attachments, all uniquely customized for their purposes, screw into the tool, along with a second pole, which he also grabs. Manipulating them both, Ned pulls a nearby branch closer and cuts it away.

As it drops, Sadie yells, "Watch out below!" Turning to Ned, she explains. "There's a woman with me."

He gazes out at the opened view. Unsure if he heard, let alone will reply, Sadie stands up to look about. The platform has just enough space to accommodate them both, but its cramped quarters makes the edges feel dangerously close. Their view extends all the way to where she found the bird feathers, around the boulder site below, and now, also out into the ocean on both sides of the peninsula. *Ned knew we were here before we did*, Sadie smiles to herself.

When he begins to climb down, Sadie follows, wondering what Ned's been doing all these years and suspects he's alone, as was his preference. She's also curious what else he's accomplished, considering his military background and his ability to stockpile goods and survive. Near the bottom rungs, she calls to Cameron, making sure the woman is prepared for the encounter.

"Cameron, this is Ned. Ned, Cameron," Sadie says, once they're back on the ground.

Ned barely acknowledges the introduction and pushes past the women. They've slowed him down enough, and before dark he intends on checking his trap line and collecting the day's water. His tall, lanky physique, accompanied by his prominent military attire, mannerisms, and weapons, makes Cameron all the more uncomfortable in his presence. It doesn't help that he's yet to speak.

Sadie motions for Cameron to stay put while she quietly follows Ned. He skirts the rock formation, pauses in deep contemplation, and then turns to Sadie, figuring, if she sidestepped his defenses, then there are gaps that need fixing. It's also feasible to assume that besides finding the traps, she's also encountered his snares.

"I got anythin'?" he asks, testing her and looking to save a walk around the entire route.

She nods. "One rat…the others…empty, but still set."

"How many?"

When she answers correctly about the number of snares she discovered, Ned nods silently, asking for more. Sadie offers what she knows.

"We sprung the pit fall, but everything's still secure before the bridge."

He nods once again, easing into her presence. She efficiently details how they evaded his trap and then explains where his catch is located. Afterwards, they walk in silence. When he begins to gather his water, Sadie observes the process and aids in the effort. Between the two sites, they gather nearly three gallons, but leave the jugs to carry for when they return. Before moving on, Sadie has questions about the dead birds, but is careful with pursuing information. She kicks at one of the piles and gestures to another.

"Good eatin'?"

He nods. "Keeps 'em outta my water, too."

"You shoot 'em? she asks, doubtful he'd risk the noise but uncertain of his method.

Ned shakes his head negatively. "Fishin'…but…ain't many 'round these days."

Sadie, confused, envisions casting a line at the cliff's edge and hooking seagulls flying by. Then, she considers bait and getting the birds to swallow a hook. Figuring that, at some point, she'll learn, Sadie follows Ned and helps him reset the sprung pitfall trap. When he asks how they managed getting the bridge across, she answers quickly, wasting no words. Staying on task, he collects the snared game, resets the wire, and heads back, checking the other snares along the way.

"This is what I was lookin' for," Sadie says, pausing when they pass the antenna tree.

Ned doesn't stop or slow until approaching the rock outcropping, where he winds clockwise in a spiral path. Sadie matches his every step, being careful to mind the exact places he walks, assuming it's rigged with mines. Cameron, comfortable at a distance, stays put, keeping watch beneath the tree—curious to discover where the hidden entrance to his place is located. Reaching the first stone, Ned steps upon it, then moves to the next, and then the next. At each level, he points to hidden hazards, ensuring Sadie's safe passage. Climbing over the final boulder, they drop into a space where a manmade stone facade, tucked between a couple of monstrous boulders, becomes visible.

A small passage, accessible from a crouched position is maneuvered open and they enter a steel-caged interior chamber that leads downward to a stout door. The short passage is lit, and seeing the exposed exterior wiring, Sadie realizes the antenna tree has a dual purpose.

"Same tree. Smart," she mumbles, knowing Ned heard perfectly well.

He exposes the locking mechanism and opens the door. "The mini model," he says, turning to Sadie before entering.

Inside the underground bunker, a small studio apartment greets them. The familiarity of its design, layout, and style resonates with Sadie. Slowing looking about, she can feel and see her father's presence in every detail.

"This was...his first design?" she asks Ned without looking at him.

"Uhhhh huh," he mutters, watching as she observes the surroundings.

Flashing images, complete with sound bites of her dad's voice, unravel in her mind. Sadie realizes that her father had provided minimal clues about what he was doing, but at the time, she misinterpreted them. In his final years, he had spent a great deal of time with Ned, and all these years later, she's finally learning what those two had been up to. The bed, kitchen, bathroom, and work desk are nearly identical to those in her father's studio. The bunker even looks like it's designed to hide a room or two, probably for storage, and she bets there's also a second exit hidden somewhere. The difference in this shelter, and of extreme interest to Sadie, is the radio station, located in the back corner, where lay a host of solar batteries and the systems they operate.

A logbook lies open along its countertop and drawn to it, Sadie recalls Ned's precise attention to detail and wonders what he's been tracking. Before grabbing it, she pauses, looking at Ned. Asking nonverbally, Sadie gets permission to look at it. (Also given without speaking.) She examines the last few entries before flipping through several pages. On the shelf above, identical books line the tight space. They, too, offer similar data. Returning to the more recent records, she studies them.

"I think...we've got much to fill in for one another." Sadie looks up, then adds, "and...it's gonna take...a while."

Ned shrugs in gist of what she's implying. "Bring 'er down...we'll eat first."

Cameron initially declines the offer to rest below, but Sadie with patience, advises differently. They retrace the entrance route, delicate with each step, and upon entering the bunker, they are greeted by the sight of Ned butchering the rat. He cuts chunks of meat and tosses the morsels, bone and all, into a heated cast iron skillet that sizzles in response to each piece hitting its hot surface. Opening a cabinet, Ned motions, picks something for himself, and then leaves the door open for them to choose. It's crammed tight with a collection of freeze-dried options which Sadie also recognizes. They're the same brands as her father's.

Eating slowly in silence, the women decline a portion of Ned's fresh meat when he offers. After the meal, Sadie goes first; to Ned, she chronologically details all the Splitter encounters she's aware of and provides details on the Yosemite colony, as well as on the settlement at the Isle of Big Sur. Though he'd never show it, Ned's impressed: She's eliminated multiple threats, confiscated several vessels, accumulated large quantities of supplies, relocated personnel, added security, and gathered credible intelligence.

He remains silent, letting her speak uninterrupted, all the while realizing that his old friend—Sadie's father—was correct in his declaration of his daughter's importance. Ned had dismissed much of what he heard as parental love and devotion, even though he respected and admired her father. Then, when meeting and interacting with Sadie during an early Splitter raid, he'd grown to understand how smart she was and how easy it would be for a dad to think that way; but now, Ned feels differently. Finding himself in appreciation of the military sense of her strategies and confident with Sadie's abilities, he's prepared to offer more than just a night's accommodation.

When she finishes her stories and before he begins his line of inquiry, Ned gets up, retrieves his logbooks, and sets them before her. Secure below ground, his bug-out shelter, which started as the prototype for two larger projects, evolved. When he repurposed the cell tower into a radio antenna, along with installing solar panels, his shelter flourished as a communications hub, even though he's only ever listened. Almost manic with the task, he's tracked numerous radio channels, monitored traffic, and kept accurate records for years, and now—the reason's become obvious.

Sadie, finding him in seemingly the perfect time for the ploy she already has in play, provides Ned with enough incentive to offer her everything he can.

Together, they verify various encounters with the Nation, creating a clearer timeline that matches the radio transmissions he logged with the firsthand knowledge acquired by Sadie. His records precisely detail the increased radio usage on IBS, including the communications Sadie was present for and the schedule they maintain. His few questions lead to further revelations, and late into the night they discuss strategy. Tired of only listening and no longer following their interactions, Cameron politely nods her departure and finds a space to curl up and rest.

When morning arrives, neither Sadie nor Ned has slept. Stationed at the radio controls, Ned adjusts the dial, getting ready for the morning transmissions. They start with IBS Command Central beginning the morning rounds. IBS Ranch and the IBS watchtower respond accordingly. Then, in sync, Ned takes his turn as Sadie had instructed and planned.

"This is IBS Watchtower II, reporting operational. Repeat…this is I…B…S…Watchtower…II. Status operational."

Sadie's breath catches in the delay and the silence that follows. Ned swivels his chair around, watching Sadie for any signal.

"Copy, Tower II. This is IBS Command Central. We hear you loud and clear! Please confirm full status, over."

"Operational and all-clear. Over," Ned replies.

"Copy that. Glad to hear! Over and out."

Ned and Sadie stare at the now silent radio. Its connection provides the incentive for them to finalize their plans and continue working. Cameron joins them when Sadie calls to her.

"Ned's gonna show you around and…make sure you know all the safe passages," Sadie begins, to Cameron's dislike.

The rest of the news sits even worse with Cameron, who's not comfortable around the old recluse. Instead of a solo existence, maintaining the rounds she's agreed to, she'll have the added duty of connecting Ned's place and more importantly, the radio, to the others— at least until the rest of Three Sisters can establish its own network.

"Can we count on you?" Sadie asks, feeling Cameron's hesitancy. "It's not permanent. It's just until we can change it. Okay?"

Cameron calculates all she's been through in her life. Realizing this is minor in comparison, she nods in acceptance of the responsibility. Sadie thanks her and turns to say goodbye to Ned, who offers a quick salute in response. He could always recognize when someone deserved a higher rank, and in his mind, Sadie should be revered like the general that she is.

"Sadie," he calls, louder than intended, while she nears the bunker's exit. He pauses and then lowers his voice. "Hold on." He digs through a few drawers. Finding what he's searching for, he hands over an envelope with Sadie's name on it.

TWENTY-FOUR

Her thoughts lingering on the unopened envelope tucked away in her pack, Sadie walks her island as Clara's canyon home comes into view. A fragrant and mouth-watering smell greets her. When she's seen, shouts of joy precede a slathering of hugs. Anna is ecstatic. So is Clara, but the older woman isn't fooled; she can tell Sadie hasn't slept, has news, and...

"Again?" she asks, seeing the look Sadie's trying to avert. "Now where to?"

Sadie diverts Clara's question. "How 'bout, first..." she inhales deeply, "let me eat some of whatever smells so good. I'm starving."

Anna talks excitedly about the stew she's been cooking, anxious for Sadie to try it. Walking the last few strides toward the cabin, Rika joins them with a basket of produce as she leaves the garden. She greets Sadie, excited with what she carries and the opportunity she's been given.

"Thank you, thank you, thank you!" she repeats, hugging and greeting Sadie. "I love it here! It's better than I ever imagined!"

Clara beams with delight as she loops an arm through Rika's. The old woman's eyes sparkle with a contented happiness, and it pleases Sadie as they move toward the fire and its aromatic soup caldron. The stew warms, nourishes, and impresses. Sadie compliments Anna repeatedly.

After a second serving, Sadie's weariness from a sleepless night followed by a long hike begins to set in deeply. Before succumbing to the desire to rest, Sadie shares the story of discovering Ned. Without getting too detailed, she explains the history they share and his connection to her father.

Only Clara knows the horrific details of what Sadie hints at, and the life-changing effect it had on her. Even so, Sadie does well hiding the emotions of her first Splitter encounters when, for her, the killing began. Getting to Ned's radio tower and their newly acquired ability to commute with the Isle of Big Sur, Sadie removes a notebook from her bag. She outlines the detailed records, tracking methods, and channels Ned's monitored, then, finding the correct pages, shares what the two of them spent most of the night doing.

Talking slowly and providing examples, Sadie helps decipher the radio codes they'll use and teaches the appropriate responses, along with how they'll piggyback Three Sisters' communications with the IBS radio schedule. Each site has its own call signs, consisting of short, but precise, bursts of what's intended to sound like random radio static and distortion.

"Anna, I need you to make a copy that'll stay here," Sadie says to the young girl, then, turning to Rika, "When she finishes, check and verify it's correct." Addressing everyone, she adds: "Tomorrow mornin'...we'll hike up the ridgeline and give it a try."

A couple more questions are addressed, but as the group observes Sadie's fatigue, they retire indoors where she removes her shoes and outer layers before going straight to bed. Wiped out from the past twenty-four hours and knowing her pace isn't going to slow anytime soon, Sadie closes her eyes, feeling comfortable in the cabin's cozy confines. She doesn't move until morning, when she gets up to help Clara in the kitchen. The other two ladies join soon after, and with a hot tea and a bite to eat, the foursome is ready.

The small, handheld walkie talkie designated for Clara's place doesn't offer quite the range needed, but it should suffice once they climb out of the canyon. The hike isn't long. Atop the ridge, they continue, until reaching a spot that offers a patch of open sky in the direction of Ned's. They've arrived early; in preparation, and the group reviews the codes, which Sadie insists everyone commit to memory. As they practice, a faint transmission stops them. Clara carefully adjusts the angle of the radio until the sound picks up better. Hearing "all-clears" from the neighboring island, followed by Ned's transmission, Clara responds with her designated call. The coded confirmation proves a success. Huge grins spread among them.

A giddy feeling of connectedness accompanies the blossoming dynamic of cooperation that's developing on Three Sisters. Sadie allows the sensation to fully sink in before moving them along and on to what she's mentally outlined as next. Hiking back and waiting for the opportune moment, Sadie suggests they keep going past Clara's in the other direction—to find out how long it takes to reach the spot where radio contact with Anna's homestead becomes possible.

"It's important for relaying messages," she adds. "We should know...how long of a delay there is, and this way...we'll be able to spend more time together."

Clara is suddenly aware of Sadie's intentions, and realizes her visit is going to be much shorter than hoped. Sadie recognizes the old woman's intuition, and puts an arm through hers.

"Sorry, I'm not stayin' too long this time." She makes eye contact with the other two girls, who've paused. "I'm headin' to the homestead...to teach them the new code so...tomorrow morning, they'll be ready to respond."

They all figured Sadie wouldn't be staying long, but hearing her talk about leaving so soon, the mood swings.

"You just got here," Anna whines. "Can you at least spend the night?"

"Sorry, kiddo," Sadie says, meaning it. "I set a timeline with Ned... and not sticking to it would cause alarm." She turns to Clara. "I'm also sorry we didn't get the chance to chat more last night."

The old woman hugs her. "Apology accepted, but...I wanna hear the rest of what you've got planned."

Sadie nods, and the group moves again. They veer briefly into Clara's so Sadie can grab the rest of her stuff, left packed and ready by the door. Hiking northwest in the opposite direction, the women listen as Sadie shares the need to acquire more help for the brothers and the importance of spreading their newly acquired radio codes.

Anna halts. "You're leavin' again, aren't you?" she asks, alarmingly concerned and finally catching on.

Sadie nods. "I'm returning to the Yosemite Colony. We've got supplies they need, along with updates on Big Sur, and...besides teaching 'em our radio signals...they need to know the Nation's timetable for relocation."

Anna's head drops at the news.

"Until we develop a better communications system," Sadie says, trying to explain it to the youngster, "and...it's safe enough to talk freely without notifying any Splitters...I have to go."

"But why's it always gotta be...you?" the girl asks.

Clara thinks the same thing but holds her words, she knows no one else is as capable as Sadie. Even so, the old woman wishes it were otherwise and, saying a silent prayer, hopes Sadie stays safe.

Sadie is not sure how to explain it. She wraps an arm around Anna. "Everyone else…already has a job. Mine's to keep us safe."

"Who keeps *you* safe?" Anna asks, not at all satisfied.

"Caleb's going with me…he'll keep me safe," Sadie answers with a comforting and heartfelt realization that's only just registering with her.

Clara grins, watching Sadie's features lighten with the mention of Caleb. They return to hiking, and Sadie continues filling in various aspects of what's to come. From Yosemite, she'll return to IBS before coming home. It'll be at least a week, possibly longer.

As they near their destination and her place of departure, the ladies find themselves not ready to say goodbye.

With an accurate estimate on how long it takes to travel between the two radio sites, the group halts. From her satchel, Clara pulls out the food she gathered when Sadie retrieved her pack and places it upon an old blanket she spread upon the ground.

"Sit, eat," Clara says in a manner that can't be argued with.

The women listen and dig in, grateful for a little more time together. There's one thing left to share; when she gets to it, Sadie clears her throat.

"Wha d'yah think of…José joinin' us this time?" Sadie says, casually turning to Clara. "At some point he's gotta learn the routes…and, right now…there shouldn't be any Splitter vessels about. This could be the safest time to try it."

Anna stands, sits, stands again. She wants to talk but can't, and listens on as Clara speaks.

"I was afraid of this," the old woman says in a whisper. "The last trip was hard for him. That boy wanted nothing more than to go with…I'm not sure how much longer we can stop him." She shakes her head as her worry grows. "But, you're right. I don't like it…as usual, but…you're right."

To the surprise of the others, Anna walks off. But she returns just as hastily. "Can I have a piece of paper…and a pen," she blurts toward Sadie.

Opening her bag, Sadie pulls out a notebook, turns to a blank page, and hands it over to Anna.

"Don't leave yet, I'll be right back." Anna walks off again and sits just beyond the others.

At first, the girl merely stares at the blank paper, but once she begins, the words pour out, and before long she's filled the entire sheet. She re-reads it—twice—and satisfied, tears it out and carefully folds the letter.

"If you take José with you...please give him this." Anna hands Sadie the paper. "If he doesn't go, then...bring it back to me." She wraps Sadie in a hug and holds tight.

Sadie can tell the girl is crying and tries to soothe her fears while keeping her wrapped in an embrace. When she finally lets up, Anna wipes her eyes.

"Please...be careful." Anna says, and then she hugs Sadie one last time.

After their final farewells, Sadie hikes toward Anna's homestead while the rest of the ladies return to Clara's. During the entire route, Sadie replays the day's events, considering everything she thought and the emotion they evoked. Nearing sunset, she chooses to bypass the campground, knowing the kids will get too amped-up too late; besides, she'll have more time tomorrow. Taking the trail down to the homestead, the day's light begins to fade. Heading straight to the house, she surprises Trew as he locks up the animal pens for the night.

"Sadie, you scared me," he says. "I didn't hear you."

"I saw the quad. Are the brothers and Caleb here?"

"Just Caleb. Red and Lucas have one more load to move. He's gonna meet 'em tomorrow...at the Memorial Camp and help 'em bring the last of the supplies."

"Great, thanks," Sadie says and turns to leave.

"You stayin' at the house?" Trew calls out as Sadie walks away.

"No, I'll be on the boat. Let the others know I'm back...I'll catch up with them in the morning."

As she loops toward the harbor, Sadie's thoughts run wild and free. Her respiration and heartbeat quicken, a tingling sensation travels from her face and creeps downward. Aboard the *Intrepid II*, she's greeted by José, who, hearing someone climb aboard, has come to check.

"Sadie!" he exclaims, comforted to know it's her as he lowers his weapon for a hug. "I didn't expect you for another day or two. Is everything okay?"

She smiles. "Of course, I've brought news...good news." She peers over his shoulder. "But it can wait until morning. Where's Caleb?"

"He's below, cleanin' up. I've modified the water system."

Excited to share his latest work, José talks rapidly about removing a solar panel from the *Enforcer* to improve his boat's desalination process, along with the addition of hot water.

Sadie, encouraged again by the boy's genius, nonetheless dismisses herself from the conversation. "Perfect, cuz I need to bathe, too," she blurts while he's mid-sentence.

She leaves his company and heads below deck. The closer she gets to the vessel's bathroom facility, the faster her heart races. Sadie sets her belongings down and doesn't even pause at the door. She opens it quickly and immediately starts shedding clothing.

"I just got in," Caleb announces, thinking it's José barging in for his turn in the shower. "Give me a few more minutes."

When no answer comes in reply, he becomes inquisitive and sheepishly sticks his head out around the curtain. Sadie, naked as the day she was born and already pushing her way into the shower, attacks his lips. The tiny shower barely accommodates them, but their bodies don't seem to mind.

"Hey," Sadie says in between kisses.

Caleb can only stutter.

"I've been thinking 'bout you," Sadie says softly.

"I can tell," Caleb says, finally finding his voice.

Sadie turns towards the showerhead and lets the hot water wash over her shoulders and down her body. She reaches for the bar of soap on the wall.

"I'll do that," Caleb says, taking the smooth soap from her.

He vigorously lathers his hands. Starting at Sadie's shoulders, he works his way along the curves of her back with great care. Sadie arches in response, pushing back against his body. When his hands wrap between her legs, she gasps, encouraging him to continue. As the hot water clears the soap from her skin, he nibbles on her neck.

Sadie turns around to face Caleb, her chest to his. He wraps his arms around and under her to lift Sadie up as she opens her legs. Caleb enters her and both shudder with ecstasy—but Sadie pulls back suddenly, stopping them.

"I can't...get pregnant," she murmurs, surprised at the restraint she's somehow managed.

Caleb gazes at her with a look of passion and thought. "There's other things we can do," he stammers, dropping to a knee and using his mouth for another purpose. Sadie can't even respond, her entire body quivers with delight.

TWENTY-FIVE

"Morning, sexy," Caleb says, pulling Sadie even closer in their already tight bunk.

He can't help but kiss, rub, and nibble every reachable part of Sadie, who to his joy, responds in kind. There's a knock at the door, and Caleb does his best to ignore it.

"We're up," Sadie calls. "Out in five." Then, turning to Caleb: "Come on, there's lots to do."

He grumbles, but follows as she gets out of bed. Meeting José, who hands them a cup of tea, Sadie dives straight into a narration of the encounter with Ned, the coded radio signals they created, and the desire to get the homestead's and boat's radios on the same page. Heading towards the house in the morning chill, Sadie outlines how she'd like the day to go and her plan to return to the Yosemite Colony and then the Isle of Big Sur. Caleb, previously unaware of the plan, listens, but finds himself distracted, thinking only of Sadie and the night they just shared together. Noticing his lack of attention, Sadie sends José ahead.

"Caleb," Sadie begins, halting his advance. "There's something else...I want to discuss."

Observing the focus with which she speaks, Caleb worries she's changing her mind about them.

"When we leave for the colony...I'd like José to travel with us. Without the Delta guys...we need another set of eyes, and...along with his abilities, I think the experience could be valuable for him. Besides...he needs to know the route...in case...in case things around here don't go as well as we hope."

"I think he's ready," Caleb responds, a bit relieved and happy to be included in the decision. "He's been anxious to get out on the boat...and play a bigger role."

"Okay," Sadie begins with a comfortable ease. "After breakfast I'll prep him. You hurry gettin' the rest of those supplies here. I want us loaded and out, tonight...with the high tide. We'll anchor off shore, then leave just after first light. Make sure the brothers know too."

Caleb stops her as she turns to leave. Grabbing her hand, he spins her back around and pulls Sadie close for another kiss. She relinquishes to his desire, but keeps it short.

"Come on, we've got work to do," she says, backing away. "Besides...I'll see you again tonight."

At the house, they eat a quick bite before the kids arrive and Caleb leaves. Sadie reiterates her news to the crew there, and puts the young couple—Sofia and Alberto—on the task of making two more copies of the radio codes. Then, they wait for the morning transmissions. The delay between Ned's place and Clara's should be nearing its end.

When the radio message emits its series of seemingly nonsensical sounds, they align perfectly with what's recorded on their paper. The entire house reacts in one big smile. A sense of accomplishment spreads among them, as each person prepares for the day's chores with an even greater sense of pride.

Before joining the kids for their breakfast, Sadie pulls José aside. She talks in depth about the preparations she wants done on the *Enforcer*, which supplies have already been stowed there, and the desire to get the vessel out with the evening's high tide. The boy listens intently, wondering if he'll ever be more than just the one preparing others for their journeys. Trying to hide his disappointment, José asks a couple of questions. Sadie answers and then hands him a copy of the coded radio signals.

"You, too, need to memorize these," she says. "Once the boats are out of the cove and clear from the cliff's edge, their radios should pick up all transmissions...especially since we know which channels to monitor."

He takes the papers and glances over them.

"Tomorrow morning...before leaving for the colony, you'll respond when Ned transmits."

He looks up to see Sadie smiling. "So, then...I'll be using...the *Enforcer*'s radio?" he asks, uncertain.

"Yes. And, once you do, we'll leave for Yosemite."

It takes a few seconds for the information to digest; José wants to make sure he understands it correctly. Enjoying their camaraderie, Sadie stops being so elusive and shares with him her exact intentions.

"I'd like you to captain the *Enforcer*...and take us to the colony, then to Big Sur."

Surprised, excited, and elated, José wraps her in a hug.

"So, you accept, then?" Sadie jests.

"Yes! Absolutely! I'll go get things ready!"

"Hold on." Sadie retrieves the note for him. "Anna wanted me to give you this before we left."

José accepts the letter with huge eyes. He leaves to read it in private. It reminds Sadie of the envelope she's been given, but it'll have to wait—the kids have finally arrived.

Luna's the first to reach her and the little one jumps into Sadie's arms eager to interact. The rescued firsties are more hesitant, but the teachers accompanying them seem in good spirits. After the meal and before the kids hike back to the campground, Sadie pulls Auntie T aside.

"Any progress?" Sadie asks.

"Most of them are still pretty traumatized...and barely speaking...it's gonna take a while, but we'll keep working with them."

"I know you will, and...I can't thank you enough," Sadie says, feeling grateful. "I'm leavin' again...headin' back to the colony and...I wanted to ask if...it's okay to use your place, when we get there?"

"Of course, you don't even need to ask," Auntie T says before turning to address one of the kids calling to her.

Sadie waves goodbye as the troop of children begin their trek back. When they're gone, she returns to the house to help with clean up and to check on the progress that's been made in her absence. By afternoon, the sound of the approaching quad draws her attention; as Caleb parks, she's there to help unload all the goods carefully loaded and packed on the machine.

"Impressive," she compliments Caleb, amazed by how much he managed to fit in one trip.

Caleb kisses her cheek. "Red and Lucas will be here by dark, they know we're leaving tomorrow."

Sadie removes the chainsaws and mill attachments. "How much they get done?"

"Not as much as hoped, but they'll run the mill here while we're gone, then finish at the campground once we return."

After numerous trips of moving goods among the work shed, the house, and the boats, Sadie and Caleb, joined by José, put the last of the items away and retreat to the *Intrepid II* for their final preparations—which include selecting the Splitter attire they'll wear for the journey. José grabs what he needs, goes aboard the *Enforcer*, and waits for Sadie and Caleb, who plan to meet him there. Before they join him, Caleb pulls Sadie aside.

"Time for a quick shower?" he asks enticingly.

Sadie smiles and takes him up on the offer. When they meet José a bit later, they're still grinning, and the young man thinks he knows why.

Before manipulating the *Enforcer* out of the harbor, the trio reviews protocol and prepares for the cautious departure past the sea stack that looms at the cove's entrance. José plays the tide and the wind, maneuvering the vessel just west of the sharp feature. Sadie reaches out from the starboard side and almost touches the rock, mainland not much further away off the port side. Once past the coastal feature, they head around the eastern side of the island and drop anchor just as the sun sets. Manipulating the radio dials, Sadie finds the correct channel in time to intercept the last of the IBS evening checks. When they come across, the group smiles, hearing the cloaked reporting of "all-clear" from their neighbor to the south.

Though the cover of darkness offers some security, they decide to keep watch on a rotation and Sadie takes the first shift. José heads below to rest but Caleb lingers, wanting more time with Sadie. She stops his advances, though, warning him that the time isn't appropriate and making sure they stay focused on what's at stake. Disappointed but understanding, he too retreats below. The evening proves uneventful and by morning, all three stand around the radio console, anxiously waiting for the morning transmissions.

Again, they hear the IBS radio calls, Ned's response, and Clara's signal. José replies appropriately with the boat's coded call sign. The yacht moves out, everything in order, and heads toward the Yosemite Colony. Along the way, each of its passengers keeps careful watch, hoping to steer clear of any Splitter boats that could be patrolling the waters. The trip is long. As the day progresses and land nears, the fog thins gradually until the sun, in its full force, emerges. When the shore becomes visible and things appear normal, Sadie nods to Caleb. He waves both arms in the air, signaling so they don't get attacked.

Anchored near the *Maji Wanga*, José's instructed to stay aboard as Caleb and Sadie take the zodiac ashore. Confirming their safety and being greeted warmly by the workers, excited by their return, Caleb retrieves José and the first batch of supplies designated for the Oceanside community. The boys shuttle additional loads while Sadie finds the Professor, who does no more than glance up from his work as she approaches. His one-armed assistant greets her warmly, repeatedly thanking Sadie for saving his life.

"I'm glad you're okay and doing well," Sadie says before the Professor sends his assistant away.

"Back so soon," the Professor grunts at Sadie, then turns back to what he's doing.

Sadie doesn't take offense at his curt mannerisms, but sits patiently, watching him maneuver a piece that's been repaired multiple times. When he gets it in place and sets down his tools, Sadie takes the opportunity to speak.

"I brought those supplies you needed," she starts, "plus a few things I'd thought you and the colony could use. They're being unloaded now...and divided into what's to remain here and what needs to go inland."

Finally getting his full attention, the Professor stares at Sadie. "You had everything...back on your island?"

"Not exactly," she replies.

As intended, her comment intrigues the aged professor. "Alright, fill me in," he says, sitting across for her.

Sadie wastes no time and, keeping things simple and brief, tells him what's taken place since she departed. She outlines the events that happened on the Isle of Big Sur, the number of Splitters they encountered and removed, the rescue of the firsties, and the two vessels that arrived while they were there. He listens carefully; with each detail, he finds himself growing more and more impressed with the woman before him. Pulling out her notebook, she hands over the coded sequences and the communications protocols that she and Ned developed, along with communicating the intention to include his site.

Sadie continues outlining her plans, further impressing the Professor with her precision to detail. After Sadie finishes, the Professor asks questions that get answered without hesitation and with an efficiency he appreciates. Satisfied with all that's been shared, he gets up and walks with Sadie to check out the pile of goods building on the shore.

He assigns workers to move the various items and gives approval for the use of the water cart to haul what remains to the colony.

Already contemplating the potential increase in their fresh water production, along with added safety measures, the Professor departs without saying goodbye or meeting José. Uncertain of what to think about the strange man, José looks to Sadie who simply shrugs her shoulders.

"It's just how he is," she says, ruffling his hair. "Come on, let's get some food and turn in early. We've got a long and hot journey ahead."

The mood is fun and celebratory as they eat around a campfire with the locals. They hang on Caleb's and Sadie's every word, finding solace knowing that the Splitter Nation has suffered more losses, and that the children have been rescued from their clutches. They ask multitudes of questions, eager for any news and hopeful for the future. Even José gets asked about his escape, about his brave decision and the steps he took to stop the crew of Splitters that enslaved him. Sadie brags of him like a proud parent, and when she gets up and leaves, the boy asks the others a few questions of his own.

He learns more about Sadie's first encounters with both the *Enforcer* and the *Maji Wanga* on her first trip to the colony and the gory details she left out when explaining what happened. He's surprised to discover how close she came to dying—the risk she'd taken to secure the safety of those living here. As Sadie returns, she interrupts the storytelling, stating their need to rest for an early start tomorrow. Reluctantly, José dismisses himself from their company and follows Sadie and Caleb back to the boat.

Still dark and quite early, they begin the two-day trek to the colony, accompanied by a couple of workers, a heavily-burdened cart, and several goats that labor hard, pulling the heavy load. As the sun heats the scorched landscape, they find themselves missing the shade of the redwoods back on Three Sisters. Sadie tells José of the days when the park's majestic scenery called to artists, poets, and naturalists.

At the end of the day, sweaty and hungry, they approach the Mid Valley checkpoint and are greeted by the patrol unit stationed there. At first, there's concern by the patrol guys that the caravan is larger than normal, but then they see who leads it.

"Caleb! Sadie! We didn't expect to see you so soon!" one of the patrollers hollers.

"Alpha pack," Sadie says, smiling, happy to see it's them on duty.

They lower their weapons, gather around their guests, and are introduced to José. The men, still smitten with Sadie from her previous visit, comment about her new short hairdo and listen intently as she spreads what news they've brought. Feeling a masculine jealousy build, Caleb offers Sadie a drink and stays close to her side. When she mentions there are supplies to be left here, the men on duty jump to help and wonder if she's managed to bring them some beer like last time.

"Sorry to disappoint fellas," Sadie responds. "No suds…just food, weapons, ammo, and…" She stalls while finding the box, then, opening it, lets them peer in.

"Hot damn!" exclaims one of the Alphas. "Sadie brought us new gear!"

"Compliments of the Splitter Nation," Sadie says mischievously. "We confiscated an entire cargo ship."

They dig through the clothes, shoes, and daypacks, finding what fits them best and leaving the rest for the other patrol units. Then, watching Sadie find another package, they grow even more curious.

"It's like Christmas," one of them says.

"These are from my personal stash," she says, handing over the container. "Might be a little stale but…"

"Holy shit! Potato chips!"

They tear open a bag, put one of the salty treats in each of their mouths, and then, in turn, hug Sadie.

"Woman, you're amazing. Thank you," says the last member of the patrol unit, breaking from his embrace with Sadie.

"Don't thank just me," Sadie starts, noticing Caleb's expression. She grabs his hand and gives him a kiss on the cheek. "He's the one who helped move all these goods."

Seeing the look Sadie gives Caleb, the Alphas drop their jaws.

"Lucky bastard," one of them jests, popping another chip in his mouth.

"Yah know, if yah ever need more men…" another Alpha begins, then pauses, looking at his comrades. "I think we'd be willing to relocate, too…huh fellas?"

A general nod of agreement circulates among the team. Sadie thanks them for their generous offer, stating that there are in fact such possibilities, but that Gus and the leadership council need to be involved with any decision making. Then, all together, the Alphas remove what's designated to stay at Mid Valley, take their ration of water from the cart, and help their guests settle in for a night around the fire with salty chips and laughter.

TWENTY-SIX

Arriving at the outskirts of the colony, Sadie and Caleb are met by a hug that nearly tackles them.

"Thank you, thank you, thank you!" the woman begins, "if it wasn't for you two...I would've..." She stops talking, not wanting to speak aloud of what almost happened to her aboard the Captain's boat before Sadie arrived that horrible day. She smiles, thanks them again, and then hurries to spread the news of their return.

By the time they reach the campground's structures, nearly the entire Yosemite community has gathered to greet them. The atmosphere is festive and full of excitement. Overwhelmed by the sheer number of people swarming in, José begins to fathom Sadie's celebrity status. She's delivered vital necessities, provided an opportunity for several folks to safely relocate, and she's the hero who quite possibly saved them all.

As José meets more of the colony's members, he can't believe how happy they are living in such a desperate state of existence. They're filthy, poorly clad, smell horrible, and look hungry.

As the commotion dies down and the crowd begins to disperse, Sadie makes her way to Gus, who's been watching all the interactions from a distance.

"Welcome back," the colony leader says, happy to see her. "I assume you've had success, and...from the looks of it...you've once again brought us a bounty of goods."

"And news, lots of it." Sadie smiles and then adds, "Would you have the supplies we brought taken to headquarters? And...can we get the council together...tonight?"

Gus nods yes, but isn't surprised a bit. "Straight to it, huh?"

"You know it," Sadie replies, in her version of an answer. "Let's say...in an hour or so?"

"Anything else?" he asks, partly in jest, part out of unbridled curiosity.

"Well, since you've asked, I was hoping to set up a gathering... tomorrow evening, and...I definitely want to speak with Adam. Has he been...cooperating?"

"Oh, yeah, he cooperates. I think he actually looks forward to my visits...keeps him from goin' stir crazy. As for talkin' with him... whenever you want." Gus turns to leave, but Sadie stops him. *Oh boy,* he thinks, *now what?*

"I'd like to introduce you...to José," she says.

"I was wondering why you brought a kid along," he says, intrigued.

Sadie tells Gus a shortened version of José's story and calls the boy over for an introduction. He greets the leader with a firm handshake and asks permission to view the helicopter.

"I'd like to inspect its systems and see if...maybe...I can help increase its fuel economy."

Gus looks to Sadie, and then back to the youngster standing in front of him. He stares at the boy as Sadie brags about José's mechanical abilities and the modifications he's made to his own vessel, which surprises Gus even further.

"I should've known," he says, looking at Sadie, "only you could find someone just as capable as you." He turns back to José. "You have my permission, but...you're gonna have to coordinate directly with me."

"Yes, Sir!" José's excitement builds with anticipation. He thanks Gus and politely dismisses himself.

"Am I dismissed now?" Gus jokes, looking at Sadie.

Sadie laughs. "I'll see ya shortly."

Returning to Caleb and José, who wait nearby, Sadie has them grab their gear and together they head to Auntie T's former residence. The run-down RV—nicknamed 'the Moose'—looks in even sadder shape now that it's been left unoccupied. Once inside the emptied quarters, they open the windows and ceiling vents to air out the place. They drop the dining table, transforming it into a bed for José, who plops down while Sadie and Caleb do the same on the back bed.

In the cramped quarters, Sadie fills them in with what Gus has agreed to; it's decided that José should stay when they leave to meet with leadership. The boy doesn't mind, he says, as he begins to drift into slumber after two long and hot days of hiking.

Walking through the campsites as dark approaches, Caleb finds himself reflecting on all that's passed since he, too, lived in the colony. It seems a lifetime ago. Realizing how fortunate he's been, he shares his sentiments with the woman he loves. Although she's focused on what's to come, Sadie also reiterates her happiness at being with him.

Before entering the former ranger station that now serves as headquarters, they share a brief but good kiss. Once inside, though, Sadie shifts to business mode: the gathered council sits, awaiting their arrival.

Sadie and Caleb take turns updating them on all that's occurred since their departure. They share explicit details, concerning IBS and the plans for it to become the Nation's new headquarters. Talk shifts to the number of Splitters they've encountered and eliminated, the freed locals and firsties, and the cargo and passenger vessels that arrived while they were there. Also included are the coded radio responses Sadie recently developed with Ned and the desire to link IBS, Three Sisters, Oceanside, and the Yosemite Colony via these signals—while keeping everything camouflaged and off of the Splitter's radar.

When addressed about the decision to keep the Commander alive, Sadie defends her actions, declaring the woman a "valuable asset for future encounters." She shares the plan of returning to IBS to gather more information and share the radio sequences. Leadership asks numerous questions and the debriefing lasts late into the night.

As Gus lights another candle, Sadie asks for the confiscated map they acquired during her first visit, the one that depicts the new boundaries of the expanded Pacific. Looking over its details, Caleb can tell that Sadie's considering something much bigger than what she's just spoken about.

Sadie shares that they've brought food, clothes, and additional weapons for the colony; then, she asks for several things, some of which surprise even Caleb. First off, she offers to relocate more of the Yosemite Colony—some to Three Sisters and, for those prepared to fight, to IBS. At some point, the Nation's president will try to relocate there and when that happens, he'll be walking into a trap—and additional personnel on the island will help ensure that it's a successful one.

When they leave, Sadie wants Adam released into her custody, since he's provided vital intel to their success on Big Sur. Besides taking the prisoner, she also asks to be allowed to keep the nautical chart.

At this point, the council, confused and tired, along with Caleb, simultaneously erupt in a slew of questions. Sadie patiently waits for them to return to order and then answers what seems to be their biggest concern.

"The firsties...more than likely, were abducted from these places." She points to locations on the map sprawled over the table. "With it in our possession...along with Adam, who was present during their captures...we might be able to return them to their families."

A round of murmurs, disbelief, and doubt escapes the council's mouths.

"Gentleman," says Sadie, standing. "I agree, our first priority is to secure our safety, which, so far..." she scans the room, making eye contact with each of them, "we've had tremendous success doing." She hesitates, finding it unnecessary to either remind them of the Splitter vessels she's commandeered and destroyed or to, once again, mention the sheer number of militants she and her team have annihilated. Instead, Sadie maintains eye contact, standing with a determination that doesn't go unnoticed. "I'm not askin' for any of you to go with...or for you to risk your personal safety...all I'm askin'...is for the opportunity, at some point...to gain the ability to reunite families. I mean...what if...it was your kids?"

Sadie walks slowly around the table, feeling all eyes on her. Then, returning to her chair, she pulls the map towards her and, glancing over it without looking up, adds one last point. "*Someone* needs to do it," she says, glaring at them with a fierceness that helps the council understand why she's been so successful. "If none of you are willing...at least...let me."

The room remains silent as she rolls up the chart. Caleb is stunned. He can't believe Sadie didn't mention any of this to him before now. He battles a series of emotions that range from anger to worry, and then to a sense of awe at Sadie's boldness.

"I'm takin' this," Sadie says, holding the chart. "I'll make the best copy I can, but...tomorrow morning, after I meet with Adam, I'll need your final decision. Until then...thank you." She stands and looks to Caleb. Together they depart.

"Sorry 'bout all that," she says, meaning it, once they're outside. "It's kinda been brewing in the back of mind...seeing that map again...and knowing we've got someone who's traveled to a lot of those places, just...moved me. Somethin' has to be done."

"But why *you*?" Can't you just be happy...staying home...with me?" Caleb steps closer.

Sadie wraps her arms around him. "I *am* happy with you, but... I've got this...calling that...I can't ignore. I know I'm meant to help... meant to...make a difference."

"You have helped...you have made a difference. What if what they said is true? What if...all the firsties' families have been killed and there's just no one out there anymore?"

Sadie rests her head on his chest and holds him tight. "They could be right, but even if only one kid gets reunited...it'd be worth it." Caleb lifts Sadie's head and kisses her softly. "Okay then. I'll help you. Again. But...could you please stop droppin' things like this on me?"

"Deal. But just so you know...I'm not really sure when we can make it happen. First, we've got to focus on keeping IBS safe from Splitter control."

Sadie lets go and they walk together through the campground.

Back at the RV, they go straight to bed. It doesn't seem long before the sun's up and the day begins. They eat, and with José's help, begin duplicating the map. With it complete, they start towards head-quarters, where the first order of business is to disperse the goods they've brought. Together they move all the food supplies to mess, where Marla, the affable kitchen manager, greets them with hugs and a smile that just doesn't stop. Enthralled with the delivery, she invites them to dinner where they'll be the honored guests. Declining is not an option.

Leaving, Sadie suggests that Caleb show José around while she talks with Adam. They'll reunite with her at headquarters for lunch to finish distributing the clothing and shoes.

Before entering Adam's holding room, Sadie retrieves the map, already copied and returned earlier. Then, after a quick knock, she unlocks the door and enters.

"Oh shit...I didn't 'spect it to be you," Adam says, uncertain what her presence means. "So...you're here...cuz wha' I told yah helped?"

"Sit," Sadie commands.

He does so and waits to see what this encounter will produce. Sadie sits across from him, staring, a lengthy silence between them. It has the effect she intended; as he squirms, she begins.

"Tell me...what've you learned from all this?" Sadie asks.

Adam clears his throat and looks around his tiny room. Looking from his stash of food supplies Sadie left last time, and then to her, Adam speaks honestly.

"I've had lots ah time to do nuttin' but think, and…I'd have to say…I've learned that…human kindness still exists and…even though I don't deserve it…forgiveness may be one of the hardest things for people, 'specially…forgivin' yerself." His head drops with shame.

"What if…I said you could help correct the wrongs you've committed?"

Adam's head snaps up. "Wha d'yah mean?"

Sadie uncurls the chart on the floor between them and turns it to face him. Adam looks at the map, wondering what she could possibly want.

"Show me where you traveled with the Splitters and where the firsties were taken from."

"Ummm…I've never seen this before," he begins, "so…I'm not really sure." He gets up and takes a knee for a closer examination. "But we traveled along the coast…and somewhere…maybe here," he says, pointing to a small coastal island. "And then…past this spot… there was a small group. But…I'm not that sure. It looks different on paper. I'm sorry."

Sadie hands him a blank notebook and pen. "Okay, then. From the time you started working for the Nation, I want you to detail every encounter you witnessed, helped with, or heard about. Everything you remember…'bout the people, the kids…their hair colors, land or sea features, the scenery, landmarks, the ones abducted, those murdered, and the ones left behind. Write it all down."

Sadie rolls up the map and makes to leave.

"Wait," Adam calls. "Does this mean…you rescued the firsties?"

"It does."

Adam collapses into the chair, and runs his hands through his hair. Sadie watches his response before she exits.

Outside his room, she sets the nautical chart upon the table before the men from last night gather again. Upon entering, they see the map, its copy, and the mounds of supplies she's rearranged.

Sadie doesn't hesitate to speak as the council sits. "There's a substantial amount of goods at Oceanside, too…including everything the Professor needed for improving the water system, additional

weapons, food, clothing, even some solar panels and batteries. But…
it doesn't compare to what's still at IBS. The amount of stuff loaded
on that cargo vessel…makes me believe it had to carry most of what
the Nation has left. They're preparing for the move, and being ahead
of 'em…was…well…let's just say…we delivered a huge blow…and
they're not even aware of it, which…makes it all the better."

Sadie moves around the pile of supplies and sits among the men.
Gus takes the lead and confirms that Sadie's basically getting everything she wants. The only hesitation comes when she speaks about
patrol units and shares the conversation she had with Alpha pack
about relocating, which leadership doesn't like hearing about.

"I understand," Sadie interjects, listening to them. "Losing
another unit compromises security, but…if we secure IBS…and eliminate Splitter command, then relocation of more colony members, and
the insurance of its long-term safety, becomes more than just a hope…
it becomes reality."

Before anything else can be said, José and Caleb enter. The group
halts, and Sadie suggests they break for lunch. As the colony's leadership leaves, José is introduced to all. Rather than following the men
out, the youngster, along with Sadie and Caleb, stays and eats from
the food they packed. While refueling themselves, Sadie listens to José
talk about all he's seen, about the poor conditions of the colony. He
can't believe they've survived this long without a closer water source
and finds it utterly absurd how far it has to be transported.

TWENTY-SEVEN

Sadie, Caleb, and José arrive at the mess hall for the evening meal, and the entire colony greets the guests like visiting royalty. Instead of waiting in line, their food is personally delivered with gusto and smiles. The energy of the room further explodes when it's announced there'll be second servings—as well as a gathering afterward where hot chocolate will be served.

José's never eaten goat before or met so many new people and finds both experiences wonderful in their novelty. The table he sits at with Caleb and Sadie stays packed. No one leaves, abuzz with anticipation of what's to come.

As the group transitions to the park's outdoor amphitheater, the site's fires light the area, and each person is handed a steaming chocolate treat upon entrance. Sipping hot chocolates, the locals fill the slab benches, anxious to learn what news will be shared and curiously talkative as to what's in the bins that are spread across the front of the venue. Gus stands and officially begins the event, but quickly turns it over to Sadie, who is met by a standing ovation that catches her by surprise. She blushes.

When the commotion dies down, she starts by telling José's story, how he, even at his young age, stood up for what was right and how he put his welfare at risk to make a difference. The place goes crazy with cheers. The colony stands, applauding him as his cheeks redden. Caleb stands to join Sadie, and the applause continues.

"It's gotta be the extra food...and sugar," Caleb jokes at Sadie's side.

When the crowd quiets, Sadie smiles, knowing what she's going to say will set them off again. "The last time I was here...I shared the heartbreaking news about the Nation abducting children...and their plans of turning them into soldiers at a new base...not far from here."

Boos and hisses travel through the audience.

"But...we've returned to tell you..." She pauses for dramatic effect. "That not only have we taken the island back, but...we've rescued all of the kids!"

The cheers reach a new level. The crowd jumps to their feet and begins chanting, "No more Nation! No more Nation!"

It goes on for some time and when they settle back down, Sadie and Caleb take turns sharing details of what occurred, news of the intended Splitter relocation to the Isle of Big Sur, and their intentions of using the island as a trap to eliminate the Nation's leaders when they attempt to make the transition. After sharing what they can, Sadie changes directions, stating that they didn't come back to just share news, but to also open up the possibility of relocating more people.

Before they get too excited, Sadie makes sure to clarify exactly what's intended. She explicitly explains that they're looking for folks willing to help with construction on Three Sisters and for others also willing to take a stand against the Splitters, on the Isle of Big Sur. She adds, that hopefully soon, they can offer a greater amount of relocation possibilities. While the people absorb all that's been shared, Gus takes the opportunity to present them with what leadership's been debating.

"Council's met," he starts, enticing the crowd's curiosity. "We've decided...your input is needed about making a decision that could affect all of us. So...we'd like you to consider the possibility of losing another patrol unit to relocation. We'd like to hear your thoughts about it."

People take turns standing to offer their opinions and concerns. After all who want to speak get the chance, a general vote is taken, and the majority agree that, if a unit wants to go, it should be their choice. Satisfied, Gus turns things back over to Sadie who motions to the bins.

"Clothing and shoes for everyone in the colony," she says proudly, and the crowd erupts again.

The Gathering wraps up, and lines form by size. Things taken from the Nation are passed out. People leave invigorated, and by the time the last of the items have been distributed, Sadie already has a list of the people interested in moving and taking on the newly offered positions.

The following day passes quickly and by the evening meal, it's already been decided who will relocate and when the caravan will leave. Word was sent ahead to Mid Valley and when the Alpha guys arrive at mess, they confirm with both Gus and Sadie the offer for them to go. Excited by the prospect, the men return to their quarters to pack their meager belongings. Sadie dismisses herself and while heading back to headquarters, she debates on what tactics she intends to use. Unlocking Adam's door, she finds him with notebook open and a focused look upon his face. He stops writing as she enters. Without having to be asked, he turns it over to Sadie. She scans what's been written so far, then, without speaking, hands it back.

"I'm not done yet," he blurts, thinking she's not satisfied.

Sadie moves to his food supply and begins sorting through it, which makes Adam nervous. "We're changing things up," she says, and then leaves with an entire bucket of food.

Adam thinks his time has come. He worries that once finished with writing about what he remembers, he'll be executed for his crimes. When Sadie returns, he asks her about it.

"Please, Sadie, tell me," he begs.

"You're being moved...tomorrow. Keep writing...I'll see you in the morning."

She leaves, taking two more containers, and Adam falls to his knees in despair. When morning arrives, he hasn't slept much, and believes it's his last day. Adam scribbles as fast as he can, trying to get as much written as possible, feeling it's the only way to redeem his soul. When Sadie enters, his face goes white.

"Some of this...is hard to read," she says, looking over his work.

"I'm sorry, I was tryin' to get as much out as I could before..." he trails off. Finding some composure, he pleads, "Please Sadie...I need more time."

She hesitates in her response, watching Adam's remorse overtake him. "Okay...put your stuff in this." She hands him a small pack.

Unsure of everything in his life at this point, Adam takes the bag. He only has the clothes he's wearing, the notebook and pen, and a water bottle.

"Put the last of the food in there, too," Sadie says.

Adam does as he is told. He puts the pack on and extends his hands when Sadie asks. She cuffs them together, opens the door, and motions for him to leave. Adam swallows and finds himself afraid to exit. When the door to the outside is opened, he steps out into fresh air and sunshine. Sadie leads him down the trail and towards the outskirts of the colony where he finds a small group of people gathered around a cart pulled by goats. Sadie attaches his cuffs to a chain at the back of the wagon, sticks a hat on his head, and waves to the group.

"You sure about this?" Caleb asks, looking at Adam as Sadie rejoins his side and the caravan begins to move.

She nods and the trek begins. It's slow, tedious, and sweltering. During the two-day journey through the dry, dusty valley, the only person who interacts with Adam is Sadie. Confused, tired, and unaccustomed to walking, Adam thanks her as she frees him from the cart when they arrive at the coast. He hasn't complained once, not the entire time, and guzzling the last of his water, he cherishes the refreshing effect it has. Adam absorbs the scenery, the sun on his face, preparing for what he thinks will be his impending end.

Sadie moves him towards the shore, where he sits, watching as the sun dips below the horizon—the sky aflame in hues of pink, orange, and red. The beauty of it strikes him profoundly; turning to Sadie, he hands her the notebook, which she witnessed him using late into the night and on every stop they made along the way.

"I'm ready," Adam says, at peace. He closes his eyes and silently awaits his execution.

"Alright then, let's go," Sadie replies, motioning to Caleb, who comes and joins them.

They move toward the beached zodiac and tell Adam to get in, the captive finds it fitting that this is how death will come—at the very place where his work with the Splitters started. When the zodiac stops alongside the *Enforcer* and he's helped aboard, Sadie moves him below, putting him into the smallest stateroom.

Sadie flips him his notebook. "Keep writing," she says sternly. "We're takin' you back with us."

Sadie leaves and locks the door behind her, and Adam crumbles to the floor, overcome by his gratitude for the human ability of forgiveness.

"You think he'll try to get out?" Caleb asks.

"No, he's gonna be alright," Sadie says. "I think he'll end up being one of the hardest workers we have. He'll do whatever it takes to redeem himself."

Returning to shore, Sadie leaves to give the Professor his copy of the radio codes while Caleb and José shuttle people and their belongings. Once everything and everyone is loaded, Sadie has a sense of déjà vu as she preps the crew and passengers. Alpha pack, Caleb, José, and Sadie, all dressed as Splitters, will be the only ones permitted free range around the yacht; once they leave in the early A.M., everyone else will stay hidden below.

Before sunrise, the crew hustles about, preparing the *Enforcer* for departure. Once they're out to sea, and after hearing the anticipated radio transmissions and proper responses, the calm conditions and clear morning sky lift their already high spirits. Sadie, though, worries about the uncharacteristic conditions and hopes that, at some point, the fog returns to hide their passage.

The radio crackles to life! It emits a message that causes fear and a sense of panic as they desperately scan the ocean around them for the hailing vessel.

"Should I reply?" Caleb asks, as the radio calls continue.

"No, nothing yet," Sadie commands, peering through her binoculars, then pointing off the port side. "There!" She turns to José—who's captaining the vessel. "Keep our speed and course constant," she orders.

"They're closing," exclaims a worried Alpha patroller, unsure of what he's gotten himself into.

As the boat gets closer, Sadie, to everyone's shock, has José slow the boat's speed and sends Caleb out to wave the Splitter vessel down. When Caleb comes back, she quickly outlines a strategy, assigns positions, and moves the men to advantageous positions. As the boat slows even further, she joins Caleb, praying for the strength and luck to pull this one off.

"Why didn't you respond?" yells one of the Splitter men from the hailing vessel as it pulls alongside the nearly stopped *Enforcer*.

"Radio's down, been havin' all kinds of problems wit it," Sadie yells back, disguising her voice.

"Where's the *Maji Wanga*?" the same man asks.

"Anchored along shore…entire electrical system's down. Rats chewed the wires."

The man turns to his crew and listens to something that not's audible to Sadie or Caleb.

"Where's the Cap'n?" he asks, turning back towards them. "And… where you headin'?"

Caleb responds with a throaty chuckle. "He's below, wit a couple new...playmates..." He cups his hands in front of his chest, mimicking huge breasts. "He doesn't want to be disturbed."

The man laughs, knowing the Captain's reputation.

"We found a couple more firsties, so...while the *Maji Wanga*'s down, we're delivering 'em to IBS." Caleb offers.

Caleb glances at Sadie, who gives him a subtle nod, pleased at how he's playing his role.

Again, the man turns away from them, but this time, he participates in a lengthy dialogue; the wait to find out what's happening threatens to ruin the calm they're trying to display. When the Splitter finally faces them, it's to announce they've been ordered to follow them to IBS. Sadie and Caleb each gulp before returning to the helm as the vessel steers clear of them.

"Shit!" Caleb says once inside. "Now what?"

Before Sadie can answer, José points at the radio and lets them know he was able to overhear everything the other vessel communicated with Splitter headquarters. He shares their dialogue, the radio handle the vessel used, and the Nation's relief about them finding the *Enforcer*.

"Nice work," says Sadie. "Let's move. We'll have to figure it out on the way."

Moments later the radio picks up more chatter; this time, their escort is attempting to contact IBS.

"Oh...this ain't good," observes another Alpha.

Sadie corrects him. "No, it'll help. Now our friends will be prepared."

Listening and waiting to see what happens, the worried crew wonders how long it will take IBS to respond. Keeping it short and simple, the radio operator on the isle confirms and asks for an ETA. The Splitter boat replies appropriately; then it sends word that it's also accompanying the *Enforcer*, who is delivering another batch of firsties but their radio is down. A lengthy pause follows. Worried, Sadie feels her gut clench.

"Copy that, IBS Command Central out."

Sadie inhales deeply. Their cover hasn't been blown—yet.

TWENTY-EIGHT

"Alright, everyone ready?"

Sadie speaks as she returns to the front line of the deck from the recesses below, where she informed the rest of the crew what to expect.

José changes course as the Isle of Big Sur becomes visible, and then relinquishes the helm to prepare for his role. The boat slows along with its enemy vessel, allowing Sadie and Caleb another chance to determine how many Splitters may be aboard. They estimate a small crew. When the watchtower comes into view, they move outside, this time with the intention of clearly being seen. Their plan is full of risk—the first being blown up by friends on shore who mistake them for Splitters.

Unable to radio their true identity without tipping off the actual Splitters, Sadie and Caleb stand in full view of the tower, praying they are recognized as friend and not foe. Sadie removes her hat in what she hopes looks like a casual overhead stretch; she uses the hat to point at the other boat. But her attempt to get the rocket launcher fired on it doesn't work, and the Nation's vessel continues its approach.

As the *Enforcer* drops anchor, so does its escort, precariously close to theirs and endangering them if their teammates on shore do attack. Sadie moves to the next step of the plan.

"You're on, kiddo," she says, grabbing the boy and dragging him into view.

José's removed any semblances of Splitter attire to look like a captured firstie. His hands are bound loosely behind his back and a gag keeps him from being able to talk.

"Da Cap wants this little bastard outta here first," Caleb yells to the two Splitters watching from across the gap between the two boats. "Then...he says I'm ta get yer crew to shore."

A collective breath holding follows his comments. The crew aboard the *Enforcer* hopes their escort's lack of visible transportation to shore is an accurate observation, as a major part of their plan hinges on it.

One of the Splitter men gives a thumbs up, and a sigh of relief escapes the team's lungs. Sadie and Caleb position the zodiac with

José playing his role of the meek and scared little kid. They shove José aboard and zoom towards the twisted rebar and concrete remnants of the Bixby Bridge. Another sigh of relief escapes when Dominic's and Devon's confusion turns to recognition as they come to greet them on the makeshift dock.

José is pushed along roughly as he's taken into custody by the two Deltas. Sadie provides the duo quick instructions before leaving with Caleb. Being dragged from sight, José fills Dom and Devon in on the series of events that put them into this position—along with their strategy to combat it depending on how the next few moments play out.

Out of sight of the boats, José is untied. He hustles to gain a better vantage, crouching low while battling an uneasy anxiety that builds in his gut.

Caleb slows the zodiac as he approaches the enemy vessel so he and Sadie can gain a better perspective on exactly who they're up against. Two men look on, eager to leave behind the confines of the boat and get on shore.

"Just you?" Caleb asks the men, trying to hide his concern as they lower themselves aboard.

"Naw, the other two wanted a little quickie," one of the Splitters says, taking a seat in front of Sadie. "Da Cap'n...ain't the only one 'round here who can git some."

"You two wanna piece before we leave?" his buddy says, misinterpreting the look on Sadie's and Caleb's faces.

Sadie feels her anger threatening to take over. She glances at Caleb. Before the opportunity lapses, she responds, "Yeah, I'm in," in a deep, male voice that Caleb recognizes all too well.

Unsure about Sadie going alone, Caleb looks to disagree. But the two Splitters on board, laughing wildly, don't give him the opportunity.

"You?" one of them says to Sadie. He laughs again and turns to his friend. "This little swingin' dick...this...youngin' thinks he's ready for some man's work."

"Boy...you even got any hair on ur balls?" the other asks. Both Splitters laugh.

Sadie's eyes grow dark and distant. "Don't worry 'bout me or my balls. I kin handle my business."

"Ohhh, shit...little boy's one cocky son of a bitch. What's yer name big man?"

"Zaid," Sadie answers, all serious. "Jus' tell me...where ta find what I'm lookin' for."

He answers and Sadie starts to move.

"You sure 'bout this?" Caleb asks through the side of his mouth.

"Oh yeah, you get these two to shore. I'll take care of business inside." Sadie climbs the ladder up to the other vessel.

Below deck, she runs into a man buttoning up his pants as he closes a door behind him.

"Wha' the fuck do you think yer doin'?" he stammers, surprised by the company.

"Yer not the only ones wit needs," Sadie snaps back.

He hesitates as he hears the zodiac take off. "Aw righty then, there's a sweet little piece of ass down there...nice en young...en tight."

The man passes by Sadie and opportunity presents itself. Removing her knife, she strikes twice from behind and then finishes by slicing his jugular. Blood spits everywhere as his body hits the ground. Zaid moves to the door. The activity behind it is inaudible. She pushes open the door and hatred fills her veins. The sight reminds her of saving Gabby all those years ago; images of rape ignite a rage that scares even its owner. When the rage subsides, Zaid's face is covered with blood and a motionless body lies slumped against the wall. Heavy breaths and long moments later, the persona of Sadie finally returns to her face; the terrorized eyes of the young girl, bound and spread, shake Sadie back to herself.

"I'm so sorry...I'm gonna cut you lose," Sadie says in her normal voice as she removes the hat from her head. "I'm not a Splitter...I'm just wearin' their clothes."

Sadie moves closer and the girl bucks. Almost in tears, Sadie removes her outer shirt and uses it to cover the emaciated young woman.

"Look," she says, removing another shirt and the wrap used to flatten her chest, so only her sports bra remains. "See, I'm a woman too... I'm not gonna hurt you. I'm just gonna cut you free."

The girl's sunken and hollow eyes follow the knife as it cuts the bindings at both wrists and then her ankles. She has barely enough strength to sit, and when Sadie tries to help, she flinches and falls backward. Heartbroken, Sadie catches her and offers a soft word. Then Sadie says she must leave, but promises to return quickly.

Rummaging around the ship, she returns with water, a bit of food, additional clothing, and an old tarp, which she tosses over the bloody corpse left from her rage. The girl drinks and, painstakingly slow, attempts eating a few morsels.

The sound of the approaching zodiac draws Sadie's attention; she runs out to see Caleb. He boards, rushing to Sadie, worried about the blood covering her, and he makes sure she's okay. His fears placated for the time being, Caleb shares with her that the two men he took to shore have been bound and are in the watchtower guarded by the two Deltas. Sadie asks him to get the others from the colony off the *Enforcer* and to bring Rowin, Mee-Maw, and José out to her. She'll stay with the girl until then. By the time they reunite with Sadie, the abused girl has barely moved from her place of imprisonment and has yet to speak.

Sadie turns the girl's care over to the women. She uses the vessel's radio, along with José, and his knowledge of the radio transmissions earlier in the day between it and Splitter headquarters, to confirm the boat's safe passage and arrival at the island. They're instructed by the Nation to examine the progress on IBS, help with the relocation, and then continue on in their searches. Acknowledging the orders, they sign off—quietly confident the Nation still has no idea of what's actually happening.

On shore, Sadie heads straight for the watchtower with Caleb. Inside, she violently cuts away the prisoners' clothing until both men are naked and bleeding in a few places. When Sadie pauses in her attack, the men realize she's the one they mistook for a boy; but before they get the chance to speak, she begins another assault. She lashes out, striking them repeatedly, cursing their evil actions until the knuckles on both her hands bleed. Out of breath, Sadie gathers herself.

"How many more boats were out lookin' for the *Enforcer*?" Sadie finally asks.

"Fuck you bitch. You…"

Sadie delivers a kick to the man's groin that abruptly stops him from finishing his statement. Turning to the other, she asks the same question.

"Just us," he stammers, afraid of the same fate.

Sadie leans in closer. "You sure?"

He nods yes.

"How many of you bastards are still at Tahoe?"

"Don't say...nuttin' else," the other groans, barely able to speak.

Sadie delivers a second kick. "How many?!" she asks, turning back to the other man.

He hems and haws, stalling.

"Not good enough," Sadie says, motioning to kick.

"Wait!" he yells. "I'm not sure."

"You'd better stop wasting my time."

"Uhh...all kinds, maybe...a couple thousand or so.

"Bullshit." Sadie delivers the kick to his torso. "I know you're lying."

Frustrated and sickened by both of them, Sadie knows it's pointless to continue. *They're not going to provide anything of value, unless...*

"Move them outside," Sadie commands.

Caleb, standing timidly by, retrieves the Delta Team just outside and together they secure the prisoners with a rope to a nearby tree. Noise of the returning zodiac distracts Sadie, who leaves the prisoners to see if the rescued girl is any better. Mee-Maw and Rowin return, carrying the body of the freed teenager wrapped in a blanket.

"Ith was...twoo wate," Mee-Maw sadly states through her toothless frown.

Sadie's head drops and tears fill her eyes. "Take her up to the house...we'll bury her tomorrow."

José hangs back, but Sadie sends him along to help, then—fueled by intense hatred—she storms back to the captured Splitters.

"I'm gonna ask...one more time," Sadie says, her knife readied. "Tell me what I want to know."

"I ain't givin' you shit," the first man states.

Sadie grabs his penis and testicles. She yanks aggressively with one hand while slicing everything off with the other. The stream of spurting blood and screams of pain escalate his comrade's fear.

"There's not many of us left," the other blubbers. "Maybe less than fifty. Most of us were sent out scoutin'...only the highest-ranking officers are left...plus their guards." He quivers as Sadie approaches.

She stares at him eye to eye to determine whether anything he's said is true. "For your crimes of rape...and murder..."

"No! No! No!"

Sadie yanks and strikes the same emasculating cut. Caleb gulps and goes to her side, scared by what he's witnessed. But Sadie just walks away.

"We can't just let 'em...bleed to death," he says, turning to follow her. "Even if they deserve to."

"I know," Sadie responds, still disgusted. She returns to the men bleeding in agony. She reaches for her gun and extends her arm. Without hesitation, from point blank range, she fires a bullet into each of their heads. "Burn the bodies," Sadie says to the Deltas before walking off alone.

Out of everyone's view, she falls to her knees. Intense sobs rock her body. Trembling, she vomits, sickened by all of it.

Caleb finds Sadie and carefully lifts her from the ground.

"We've gotta...stop...all this," she says, sobbing against his torso.

He slowly moves them towards the ranch house where they'll spend the night. Even though she's secluded from the others, it takes a long time before sleep finds Sadie; and when it does, it's unsettled and riddled with nightmares.

*   *   *

Running in the dark, Sadie stumbles and falls. Suddenly in an old barn, she peers up to discover the rafters are full of bodies, stripped naked and hanging by their necks. Trying to escape the blood raining down from the corpses, she turns, only to discover a raging fire moving towards her that blocks the exit. Backpedaling, Sadie can't move her feet. Looking down at what slows her, she sinks shin deep into the rotted and burning flesh of a mass grave. The harder she struggles to free herself, the deeper she sinks and the closer the flames come.

Screaming, Sadie looks up as the scenery shifts. She's being chased! Running into a worn-down house, she storms up a steep set of stairs, which lengthen without end. The harder she pushes, the more steps appear, until a doorway emerges at one side. Sadie dives through it and smacks face first onto a stained and foul-smelling mattress. Scrambling to her knees, she looks up to find Gabby, her friend from long ago, limp and chained to the headboard. No matter how hard she tries, Sadie can't wake or free her.

Frantically looking for something to help, the scene shifts again, and Sadie's trapped below deck in the engine room of an extremely small vessel. A foot protruding from behind a fuel tank draws her attention and, moving closer, the image of the withered and beaten young girl from the day comes into view. Sensing a Splitter getting ready to attack her from behind, Sadie prepares to defend herself. *I will not fall prey.* She turns. With the webbing between her thumb and index finger, Sadie strikes to crush the militant's trachea.

*　*　*

Caleb rolls over to put his arm around Sadie. She's been quivering while she sleeps, and he barely gets a protective arm up in time to shield her deadly strike.

"It's me! It's me!" he says until Sadie gathers her senses.

It takes a few moments for the nightmare to settle before Sadie can speak.

"What...have I become?" she whispers.

TWENTY-NINE

Groggy and unsettled from the rough night of haunting dreams, Sadie starts the day well before sun up. It begins by spending time with the dead teenage girl. She washes, dresses, and wraps the girl before saying a silent prayer and wishing her soul peace. Then, shovel in hand, Sadie hikes to a secluded location under a massive oak tree where murdered locals were buried when the Nation first came to the isle. Sadie breaks earth. The labor helps ease her mental unease. Just before sunrise, José, who also struggled with sleep, joins her.

They work together in silence. As the mound of dirt builds, José's mind strays to Anna. The dead girl's hair color matched Anna's, and he can't help but think, *what if it had been her?*

When Caleb appears, he hands them water and takes over for Sadie who he hadn't even known had left their bed. After her nightmarish episode, Caleb eventually fell back asleep and thought she'd done the same. As the grave nears completion, Sadie climbs from the hole and sits alongside José.

"After we bury her, return to that boat...take the Alpha guys... scavenge everything you can. Siphon all the fuel, empty the back-up tanks, and take whatever you'd like for the *Intrepid II.* Strip it completely. Then, sink it... far off shore." Sadie stands, places a hand on his shoulder and turns to look at the rising sun. "Check out the cargo ship too...I'm sure there's a few things you'd like from it."

José nods, and together the three of them head back to the ranch house for the morning meal and to clean up before the burial. Sadie keeps her distance from the others and retreats into a few minutes of seclusion. When it's time, she carries the body, with help from Caleb and José, before presiding over the simple ceremony.

Afterwards, Mee-Maw and Rowin place a wreath around the small cross and wait for Sadie, who has taken it upon herself to fill in the grave. Sadie mounds the stones they uncovered while digging, and the two women sense she doesn't want to interact—but they silently help anyway. When finished, Mee-Maw and Rowin shed tears for the young woman; they know all too well the brutality of the Nation.

Leaving the site, the three women walk toward the barracks. Before departing, they each wrap Sadie in a lengthy embrace that speaks more than words.

Returning to the ranch house, Sadie connects with Leon, to whom Caleb's been teaching the new radio codes, while making additional copies.

"You 'bout ready," she asks Caleb, examining their work.

Caleb nods. They retrieve their belongings and head out, hiking further into the island and towards Command Central. Approaching IBS's water source, the boys, excited for the return of the very people who rescued them, extend their greeting, happy to see that Sadie and Caleb are safe. They are relieved after being informed of the confusing radio transmissions the previous day, and the kids are glad to learn everyone's safe. Sensing the heaviness with which the two adults travel, the boys return to their water-gathering chores, realizing their visit is for business and not pleasure.

At the house there is more excitement, but it fades quickly with Sadie's serious manner. She immediately asks for updates concerning Russo and wants an outline of all the interactions that have occurred in her absence, along with details of the radio contact they've had with the Nation's Tahoe headquarters. As information is shared by the two men, Sadie asks clarifying questions. Once satisfied, she switches to the updates she's brought. She speaks of relocating more people from the Yosemite colony and the radio signals that will be used to set up communications among all of them, completing the circuit. At the conclusion of the discussion, Sadie stands and moves towards the room where Rene is kept, followed closely by Caleb.

"I'm gonna find out everything I can, then..." she leans into Caleb, "I'm ready to go home."

They stay partially embraced as Sadie gathers her strength and wits, knowing how the woman on the other side of the door can sense weakness.

Caleb gives her a kiss. "Hurry back."

Sadie straightens her shoulders and enters, finding Rene in the midst of a set of pushups. The former MMA champion is drenched in sweat, doing what she can to stay in fighting shape within the confines of the small space.

"Well...looky, looky," she says with murderous glee, finishing her set and standing. "I would've cleaned up...if I knew you were visiting."

Sadie locks the outer door, enters through the second, and stops just out of Rene's ankle-chained reach. The bold, red coloring of her hair is beginning to fade, and there are hints of blond roots showing, but overall, she still looks fierce in nothing but an old sports bra and shorts.

"You treatin' everyone okay?" Sadie begins, trying for nonchalance.

Rene laughs. "They're scared shitless...you should see them when they rotate my chains."

"You know...you gotta stop intimidating them."

Russo laughs again. "It's the only entertainment I got. I'm goin' stir crazy in here...I'd kill for the chance to go for a run."

"Careful. It's talk like that...that'll keep you locked up...or..." Sadie doesn't finish, knowing her point's been made.

"What about you? Seems you've been...playing rough." Russo motions to Sadie's torn and swollen knuckles. "That's serious damage...How's the other guy look?"

"*Guys.* And they're not lookin' at anything anymore," Sadie replies, unpleased with her loss of control.

"Been on a bit of a terror, have you?"

Sadie pushes the small table from against the wall so it rests in between them. On it she sets her notebook that Rene recognizes from before. Then Sadie uncurls the map she's brought. Taking the chair across from her, the former Commander takes a seat and looks over the chart.

"Alright, Sexy," Rene says. "Exactly...whad'yah want?"

"Everything," Sadie responds, straight faced. "Let's start...with your journey around these waters." She taps the map. "And what you know about...where the firsties were taken from."

Rene glances over to the picture of her younger self and twin sister—exactly what Sadie hoped she would do. Russo's torment concerning her sister's disappearance is the catalyst Sadie's using to gain valuable information as the warrior works to redeem herself.

"The Captain may have been a real pig," Russo says, looking at the map. "But his attention to detail sure was exquisite."

Sadie is not surprised that Rene recognizes his work and asks how often the two of them interacted.

"Hardly ever and...not at all like he wanted," Russo sneers. "The bastard thought he was God's gift to women, and it took...let's just say...I set him straight. Afterwards, he steered clear of me...wouldn't even come aboard my vessel." She scans the chart. "But I'm afraid I'm not gonna be much help. We didn't travel together. I was scoutin' base locations while he and Cookie were out collectin' firsties."

"You mean...kidnapping them," Sadie corrects.

Rene looks up, feeling her stomach drop, knowing she was in charge of the operation and led the way in pushing for an army of children. Sadie lets the weight of Russo's crimes sink further, then demands what other information the fighter can provide. Meticulously, Russo retraces the route she traveled and the locations she personally examined, along with any and every encounter she recalls. Sadie records the details without interrupting. When Russo reaches the point of her arrival at the Isle of Big Sur, their first session comes to its conclusion.

Sadie stands to stretch overhead and shakes out her sore hands. Between the abuse they suffered from the day before, accompanied by all the digging and the writing, they feel arthritic and unresponsive. Rene also stands, feeling a new lightness about her; due to the steps she's begun to take in righting her wrongs. She wonders what else Sadie's after. It doesn't take long before she finds out, as Sadie returns to her notebook, scans through the notes taken during their last visit, and then turns to a blank page.

"Okay, Commander..." Sadie begins, "I need more details on the Splitter fleet."

Rene stares straight ahead maintaining eye contact, but doesn't answer.

Sadie raises an eyebrow. "You know...reuniting the kids with their families...if...they're still alive...is gonna be a huge challenge. If we're gonna make an attempt, it'd be real helpful knowing more about who else...and how many boats are out there."

Sadie looks to the childhood photo of Rene and her sister and then back across the table. Rene doesn't miss the implication. For years, she wished her sister had been returned, even now she still does.

"What exactly do you wanna know?" Russo finally says, acquiescing to Sadie.

"Everything," Sadie states again, "starting with the fleet's size and the boats you personally know or heard about."

Russo shares what's been asked. She estimates its size, reiterating that the motorized section of the fleet stayed in the vicinity, while the sailboats were sent on further explorations. With an impressive memory, Rene produces an extensive list, complete with what she recalls about crew sizes, adding any additional details when possible. Sadie has her skip over the boats that have already been destroyed or confiscated. With each one, Rene gauges the extent of Sadie's abilities, and how far she's already gotten.

As the pages fill, Sadie's even more intrigued by the woman before her. Besides being an incredible athlete, warrior, and survivor, she has an intellect that deserves its own validation. By the time they've exhausted Rene's knowledge, Sadie's hand aches, and her writing has become sloppy. Sadie doesn't ask anything further, allowing her captive to divulge things at her own pace, but there's something she's been curious about.

"What about fuel?" Sadie finally askes. "How's the Nation keepin' the boats gassed?"

"Figured you'd get 'round to that," Rene responds. *"Texas Hold 'Em."*

Sadie shoots her a look. "You gonna make me ask?"

"It's an oil tanker...from the Gulf of Mexico. At least...what used to be the Gulf. Now, just beyond here," Rene says, pointing to a place on the chart where its details end, "there's nothin' but one huge, open expanse of water...reachin' all the way to the Atlantic. From what I've gathered...the tanker was off the Florida panhandle when the Tri-Nami hit. Not that Florida exists anymore. But...at the time, the Gulf Coast was our only coastline the Enders didn't crush. But as the ocean kept rising, that tanker continued west until the Nation got a hold of it. Now...it's permanently stationed a few hours south of the Tahoe headquarters...and guarded fiercely."

Absorbing the fact that you can now sail from the Pacific directly to the Atlantic, Sadie ponders what intel of Russo's is a primary source and what she has heard from others. Intrigued by this information, she questions the Commander further about her experiences.

Then, Sadie switches back to asking and learning about the oil tanker. She wants details on fuel rationing and delivery, and numbers of men working and guarding it. Sadie learns details concerning the refinement station setup along its shore. Russo provides what she can, complete with an estimation on how much fuel is left and the pace of the Nation's usage.

Pleased with the session, Sadie closes her notes and stands to once again stretch her limbs. She's stiff from sitting so long and her poor hands feel tortured. Rene watches, also pleased.

"Join me for dinner," Russo says more than asks. "After all this... it's the least you can do."

Sadie contemplates her options. To Rene's pleasure, she accepts. She leaves, and returns a half hour later with food for two. Rene, who washed as well as she could considering the small amount of water rationed for her, has changed and tidied up her small confinement space. Sitting together, their eating starts in silence as both women are genuinely hungry. But after several bites, it's the Commander who strikes up a conversation. It begins with casual chatter, but quickly moves to exactly what she had in mind.

"I'm glad you're back around," begins Rene. "It's nice havin' company."

Sadie nods, then finishes the last of the food in her bowl before looking up and sensing there's more to come.

"I think...I've been the most candid, honest, and informative with you...since..." Rene looks at the photo of her sister, then slowly returns her gaze to Sadie. "Since *those* days. She would've really liked you." She takes a drink from her cup. "But if *this* is ever gonna work, I mean...really work, then...we gotta work on bein' teammates. And that means information goes both ways."

Sadie tries to get a read on Russo.

"Relax, no games...just the two of us talking." Rene leans back comfortably in her chair. "Tell me somethin'...somethin' 'bout you. I mean...you've had a rough go of things...that's obvious, and...from the looks of it now...somethin' real recent has taken quite a toll on yah."

Although doubtful of her captive's true intentions, Sadie is still impressed. Rene Russo continues demonstrating multitudes of ability. Taking a deep breath, Sadie knows it'd be good to talk some of it out, and Rene's right: It'd help create a stronger sense of connection between them, which, at some point they may need. Trying to keep it short, Sadie unloads the details of the young girl she tried to rescue. She talks about her sunken, hollow eyes, bruised and bone-thin body, and the deep gashes under the restraints that kept her exposed for easy access.

"I think…" Sadie's speaks, her heart lurching. "I think…her hip was dislocated." Her head drops, and her voice weakens. "Those bastards forced her legs too far apart." Sadie looks back up. "She was only a few years older than Rachel."

Hearing her sister's name, the sin and cruelty of the crime hits Rene's core. She reaches over and clasps Sadie's hands, turning them knuckle-damaged side up. "I assume you punished the guilty."

Sadie pulls her hands back. "Savagely."

A long silence ensues as emotions settle. Trying to shake the haunting images of the girl and what she'd done afterwards, Sadie gets up and walks about the space. It's the first time she's moved within Rene's reach. Going to the picture, Sadie picks it up, stares at the image of the two smiling twins, and sits upon the bunk. Touched by the gesture, Russo moves and sits next to Sadie. Exhausted with physical and mental fatigue, Sadie hands the photo back to Russo, who returns it to its place. When she turns back around, Sadie's closed her eyes and has rested her head against the wall.

"You're more than welcomed to…stay here with me tonight," Rene offers, feeling a greater connection, closeness, and attraction to her.

Sadie doesn't respond, making Rene unsure whether she even heard. Russo sits down next to her, creating the catalyst for Sadie to finally answer.

"Thanks, but…how 'bout…we get back together first thing in the morning?" Sadie says, opening her eyes and sliding towards the edge of the bed.

Russo—disappointed but not surprised—watches Sadie get up. As Sadie gathers her notebook and begins collecting the dishes from their meal, Rene joins to help her. Handing over her bowl, she lightly brushes Sadie's hand.

"Take care of those knuckles," Rene whispers. "And yourself."

After another rough night of unsettling dreams, Sadie, true to her word, is up and back with Rene before anyone else in the house is even awake. The warrior rolls from the bunk and looks over her visitor, who appears sweaty from a predawn jog.

"What a tease," Russo says as Sadie removes her sweatshirt. "Take a little jog, did yah?"

Sadie nods. It was a short run—barely enough to clear her mind and organize some thoughts—but the post-exertion effect is uplifting, even with her lack of sleep, which is apparent.

"Bet yah would've slept better here...next to me," Rene begins, noticing the dark circles still under Sadie's eyes, "than out there with... Caleb." She removes the thin tee she slept in and, standing completely naked, looks into Sadie's eyes while judging the accuracy of her observation. She laughs. "Thought so...I can sense him all over you. Didn't think he'd let you come all this way alone."

Sadie is ashamed of being so easy to read. She ignores Rene, who dresses in workout clothes and begins her morning routine. The athlete moves about the tiny space with a variety of movement, doing what exercises she can within the confines of her prison.

"Wanna join me?" Rene asks, feeling her body warm up.

"Not this time, Champ," Sadie replies. "Just a light sweat and stretch for me today."

Sadie watches briefly, then, needing movement, goes through a series of yoga poses, deciding it'd do her more good than getting straight to business. As Rene wraps up her workout, Sadie retrieves her notebook out of the small bag she brought along. Before starting her next round of questions, Sadie begins emptying out some of the bag's other contents.

"I brought ya a few things," Sadie says.

Rene moves to the table while downing a glass of water. About to make a comment about only wanting her, Rene stops abruptly at what Sadie's spread across the table. "No way!" she says.

Sadie smiles, watching Rene immediately stir a scoop of powder into another glass of water.

"Figured you'd like a little post-workout protein," Sadie says. "I know you're not gettin' the calories you're used to...besides...looks like...you're losing some mass."

This time, it's Rene's cheeks that flush. She has lost some muscle but didn't know it was that visible. Using the other gifts as an excuse to look away, Russo gathers the new toothbrush, toothpaste, and tampons, along with additional clothing, two towels—and, hidden beneath them, a bar of chocolate.

"You kiddin' me? Even the Nation doesn't have chocolate." She picks up the treat and examines it like a priceless relic. "Where'd you? Wait...if you're giving it to me...then yah got more?"

"You could say that," Sadie laughs, keeping knowledge of her life-time supply to herself. Still smiling, she takes a seat, signaling that free time is over. Her demeanor turns serious. "Tell me about Tahoe... and tell me about...this...President X."

THIRTY

Sadie keeps her word and returns to Russo's room after breakfast. She's brought company, and the two local men, accompanied by Caleb, wait for Sadie's cue.

"Knew you'd be good on your end of it," says the captive.

"To make this happen...it's gonna be...a bit..." Sadie searches for the correct descriptive. Then, thinking how she'd feel if it was her, she continues. "It's gonna be a bit degrading, but...the caution is out of true respect for your...abilities."

"O-kay?" Rene responds, confused, but ready. "Whatever, just let me outta here already?"

"I'm here only to observe," Sadie says, "and make sure things go...smoothly."

Russo doesn't miss the implication. Sadie's made it perfectly clear, even chastised her more than a bit about messing with the guys. *Empowered, not coward*, Rene thinks, Sadie's catchy little phrase sticking.

Russo turns to the two locals who've been in charge of her watch as Sadie and Caleb step aside. Moving forward, the men begin the practiced procedures they developed when Sadie returned yesterday from her last session with Rene. The captive is ordered to stand with her arms extended out in front of her body. With Russo in position, the men take full precautions and begin moving their prisoner.

Alternating between two chain attachments, they transfer the Commander, one length at a time, never removing one restraint until the next one is secure. Each change requires Rene to be seated in one of the chairs that are also alternated with the moves. Their route, out of the confinement cell and through the backdoor, has been modified with anchor points along the path, where the chains can be secured. It's a slow process. Once outside, the last attachment connects to an old, resurrected dog run. Russo's eyes dart to Sadie during the last transfer.

"I told ya, degrading," Sadie says. "But all out of respect. You're outside...like you asked...and as promised." Sadie smiles, concealing a laugh, satisfied with the process and Russo's cooperation.

The warrior breaths heavily, running and moving about back and forth between the restricted length offered by the cable. She does short sprints, lunges, squat jumps, and a series of pushup variations that have her moving on her hands along the entire length of her range. After the hour, she's returned to her cell in the same, precise manner, undertaken in the opposite order.

"Thank you," Rene offers to each of the men as she's returned to her room. "This was fun…we should do it again."

The men look confusingly at Sadie, who simply offers a nominal shrug. The two local men finish by locking the inner door and then the outer one. They regroup, as planned, to debrief and talk about the process: how it went, its success, and the possibilities of its continued use to foster positive interactions with their captive.

After a long conversation led by Sadie, she's ready to move on; she initiates her departure by saying goodbye. Caleb—looking forward to spending more time with Sadie now that Russo's not occupying all her energy—does the same. He, too, looks forward to returning home.

Hiking back to the ranch house, Caleb senses Sadie's lingering fatigue and feels slightly guilty of all the sleep he's managed. When she eventually joined him late at night, he didn't even stir; when he awoke each morning, she was up and already long gone.

Before reaching the ranch house he takes her hand. They haven't talked, but he knows she has a lengthy list of things to do, and she'll put everyone else ahead of her own needs. Caleb finds it difficult to imagine surviving like Sadie had done, in complete solitude, without a single person to talk with or be there for help. He knows it's going to take more time for Sadie to adapt and break her distant habits, but he wants her to know she's not in this alone.

"Hey…" Caleb pulls her close, "I just wanna say, you're doin' great." He kisses the top of her head. "You've saved a lot of people."

At first unpleased by stopping, Sadie acquiesces by closing her eyes and allowing her emotions to run their course. With her head rested on Caleb's chest, she drops all guise of strength and control. Silent tears streak down her cheeks as Caleb holds her.

"Because of you," he continues, "we have hope."

They stay entwined until Sadie recovers. Straightening up, she pulls away only to wipe her eyes. She kisses Caleb.

"I'll help wherever you need me, okay?"

"Thanks," she offers. Then, just as quickly, Sadie takes his hand and gets them moving again.

At the ranch, they head in opposite directions, each with a list to accomplish. Bouncing among all the people and sites, Sadie pushes aside the desire to rest; by the evening meal, she's gotten just about everything checked off her list. Sitting next to Leon, she decides to wait until they've finished eating before moving on to him. She can't interrupt the adorable interactions between him and the little girl he's adopted.

When they move inside and the youngster lies down, Sadie pulls out what's become a well-worn and full notebook—and begins outlining the Nation's expected timeline according to the most recent intel she's gathered. Included are what communications will be needed, and when, by Leon, to keep the Splitters unsuspecting of what's actually going on. It's a vital part of Sadie's plan—for the island itself and the safety of everyone on it. Besides a high level of responsibility, she is placing a substantial amount of trust upon Leon to continue these necessary communications.

Though he started in a rather questionable position with the Splitters, Sadie has a strong sense concerning his abilities and loyalties. After numerous run-throughs that leave Leon weary, they finally wrap up for the evening. Sadie is mentally and physically exhausted. She makes her way to Caleb, who's made it a point to stay awake. He greets her with a hug and a shoulder rub that eases Sadie into slumber.

By morning, Caleb is once again alone, but this time, at least Sadie is near. Hearing her and Leon practicing at the radio, he approaches as the morning transmissions begin. All the coded responses from various locations are finally in sync. Sadie smiles, acknowledging the accomplishment. She can't help but think how wonderful it'll be once they can talk freely, without fear of Splitter ears and Splitter retaliation.

After a quick round of goodbyes, Caleb and Sadie reunite at the barracks with the trio of Yosemite locals who'll return with them to Three Sisters. The departing transplants say farewell to their friends, who'll be staying to help on IBS. Excited and a bit anxious to finally arrive at their new home, they listen intently whenever Sadie speaks. At the ships, an exhausted crew carrying random pieces of boat machinery greets them. José, Delta Force, and Alpha pack pulled an all-nighter, after back to back days of heavy work.

"Capin' Gutiérrez " Dom drops a hefty load. "Is a bit of ah worka-holic." He sits among a mound of materials and chugs gulp after gulp of water. "A real slave driver." He smiles, wiping his mouth while looking at José.

The young captain, filthy in grease, dirt, and sweat, sheepishly shrugs and looks at Sadie. "You said strip it, take what I can."

"Yeah...and he wants...ev-er-thang!" hollers Devon, also taking a seat.

"One more trip, then...it's ready." José pipes up, responding to Sadie's glance toward the still-present boat. He turns to look at the rest of the arrivals. "It'd go faster with more help."

Sadie nods, communicating that everyone's got a task, including her.

José repositioned the confiscated boat days ago so it was anchored closer, but still, transferring the items using the zodiac is painstaking. Shocked by the gutted interior, complete engine removal, and stripped controls, Sadie is impressed by José's team and their work. Before tow-ing the foul boat out to sink it—José's very last item in a well-thought-out order—has him pulling up the now detached anchor. With it on shore, the boat drifts briefly before being towed out to sea. A single, precisely placed grenade finishes the job, and the vessel of hate disap-pears below the big grey ocean.

The little zodiac continues its relentless pace, zooming passengers out to the *Enforcer*. Before Sadie makes her final departure, she spends time communicating with the patrol units staying behind on the isle. Both Delta Team and the Alpha guys will remain, and it's important for them to understand their roles and responsibilities. At first, Sadie shares her gratitude; she then offers encouragement for the work that lies ahead, providing an overview of what she's learned from Russo on the expected Splitter timeline and strategy.

Caleb's arrival back to shore signals that everything on the *Enforc-er*'s been readied. He listens intently as Sadie shares her final words with the men and then, he too, offers them well-wishes and a sincere farewell. Just as quickly as Caleb and Sadie return to the *Enforcer*, the boat heads out, its course set for Three Sisters.

Sadie's the last to change garb. Appearing at the helm, back in her Splitter disguise, the crew of six gets their assignments and falls into place. Scanning the waters and carefully monitoring their course, José captains the *Enforcer*.

By sunset, their home island has lay at starboard long enough to anticipate the end of their trip. During the journey, the energy of a building swell was concerning, but as they near the northern edge of Three Sisters, it's just safe enough to begin the final phase of returning home. Not until protected in the safety of the harbor do they relax. By the time feet are put to ground, it's in darkness. But it doesn't deter those at the homestead from waiting up to welcome them back.

The three Yosemite transplants get reacquainted with the other colony members who arrived before them, and then, while they're instructed where to put their things, the brothers—with whom they'll be working—prep them on the labor that'll begin first thing in the morning. Before they leave, Sadie asks Red and Lucas to accompany her back aboard the *Enforcer*. She preps them in detail about Adam; and together, they go into his room, where he's been staying, locked away.

Upon Sadie's entrance, Adam gives her his completed work. He looks at the two men and takes a nervous gulp. A long silence follows as Sadie sits aside, flipping through the notebook pages he's written, leaving Red and Lucas to eye Adam. Sadie finally informs Adam that he's being sentenced to hard manual labor—and will be under Red and Lucas's watch until informed differently.

"Don't get too happy," Red warns. "We're gonna work yah to the bone. You got a lot to make up for."

Adam's hint of a smile disappears. "Yes sir."

"You start before sun up. Make sure you're ready when we come get yah." Red motions to his brother and they exit together.

"A lot of these pages are too sloppy," Sadie says, handing back the notebook and beginning to depart. "Rewrite 'em."

"Wait," Adam says. "Thank you…thank you for this chance."

"Just make sure no one regrets it."

Before joining Caleb and turning in for the night aboard the *Intrepid II* in the harbor, Sadie finds José re-reading the letter from Anna for the umpteenth time. Seeing her, he carefully refolds the paper and tucks it safely away. Reminded of the letter still unopened from her father, Sadie must set aside the thought to address José.

"You did a really great job," she says. "I wanted to let you know how proud I am of you."

The compliment buoy's José. To his surprise, Sadie doesn't stop. Instead of learning what work she expects from him next, Sadie informs José that she'd like him to visit Clara's to communicate in person the news of their safe return. The young man beams with emerging maturity and catches Sadie off guard when he jumps and wraps her in a giant hug. Breaking from the embrace, she adds a few more things, making sure he knows how long he can stay and what's to be done when he returns.

"Tomorrow, early...find me before you leave," Sadie adds in thought. "I'll have a letter of my own ready to deliver."

THIRTY-ONE

The sounds of heavy work and chainsaws provide the early morning soundtrack to Sadie's and Caleb's departure on foot. Sadie plans to reassess all that's occurred while en route, and then, in the comforts of her home, recuperate—before another round of travel among the island's inhabitants is required of her. The journey to the Memorial Campground, then to her cave, and finally all the way back to her main bunker, will provide plenty of opportunity to fully digest all that's occurred.

During their travels, Sadie rarely talks and Caleb respects her silence. They've been through much and both desperately need the time to decompress as they struggle to navigate their tormented and introspective thoughts.

Arriving at her home, and in its secluded privacy, Sadie finally makes the decision to read the letter her dad left for her all those years ago. Not sure why it took her so long to do so, and apprehensive about what it may contain, Sadie opens the envelope. In slow motion she unfolds the paper, and begins to read.

Sadie Pie,

The words have her catching her breath. Her father is the only one who ever called her that. She hears his voice as she reads.

Sadie Pie,

This letter, finding you now, means I'm no longer physically with you. But right now, at this very moment, please know I am smiling down on you with the biggest grin, love, and pride that any father could ever feel. You are that shining star I've always known and felt you'd be.

Sadie's shoulders twitch uncontrollably as she sobs. When her vision refocuses, she continues reading.

I left this note behind for safekeeping and as a precaution in case things don't go as we've planned. With it in your possession and without me communicating what it contains in person, it means, that at the very least, you still have Ned, who, albeit an odd one, is an incredible resource. He and I shared a vision that most didn't understand or want any part of, but please realize everything I did, I did for you.

You're destined for something bigger than all of us and with each passing day, the feeling I have about this grows stronger. It so overwhelms me that I feared losing you, which is why I started hiding much of what I was doing, and I'm sorry for that. I know you worried and thought I was losing my mind, but be reassured, you did incredible! You were so strong, so brave, so patient. Showing all the qualities of a true leader.

My dreams and visions haunted me for years. They were always the same: you leading others back from the brink. I prayed things would never come to what I saw in my dreams, but sensing such a tremendous importance in them, I prepared anyway.

This intrusion of evil men into our community, and the harming of the ones we love finds me worried that the signs I was given were indeed a warning. There's much I've still kept hidden, and suddenly I'm forced to face the errors of not communicating things with you sooner.

Tomorrow, we set about to end this horrid plague released upon us. First and foremost, I worry for your safety. For that reason, I've chosen this route of communicating because I didn't want to overwhelm you with all I have to share. I've feared that, if I did tell you everything now, it would cloud your focus—which is of the utmost importance for what's required.

Sadie closes her eyes and remembers the days of which he spoke, her initiation into the world of the Splitters, of killing, of terrors that still haunt her. She blinks away the images, and returns to the letter.

I've failed to share so much with you, especially, the extent of resources I've been stockpiling. My tool shed, with its hidden apartment, has so much more to offer and I hope to show you in person, but, if not, I'm sorry, I've failed you.

Its secrets will have to be revealed by using the access panel at the back wall where the wood seams butt together. With careful inspection, you'll find a notch that becomes apparent along your right side. It opens to a passage that leads to a door you already know how to unlock. Inside, I've left blueprints and detailed instructions for everything you'll need.

If I survive what these next twelve hours will entail, I promise there will be no more secrets. If I don't make it, I'm so sorry. I can't apologize enough, and, with all my heart, I regret having this be the way you have to learn about these things.

Sadie's heart clinches with the vision of her dying father and his final words as he fought for each breath, of him trying to share what he'd hidden from her. Tears fall and blur her vision. She wipes them away with the back of her hand.

There's more. I've also hidden items (of a more extreme nature) and what you're going to find may be overwhelming at first. Remember, I've tried to prepare for any scenario you may encounter, but may most of what's stored beneath my shop never be needed. Trust your gut, save those you can, and live knowing that I'm watching over and protecting you.

The day you were born, besides being the most joyous occasion of my life, will also gain you entry to these stores. Check the barn's extinguish-ers, turn the red one to the right, then, the white one left. Please use the utmost of caution, and by all means, listen to your heart.

I hope this letter never needs to find you and that I get the chance to share what I've been keeping from you in all its absurd details. There's so much more I want to say and do. I pray time gives us the opportunity and the longevity to see it through. If not, you need to know that my heart fills every time you smile. Even if I'm watching from above, know that your joy still reaches me up there and brightens my day.

I love you my little... Sadie Pie, Sadie Pie,

Brightest Star in the Sky.

XOXO,

Dad

Sadie's eyes overflow. She hasn't thought about her father's silly rhyme for years; she didn't realize how much it could be missed. After several minutes, she sits upright and sets the letter aside. She leaves her room, surprising Caleb by her sudden appearance.

"Come on," she blurts, quickly preparing to head out to check her father's hidden storeroom.

Holding back his questions and hoping soon she'll share what she's read, Caleb follows behind as Sadie takes off at a near run to the barn. She's caught by surprise at the absence of the horrid log near the barn's entrance. All that remains is a mound of sawdust, scraps of wood, and a neatly-stacked pile of drying lumber.

"Thought you'd like it gone," Caleb says.

Sadie doesn't have the words for what it means to her. But with such a strong sense of curiosity about what's hidden under the barn, she can only offer a brief thanks and a kiss on his cheek before hustling to the entrance. She pulls open the large door. Inside, she heads straight to the fire extinguishers and turns them in the order instructed by her father's letter.

The entire cabinet they're housed in opens up, releasing from the wall—and a vault door appears, complete with combination dial. Sadie enters the numbers of her birthday. She unlocks and opens the door. An extra-wide spiral staircase is revealed, descending into the darkness below.

Grabbing a light, she leads the way, Caleb at her hip. Goose bumps crawl along their skin as they take small steps. At the bottom, two large cranks protrude from the wall. Knowing at once their purpose, she turns one rapidly while telling Caleb to do the same with the other. When enough energy has been produced, a progression of lights clicks on, illuminating the space.

"Holy shit," Caleb says low and slow, his eyes widening and his goose bumps stiffening. He bounds off, excited to get a closer look.

Sadie eyes the expanse. She looks at the stores. Under her breath and without moving, she mumbles to herself.

"So, this is where it's all led." Shaken, Sadie now knows precisely what it all means.

ABOUT THE AUTHOR

Nikki Lewen looks forward to binge-reading everything—and any-thing—after years of idiotic, self-imposed literary deprivation to avoid sway over her writing style and storyline. Whether this tactic proves accolade-worthy (or naïve) is yet to be determined. Her absen-teeism from the pages of fictional works nears its end with the release of the final installment of the *Three Sisters Trilogy*: **Destined**, due out August 2020.

THANK YOU!

A huge THANK YOU to all of you who've bought, read, cheered, and supported the first two books of the *Three Sisters Trilogy*.

I hope you enjoyed **Return to Three Sisters** and that you're eager to find out how it will all come together for Sadie Larkin in the final installment of her saga: **Destined**.

It would be super helpful and much appreciated if you could write a short review of this book on Amazon. Please keep spreading the word about *Three Sister's* Sadie Larkin to any and all — in whichever manner you choose.

A million and one thanks!

Nikki Lewen

RETURN TO THREE SISTERS

Book Club Questions

1. The novel's environmentally-devasted, post-apocalyptic world expands upon real problems the world faces today. What measures do you and your family take to ensure a sustainable future for yourselves, your community, and the planet?

2. What qualities do the main characters possess that drive them to put others before themselves?

3. What factors and life experiences shaped Rene Russo into 'the Commander?' Do you believe her loyalty can be trusted? Why or why not?

4. How has Caleb's and Sadie's relationship evolved? What roles do they fill for each other as they struggle with the physiological and psychological trauma they endure?

5. When battling the Splitter Nation, Sadie hides her sexual identity. Why does she find this necessary? Additionally, what current societal inequalities and global abuses mirror what the women in this new world face?

6. Sadie's determination to help others continues to escalate. Why do you think this is so? What roles have other characters played to aid in her successes?

7. Why do you think the rescue and education of young children becomes such a prominent theme?

8. Sadie's father had the foresight to plan, prepare, and stockpile goods to ensure his daughter's survival. What steps have you and your family taken to prepare for various types of emergencies?

9. What do you think Sadie discovers under her family's barn? And what do you think she'll do with it?

Made in the USA
Middletown, DE
30 October 2023

41676133R00126